ADVANCE PRAISE FOR OUT OF WATER

"Sarah Read's short stories are wonderfully creepy, heartbreaking, scary, and delightful! Highly recommended!"
—Jonathan Maberry, New York Times bestselling author of *V-Wars* and *Glimpse*

"In Sarah Read's *Out of Water* you will find monsters with human faces and humans with monstrous hearts. There are secrets dark and deep, and dreams darker and deeper still. And there are characters who stretch their hands from haunted shores in hopes of reaching a happier one. Read's collection is filled with grim humour, heart-wrenching horror and, sometimes, dire hopes."
—Angela Slatter, author of the World Fantasy Award-winning *The Bitterwood Bible and Other Recountings*

"Sarah Read is one of my very favorite voices in horror and dark fantasy, and I've been waiting a long time for her to release a collection. So let me say this loud and clear: that wait was absolutely worth it. *Out of Water* is a gorgeous, sinister, and incredibly lovely dive into all the darkness the horror genre has to offer. Sarah knows exactly how to draw the reader in and then send chills up their spine, all while breaking their hearts. Whatever you do, don't miss this book."
—Gwendolyn Kiste, Bram Stoker Award®-winning author of *The Rust Maidens* and *The Invention of Ghosts*

"Read's stories left me emotionally wrought and viscerally disturbed. With unforgettable imagery and characters that come to life on the page, *Out of Water* is one of the best collections I've read this year."
—Kaaron Warren, Aurealis and Australian Shadows award-winning author of *Tide of Stone*

OUT OF WATER

SARAH READ

TREPIDATIO
PUBLISHING

ISBN: 978-1-950305-05-6 (sc)
ISBN: 978-1-950305-06-3 (ebook)
Library of Congress Control Number: 2019944108

First printing edition: November 1, 2019
Printed by Trepidatio Publishing in the United States of America.
Cover Design and Layout: Mikio Murakami
Interior Layout: Lori Michelle
Edited by Scarlett R. Algee
Proofread by Sean Leonard

Trepidatio Publishing, an imprint of JournalStone Publishing
3205 Sassafras Trail
Carbondale, Illinois 62901

Trepidatio books may be ordered through booksellers or by
contacting:
Trepidatio | www.trepidatio.com
or
JournalStone | www.journalstone.com

For Sweet Grandma Lou, for the words in the first place.

OUT OF
WATER

TABLE OF CONTENTS

Introduction by Gemma Files i

Endoskeletal 1

Making Monsters 17

Dead Man's Curve 25

In Tongues 37

The Eyes of Salton Sea 47

Underwater Thing 63

Tall Grass, Shallow Water 81

Intersect 95

Grave Mother 99

Thorn Tongue 103

Through Gravel 115

Still Life with Natalie 131

Golden Avery 139

Scavengers 145

The Eye Liars 157

Magnifying Glass 171

Crosswind 181

Renovation 197

INTRODUCTION

GEMMA FILES

TEACHING IS ONE of the great joys in my life, though it wasn't always that way. Once upon a time, it was "just" a job—something I clung to desperately as my film criticism career ebbed away, always aware that my sole university degree was in journalism, not education. In a way, it took losing a full-time teaching position, as well as using that loss to (eventually) jump-start my the next phase of my professional fiction-writing career, to reconnect me with the quote-quote simple joys of helping someone else nurture their own creative spark by spinning a moment's absent thought into something entirely different, black on white, words on a page. A beautiful, tumorous blossom of metaphor run wild with narrative for blood, referential imagery for bone.

This is how I first met Sarah Read . . . not in body, but mind to mind. By watching a creepy, frightening, wonderful idea she pitched me evolve, stage by stage, into something which would eventually become one of the best horror stories of the year. It was called "Endoskeletal," and you'll meet it soon enough, since it opens this debut collection of Sarah's short fiction. Let me put it to you this way: it makes me wish I'd written it, even though I know damn well I never could have.

The walls of the jar were thin enough that she could see the glow of light behind it, and the silhouette of a lumpy shadow inside. She photographed every angle, every detail, and made sure the pictures were uploaded and saved before grabbing her scalpel and tweezers. She both hated and wanted this part. Her pulse grew distracting, a pounding in her sore joints, and it would continue to rise until the beautiful thing in front of her was destroyed. And destroying the sample would destroy her career, or make it.

Now granted, any story involving archaeology is basically guaranteed my full attention, but what I love about what Sarah's doing here is the way she cross-breeds her utterly convincing grasp of methodology with sharp psychological observation, making us care deeply about both the artefact her protagonist is examining and her own bone-deep regret that the only way to confirm the ancient mystery before her—let alone

1

to understand it—is to lose even a single part of something so irreplace-able. Simple, clear, concise, human; these sentences confirm how much I love the way that Sarah thinks, almost as much as I love the things she thinks about. What I like best about this paragraph, in other words, is pretty much everything.

But man, I kind of like this one that comes a bit later on even better:

Panting, she held her hands up to the light. Her knuckles twisted as the skin pulled tighter. The grooves of her knuckles split, the fissures like small gaping mouths from which erupted bone upon bone. She shrieked at the sting of it and tried to close the split flesh by straight-ening her fingers, felt the pressure grow, pulsing under her nails—saw the white of bone pale like blisters at the tips of her fingers. She stretched her fingers further and the skin burst, springing back along the protruding shafts of bone, curling back like a blooming flower.

It's always very funny to me, the generalized received wisdom that women aren't supposed to embrace horror, when horror is—in a lot of ways—the female condition, as well as the human one: body horror, so-cial horror, moral horror. Some of the meat-suits we're born into can bleed seven days and not die, or come pre-equipped to incubate, then push forth, a parasitical proto-human only partially made from our own DNA, whom we may not automatically love simply because we're "auto-matically" genetically pre-disposed to. Politicians and religious leaders often seem bent on reducing us to mere extensions of our bodily func-tions, while the marriage-happy fairytale the media spends much of its time selling us on is alarmingly far more likely to end less in happily ever after than in violence and rancor, divorce at best, murder-suicide at worst. Turn a prospective lover down and you might get shot, get acid thrown in your face, get your baby thrown over a shopping mall balcony in order to teach you a lesson. Every woman I know doesn't have just one #MeToo story, but a handful—at the least. The very, very least.

Browse the Internet for ten minutes (or wait a similar length of time after making a Twitter post about equalized gender representation in fandom), and you'll soon find out that we're Other by literal nature, pari-ahs, witches, bitches, Staceys—hollow things made from spare parts, malign and perverse, never content to just shut the hell up and do what we're told. We steer dudes around by their parts, suck their virility dry in their dreams, prevent them from being the men they always expected to become by depriving them of . . . um, ourselves, I guess: mothers,

12

wives, sex-toys. Something permanently less, perfectly designed to make any random guy feel like something permanently more.

It's like the joke about the old Jewish man who, when asked why he kept on re-reading the *Protocols of the Elders of Zion*, replied: "Because I want to remember how powerful I supposedly am." Except in our case, the book in question is not just *Malleus Malificarum*, that Burning Times textbook on how to find evil creepy penis-stealing ladies anywhere a dissatisfied guy might glance, but almost every other myth and fairytale going back through time . . . these endless fantasies of sexual lure and betrayal, of cannibal mothers, of lying scolds whose evil words inevitably come true, spinning spells from insults. Sin on legs, constantly on the run from Eve's legacy: a tryst with the serpent that ruined a previously perfect world by letting in not only knowledge, but death.

And I have to say, after a while, the idea that every woman is a barely-disguised potential monster starts to sound pretty good, by comparison. "Baba Yaga wouldn't have to take this sort of crap," you find yourself thinking; or Tiamat, or Lilith, or Echidna, or Kayako. Pretty soon you're having fantasies of your own, ones which all too often end with you getting offered butter/a delicious life by a sexy- voiced black goat and rising into the dark air on boiled baby-fat, laughing hysterically. Or losing everything and getting burned at the stake, whichever comes first!

Sarah Read gets all this, on a very basic level, and the scenarios she comes up with to combat the all- too-mundane horrors of the world around us burn and shine with a darkness that immerses, entrances, inspires. Her anger and humour are equally resonant; science and the supernatural interbreed freely, spawning all sorts of unique and fascinating nightmares. And all of it reads with the same snap, the same flare, the same gorgeously offhand-seeming gothic grotesquerie: insects and angels, storms and spectres, curdled love, transforming grief. This book is full of awful, delightful things, and I'm so glad it exists, I can't even tell you.

So read on or don't, but never say you weren't warned. It takes a certain type of person to write like Sarah Read writes. Luckily for the rest of us, however, all we have to do in order to enjoy the fruits of her labour . . . is to develop a taste.

ENDOSKELETAL

THE FIGURES ARE *drawn in yellow ochre, their limbs overlong, their faces drawn as skulls—white with crushed calcite, eyes carbon black with a spark of red ochre inside. Each figure holds an orb-like jar beneath its chin. Umber shadows trail behind them as they march the length of the chamber, deep into the small spaces at the back of the cave, where there is the monster. A mass all in soot bone black, large as the cave wall, covered in a hundred lidless eyes. The eyes are not drawn, but etched into the stone itself.*

Ashley looked from the cave wall back to her sketch and smoothed her thumb over a figure's shadow, blending her pencil lines. Henri's camera flashed, blinding her. When her eyes adjusted, pupils wavering into equilibrium, her LED lantern seemed dimmer than before, the figures drawn on the cave walls harder to make out.

"Can you wait a minute, please?" She didn't temper the edge in her voice. She'd asked him this a hundred times already—at the office as she checked her daypack, along the Alpine trail as he led the way at a pace she could not possibly match. *You must get used to the altitude if you want to study here*, he'd said as she caught up, panting, the thin air heavy in her lungs. *You're not ready to study here*, is what she heard. What he probably wanted her to hear.

"I *am* studying here," she'd puffed between shallow gasps. "And you can't outrun altitude sickness. Don't they teach that to guides here?" She'd planted herself on a rock and made him wait.

His camera flashed again. "We don't have time." Another photo. "We've waited half the day away. Your drawings are too slow. We don't do it that way anymore."

Ashley shifted; the cold of the cave floor had crept through the sweater she'd folded into a cushion. She counted to ten, her eyes squeezed shut against the flashes. "I'm not just sketching to record them, Henri. I'm learning them—studying them."

"You can do that in the lab, unless you want to hike back in the

1

dark. You're wasting time. We don't even know if you'll be allowed to study these."

She stood then, clutching her pencils in her fist. "What do you mean?"

"You came to study bears? These aren't bears. There are bears in the other chamber you can study—we have enough of those to share. But this is special. This is weird. They will want a Swiss archaeologist for this."

Ashley hadn't considered that. When she'd proposed the expedition to explore the new chambers exposed by the receding glacier, she'd counted on finding either cave bears or nothing. Instead, she'd found a national treasure. The specters from the camera flash danced in her eyes as she added notes to her handwritten report. He hadn't convinced her to hurry. Now her notebook was more important than ever—it might be the only proof she'd have of the discovery, if the site was seized.

The cave painting showed at least twenty figures confronting the shadow covered with eyes. The skull-faced figures threw bones at the shadow, though it wasn't clear if they were fighting it or feeding it. Ashley paced the length of the chamber, back toward where she had to bow her six-foot-seven frame to fit beneath the mineral-slick stone. The eyes of the monster seemed to follow her, their charcoal-darkened shadows shifting in the weak light. It made the hair on her arms rise, made it difficult to look away from the creature—as if it would move closer when her back turned.

A dozen skeletal remains filled shallow alcoves that lined the walls beneath the drawings. Beyond the alcoves, two narrow openings split the back of the cave. One led to nothing but a cavernous sinkhole. The other led to the much-trafficked cave chamber containing the remains of several cave bears. No one had known that the loose rubble wall of the cave bear room had concealed the entrance to another chamber. No one had wanted to disturb the stones and risk a cave-in. But with temperatures rising, the ice on the opposite slope had melted away, and the true entrance to the cave had opened its dark eye over the valley below.

She looked back to her sketch and darkened the space inside an eye socket, layering the charcoal until there was no hint of cream paper beneath. She leaned further over the skeletal remains in an alcove. The bones of the legs and arms were broken, but Ashley could tell from the growth plates that he died young. *The bones are in bad condition—fragmented and overgrown with mineral deposits that will be difficult or impossible to remove without destroying the specimen . . .*

The skulls, though, were all complete: each one with its jaw pried apart and a jar shoved between its teeth. *The jars are clay or stone, perhaps dug from the cave walls? Smooth and yellowed. They're undecorated, sealed with fine leather. They are some form of canopic jar perhaps, or an offering to the dead or the afterlife?* She reached out a finger to touch the fragile leather, then pulled back. *The leather remains intact despite no apparent organic matter left on the bodies themselves. It will need to be tested for ancient preservation techniques.*

There wasn't much known about Paleolithic funerary rites. Because sites like this were never found.

Most of the jars lay in shards—the pieces tumbled toward the back of the skeletons' throats, the jaws left gaping—only fine dust remained of their contents. But there were five jars whole and tempting. Her hands kept returning to the space above the skull, hovering, as if to stroke its brow. She had never before been tempted to touch a specimen, to violate every rule that she herself had repeated incessantly to students and assistants at her sites.

"We're taking one back with us," Ashley said, tucking her book into her pack.

The camera flash paused, and Ashley felt Henri's eyes scolding her through the darkness. There was something in the way he looked at her that made her skin prickle.

"I don't think we should," he said.

Ashley pulled another kit from her pack—a small plastic crate filled with chunks of polyethylene foam, and rolls of gauze and tape. She began assembling a nest that would protect the specimen as they hiked back to the research center.

"Dr. Knochdieb won't like it. You'll lose your post for sure if you disturb this site."

"Isn't that what you all want, anyway?" She was done with their bureaucracy—she'd come here to work. And the thought of leaving without something more to study—without some way to begin answering the thousand questions storming in her brain—was torture.

Henri's scoff echoed off the walls, the drawings, the bones. "It'll be dark before we get back as it is. It'll be dark before we leave if we wait much longer. *I* can hike that trail in the dark, but you're going to get hurt if you try." He mumbled to himself in German as he changed the camera's memory card. It sounded like a prayer. His hair was the brightest thing in the cave—the sort of blond Californians paid good money for. Perhaps he'd be her beacon in the dark. She imagined she'd disappear in the dark entirely, invisible against the sky, though Henri had earlier said that her height made her impossible to lose. She felt the telltale ache in her shoulders as she'd unconsciously slouched ever since.

He was right, though, about all of it. She could picture the red-faced spluttering of the department head when he learned she had touched an unknown burial site. It would be several shades darker than when he'd learned she'd be studying there to begin with. The program hadn't accepted any foreign students since the dawn of digital record keeping. They weren't keen to break the record. And, of course, they hadn't known what she would find in the cave. Henri, in particular, was upset to lose what would have been *his* project— what now would be, at best, a third-author credit, behind her, if she stayed—and her behind the soon-to-be-furious Dr. Knochdieb.

But he'd be mad tomorrow. Tonight was her chance to learn what she could and put together a proposal to convince them to give her the project—this project, instead of the bears—or at least allow her to stay involved. An underling, even. She'd bring them coffee, up the mountain, if she could work on-site. Anything to stay with the bones.

Now gloved, she did risk a touch. Just a fingertip, above the teeth, where the lips would have been stretched back around the bulbous jar.

She draped sheets of gauze over the skull as carefully as if wrapping a newborn. Its face—its gaping jaw and strange jar— vanished behind the layers of soft white. She set the bundle in a ring of foam inside the crate and layered more around it. She scoured the alcove for any small pieces or artifacts she may have missed. *Nothing. Not even a bead. All they have is their jars.*

The camera flash had returned, throwing her shadow in front of her, up the cave wall and across the skeletal drawings, as if she were another soot monster swallowing the stick-like figures whole.

But Henri wasn't documenting the remains anymore. He was documenting her, just as he'd probably been told to do from the beginning. More of a spy than a guide and assistant. But he didn't have the authority to stop her. And even if he went straight to Dr. Knochdieb, she'd have a few hours to study her sample and make her case. There was little hope either way, but at least she could learn something about the bones.

~

Ashley's body ached as they reached the foot of the mountain. Every knuckle was skinned and bleeding, the tendons in her wrists and ankles throbbing from every twist and fall. But the specimen was safe, its crate wrapped in her blanket in the padded compartment of her pack. She'd been careful to pitch her weight forward when she fell. Her palms, her elbows, even her face took the brunt of her falls. After the first few, Henri had stopped helping her up, leaving her to the natural consequences of her decision to keep them in the mountains past dark. The mountain dark of the Alps was as black as the inside of its caves, and her dimming lantern hadn't shown every peril on the path. She'd embarrassed herself. But she tried to focus on her project—the specimen in her pack—her future.

She nearly wept at the sight of the single lamp post that illuminated the door to their isolated research center. It was tucked in a folded valley between steep hills, along the path of an old glacier flow. The scars of its ancient passage could still be seen from the hills above. At least, in the light they could.

She wanted the close space of her drafty clapboard dorm. The antique, Alpine barn conversion had been anything but welcoming, but she'd make a home of anywhere with Tylenol and a hot bath. And a private lab.

Henri flashed his keycard at the sensor and held the door for her as she limped across the threshold. "Do you need first aid? There is ice in the kitchen."

"No, thanks." His offer seemed sincere, though she thought he might be mocking her. His accent made it difficult to discern. "I'm going to drop this off at the lab," she said, holding her pack in front of her like a baby. "We'll need to meet with Dr. Knochdieb in the morning."

"I think he'll come in early for this. I'm going to call him now."

"There's no need to wake him. The bodies have been there for thousands of years; they aren't going anywhere."

"*They* aren't. I suggest you start packing, Miss Alesso. I'm sorry."

Ashley watched him strut down the hall toward the dorms. His machismo didn't hide his own limp as well as he doubtless hoped it would. She felt a mixture of shame and wicked glee. She'd forced him to risk his neck on that trail. Her hopes of winning the friendship of her young assistant were in ashes, but at least she could count on him habitually underestimating her.

The halls were dark, empty. The few other researchers and students who shared the facility had long since gone to bed. The lab was hers for as long as it took the director to climb down from his fancy chalet.

The browned bones of the face appeared through the gauze as if surfacing through a sheet of melting snow. She leaned over it as she worked, the muscles in her back and neck knotted and angry. The soft brush feathered over the skull, sweeping away the dirt and fine white threads into the nest of packing gauze.

She studied the protrusions that lined the brow. Under the bright lights of the lab, she saw that they were a part of the bone itself—not cave deposits or applied funerary decorations, but some sort of cancer or deformity. Her heart pinched for the people of the cave. The spurs must have hurt.

She ran a gloved fingertip around the perimeter of an eye socket. They were like toothy hills crowned with needles that snagged at the latex of her glove as she pulled back.

Her fingertip trailed to the jaw and the jar wedged inside the mouth. She could see, then, that it was stone—carved from a solid piece, the walls eggshell-thin. Ashley brushed away all traces of debris and slid her fingers past the long teeth, deep into the mouth, and cupped the bottom of the jar with her fingertips. She lifted gently and felt it give, the stone scraping against the ancient teeth like squeaking chalk. An uncomfortable shudder moved down her body. The jar worked free, intact, and she set it on a pillow of foam on a tray. The skull, its mouth unnaturally stretched, appeared as if it screamed or laughed. Its empty eyes seemed accusatory in their darkness. She covered the face with a fold of gauze. The empty eyes reminded her of the eyes on the cave monster.

The walls of the jar were thin enough that she could see the glow of light behind it, and the silhouette of a lumpy shadow inside. She photographed every angle, every detail, and made sure the pictures were uploaded and saved before grabbing her scalpel and tweezers. She both hated and wanted this part. Her pulse grew distracting, a pounding in her sore joints, and it would continue to rise until the beautiful thing in front of her was destroyed. And destroying the sample would destroy her career, or make it. Her hair stuck to her sweaty brow.

She cut away the cord that secured the flap over the opening and gathered the flakes of leather as they fell, dropping them into a jar of her own—bright glass, sterile, but otherwise little had changed in twenty-five thousand years.

The leather scrap was thin and fine like the tender skin of a rodent. It had dried to something almost like vellum. *It shouldn't exist at all.*

Once the seal was pulled away, odor overwhelmed her, sweet and rancid like cherries and old cheese. She clutched her wrist to her nose until the wave passed. She hadn't dealt with fresh remains in years. This specimen shouldn't be fresh. Shining more light inside revealed dark clumps clinging to the illuminated walls. She dipped her scalpel inside and scooped out a trace of the substance, sending a fresh wave of odor down her throat. It stuck to the blade as she tapped it onto a glass slide. It was crumbly and clumpy, like wet, purple sand. She took more photographs, brightened them, and saw purple, red, gold, brown. Perhaps a desiccated organ. Or maybe the tongue, considering the placement of the jar.

Magnified under the microscope, it was a brilliant lattice of blood cells—platelets, red and white cells, stem cells, and fatty deposits. Myelorytes. Fragments of vessel. Bone marrow.

Ashley turned back to the crate with the skull and peeled back the gauze. She ran her fingers over the blossoms of bone again, ignoring the sharp snags, searching for a perforation in the bone. Then she remembered the arms and legs, each broken on every body. Not from the brittleness of millennia, perhaps, but as part of this strange funerary ritual. She wanted to get the rest of the bones—make a full layout of the body and examine the breaks. Look for manmade trauma. But she needed to finish her work with the jar. She grabbed the jar and held it directly above the light, peering into its mouth, trying to gauge the quantity of marrow collected, presumably from the man whose mouth it had filled. Though it was astoundingly preserved under its ancient seal, some evaporation had to have occurred. A slow concentration. She couldn't tell how much marrow was there, but she didn't want to disturb the whole sample.

There needed to be something left intact for her report—and some evidence that she'd be dedicated to the proper handling of these artifacts, despite her hasty removal of the sample.

She was beginning to like the smell. She breathed it in and felt certain, then, that the gaping skull smiled.

The tightness in her neck made it difficult to lift the crate onto the high shelf in the storage fridge. Her hands shook, and fresh blood had slicked the inside of her gloves. She felt the altitude again like a punch in the gut.

~

The ache in her body had deepened by morning, but she couldn't stop pacing. She limped from one end of the conference room to the other, her eyes sweeping over the board that she'd papered with her sketches. She paused, pulled a pencil from her hair, and fixed a sketch. Deepened a shadow. Added texture to the rough fracture of the bones.

She ran her fingers through her hair and pulled another sliver of shale from the dark curls. She hadn't managed a bath yet. With any luck, she'd be coated in dirt again by the afternoon, anyway.

The meeting wouldn't start for an hour, but she needed time to prepare. They'd be looking for the first excuse to kick her out, contract be damned. But she wouldn't let it go without a fight. This was the find of a lifetime, and it was her discovery. She wasn't likely to ever see anything like this again—but if she got her name on this study, it could change the trajectory of her whole career.

Her knees gave, and pain shot up her legs. Her body contorted on the floor, folding over as the cramps arced across her body. Pain twisted through her hips and up her back before it faded, leaving her sweating and panting on the floor.

She'd been distracted and preoccupied on the way down the mountain. She must have pulled a tendon. Pinched a nerve. Her breath evened, and she pulled herself up into one of the rolling desk chairs. Black spots receded from her vision. She poured herself a drink of water from the pitcher on the table, spilling as she did, her hands unsteady—her fingers weak and trembling. She choked on the water, coughing splashes down her front.

Dr. Knochdieb burst into the room, Henri behind him.

She wiped her dripping chin on her sleeve.

Dr. Knochdieb stormed past her to the board covered with her sketches and photographs. His tie was slightly off-center. He must have rushed.

"Quite the find," he said, pausing to look at the sketch of the shadow monster. "We were of course aware of Stone Age human settlements near the lake, but we hadn't yet found any in the high hills. Not in any of the dozens of caves. So tell me, scholar, why they are there?" He pulled her sketch of the cave paintings from the board and sat in the chair to her right. From this angle, she could see that he had also failed to press down his silver cowlick. The spike of hair at his crown was usually plastered with gel—a feature Henri had nicknamed the Oberaletsch Glacier.

Ashley's voice caught deep in her chest. She'd had a speech prepared, but it didn't account for this sort of question. She'd been expecting more "who do you think you are," not "what do you think." Hope made it hard to think at all.

"Well, the bones show significant funerary preparations. They're laid out, and the stone jars are inserted into the mouths. The jars contain bone marrow, which I suspect came from the arms and legs, which have all been broken—"

"How do you know that?" Dr. Knochdieb and Henri both turned to her at that, their faces masked with twin looks of alarm.

Ashley felt the cold water creeping back up her throat. "I examined the specimen last night. I wanted to provide a full rep—"

"You tampered with it?"

9

Here was the tirade she'd been expecting. His eyes roved over her in a way that made her feel inside-out. As though she was raw to his judgement.

"I felt it was my responsibility to report my findings in full. To provide enough information to justify a continued excavation and protection of the site." Her jaw stiffened as she spoke, so that her last words hissed past her teeth, sounding more impertinent than she meant them.

"Of course it will be excavated. And protected. But it's not your job to tell us that." Dr. Knochdieb's hands shook with indignation. The color of his face rose to match his tie.

"I meant to justify *my* continued excavation. Just . . . please. Please, let me work on this with you." This wasn't her script—she hadn't intended to beg. But her head was spinning. She couldn't remember what she was supposed to say—her jaw felt sealed against her words. Something about her past experience under her mentor in Peru. Something about global cooperation. She could only think of the bones—of getting back to them. *Remind them why you're here—why they said yes.*

The black spots were returning to her vision. She held herself firm in her seat, upright, eyes closed.

She caught the word "dismissed," then stumbled out of her chair, sending it rolling into the board, knocking sketches into the air. She ran from the room as Dr. Knochdieb scolded her rude departure.

Her legs buckled awkwardly as she raced down the hall to her office. She slammed the door shut behind her and sank to the cold floorboards.

Her fingers ached as though they'd been jammed. It reminded her of her adolescent growing pains—of soaking, curled, in hot baths and the aftertaste of Advil bitter on her tongue, her mother's long fingers pulling through her wet, curly hair, reassuring her that the boys would catch up to her height, that she wasn't a "freak." She felt the familiar itch of the stretch marks that lashed across her back and around her thighs—a crossed dark lattice. She remembered the eyes on her, everywhere she went—the staring, their gazes tickling up her neck. She remembered waking at slumber parties to find games of tic-tac-toe played in the crosshatch of her scars. Every dry itch of that pull of skin brought fresh humiliation. And now she felt it on her hands, her face and neck. It felt as though her flesh was a shrinking glove, curling her fingers to her palms and holding them there.

Panting, she held her hands up to the light. Her knuckles twisted as the skin pulled tighter. The grooves of her knuckles split, the fissures like small gaping mouths from which erupted bone upon bone. She shrieked at the sting of it and tried to close the split flesh by straightening her fingers, felt the pressure grow, pulsing under her nails—saw the white of bone pale like blisters at the tips of her fingers. She stretched her fingers further and the skin burst, springing back along the protruding shafts of bone, curling back like a blooming flower. Her fingernails scattered around her. Each breath, deep and ragged, felt as though it contained less air than the one before.

There's something in those jars. Something wrong. She remembered the prick of the bone spurs, the blood in her gloves. *Careless.*

She struggled, shaking, to her feet. Blood dripped from her twisting fingers to the dingy floor. She reached long, tender, bone-tipped fingers into her pocket, moaning as the rough fabric scraped against the exposed nerves, and pulled her lab keycard out. *This hurts, hurts, this hurts . . . but not as much as it should.* Half her brain was a hum of panic while half observed, fighting the adrenaline for scraps of logic.

The hallway was empty. It was still early—no one was in their offices yet. She limped around the door and down the hall, catching herself against the wall as she stumbled, crying out when her bones clacked against the plaster. *What is happening to me?* The metatarsals of her feet strained against the leather of her shoes.

She fumbled with the keycard at the lab door, dropping it, scraping it from the tiles with her bone-tips. *The bones; I need the bones; I need the marrow.* She brought the card to her mouth and used her lips to hold it to the sensor. The light flashed red. The door handle stuck, unmoving.

They've changed the locks. Dread washed over her, almost enough to erase the pain in her hands, her face, her feet and knees. There was only one other place she could study the jars. Only one place that might have an answer about what was happening to her.

The thought of the cave was like an endorphin balm. She needed the cave.

Her knees left damp patches of blood along the trail behind her. She held her lantern clenched in her teeth. Her long fingers slid through spaces between the rocks, gripping them, hauling herself more easily than she had the day before—all her weight pivoting on the levers of her long bones. The pull of the cave was so strong it felt as though it lifted her up the mountain. When she reached the top of the rise where the cave gaped open, her bones had grown so tall that she had to fold herself unnaturally to enter. She rolled inside and lay on the floor, shaking violently, shrieking as more bones popped out of her jaw and hips, spraying blood across the ancient amber bones and ochre drawings. *I'm contaminating the samples.* She nearly laughed at her impulse to preserve the cave art. *Die somewhere else. You're making a mess.*

Her hands, feet, face continued to erupt—her legs and arms extending until they were difficult to place. She tried to stand and fell over her own long legs, as she had when she was fifteen, trying to dance.

She felt eyes on her, then—angry and hungry—and turned toward the cave entrance, expecting to see Henri, maybe even Dr. Knochdieb. The opening was hidden in shadow, as if night had fallen as she lay on the floor. Shingles of bone growing from her face obstructed her view, but still she felt watched. Then the darkness moved toward her. She scrambled back, long limbs flailing against the rock and pushing her farther away from her lantern. As she squirmed toward the back of the cave, the neon-white light disappeared as if draped in cloth.

She skittered deeper into the cave, tapping with her long bones to find her way. She passed an alcove, and remembered the painted figures marching on the monster. She grabbed for the bones on the shelf and hurled them into the shadow. The pressure abated—drawing back, a flinch—a blink. The pile dwindled till she came to the skull, and remembered the jar. The sacred marrow. She reached into its mouth, to the intact orb of stone, and slipped the jar free—clutched it to her chest as she threw the skull, the final bone, into the shadow. It fell back, just enough to free the glow of her lantern. She crawled toward the openings at the back of the cave. She remembered the chamber maps vaguely—what Henri had let her see of them. One chamber led to the bear cave and exited onto the southern slope above town. The other led to a chasm. She couldn't remember which was which. *I can't think; why can't I think anymore?* It was as if the bones pulled the thoughts from her head.

She slid her long legs into the hole just as darkness drowned the lantern again, and the shadow moved toward her, all thousand eyes fixed on her bone helmet as she dropped from the chamber into the narrow passage beyond.

She slid, fell, branching fingers clutching at empty air, then landed on a haystack of bones in a frenzy of fracture and splintering. Dry, ancient bones shattered against her armor. Three of her long fingers snapped. The stone jar had crushed against her chest, the sticky paste inside smearing her with its scent. She coughed a scream.

The eyes were all around her, stripping her, driving through her armor, under her skin. The old dry bones did nothing to slow it. These weren't ritual bones. They weren't marrow bones—these bones had already been drunk dry. She found the warm twigs of her broken fingers, phalanges five inches long—she could smell the meat in them, rich and fatty. Life itself, reborn over and over, the factory of longevity. She slid the bones through the small holes in her skull mask and wrapped her lips around the jagged edges, felt the needle-like texture of their surface prick at her lips. She sucked at the marrow. It slid over her tongue, thick and creamy. Her pain faded. Her eyes began to adjust to the darkness on all sides. She threw her empty bones at the shadow and it fell back, giving her room to see and breathe.

The sinkhole was a trash heap of abandoned remains. Eyes were etched deep into the walls as far up as she could see, as though the monster slept here under its own watch. Above her, the shadow swirled like a cloud of bats, all pupil, wide and dark. She slid her long fingers into the carved grooves and began to climb. Her overlong arms and legs quivered under the stone weight of her growing bone armor. They gave, and she plummeted back to the bottom, snapping more protrusions.

13

She sucked more marrow from her freshly broken digits, and her strength increased—the pain faded further. The fragments continued to drive back the shadow. The marrow from the jar smeared across her chest made her itch again, and she felt more stretching, more calcium armor growing with a deep bass rumble deep in her core. She began to climb again. When she weakened, her body growing too heavy even for her strengthened hands, she put a finger in her mouth and bit down, breaking it off with her teeth and sucking at it, drawing more strength, more ammunition against the monster. When her fingers were stumps just long enough to press into the grooves of the stone, she broke away pieces from her face—thick wings of bone from her eyes and jaw, till her head was free again but for the jagged edges of broken bone at the tattered eruption points, her face a mask of ivory needles.

She reached the top and slithered back through the opening into the catacomb chamber. Her lantern was there, the monster no longer between her and the exit. The exposed nerves in her body sang with pain again in the open air of the chamber.

The beast emerged from a crack in the rocks. Its gaze buckled her knees and dropped her to the cave floor as she turned to face it. It bubbled up through the narrow vent, its vision multiplying as it filled the cavern.

Ashley's bones bled from fragile, ragged fractures. There was nothing left to throw. Her bones weren't growing fast enough.

She edged to the cave wall and reached into an alcove, running her fingers over the ritual skeletons till she felt the familiar curve of a skull, a jar. She pried it out of the jaw and brought it to her mouth. The neck of the jar shattered between her teeth and she drove her tongue into the opening, lapping at the gritty paste inside. Her body quaked. She screamed as bones burst from her, jutting from her hands, feet, and face. The shadow lurched, and she pitched an alcove bone at the monster. It hesitated, rushed forward.

Ashley scrambled back. She reached into the next alcove and claimed another jar, sucked its contents down, and grew again. Sheets of bone from her eye sockets crept into her periphery, growing across her face. She raked long fingers toward the shadow, swiping at it. She felt it blink—a momentary release from its boring gaze.

14

She danced on long toes across the narrow chamber to the other alcoves, and the last jar. More marrow, more bone, less darkness. Her ribs crisscrossed in front of her, a shield over her soft, bleeding center. She charged the monster. She glared into its gaze, eye to eye to eye, until it sank back through the crevasse, back to the eye-walled pit, its vision winking out, leaving her in only natural darkness. She drove her ossified fist into the stone above the fissure, pounding it into grit, her hardened hands like hammers glancing off the slick stone till it crumbled. The opening gave and the ceiling fell, thundering, sealing the side chamber shut—like the jars, like the bone closing over Ashley's face.

Her rapid breath flowed back at her in the confines of her outer skull. Her vision narrowed to the width of a single finger. She reached through the small hole and tried to pull at the bone, to break herself free. The skull mask clamped shut on her fingertip, growing over it, trapping it, shutting out all but a little light. She screamed inside her skull and the sound bounced around her ears. The expanding lattice of her ribcage lifted her off the floor.

Her breathing slowed. Cradled in her bones, with her own soft breath against her face, her panic settled into calm. It was quiet inside her bones, and no one could see her. Not the monster with his thousand eyes or Henri through his camera lens, or the thousands who had stared over the years at her height, her scars. She was hidden, shielded by armor of her own making.

They'd find her, though, she knew. Later. Long after her life was gone. She'd be a curiosity—a national treasure: the woman inside of a bone cave inside of a cave of bones. A freak. They'd take her bones away and seal them in jars. Study them. But the monster was gone. And so was the sacred marrow. Except for the sample in the lab. The open jar with its rich odor, its inescapable pull toward the cave. Perhaps, exposed, it would fall to dust. Perhaps, exposed, those who laid eyes on it would become monsters. Maybe covered with bone, maybe covered with eyes.

The last seams of her skull plates squeezed tight—only slivers of light slipping through and dancing across the inside of her skull like figures on a cave wall. All she could see was her own darkness, her own shadow, and the only eyes were hers. Nothing and no one looked back.

MAKING MONSTERS

MY THIGHS STICK to the hot seat, my fingers touch-tapping the baked vinyl of the wheel. My face tingles—feels stretched over my skull as the capillaries dilate in the hot van. The sun filters through the dirty glass. Bracelets of sweat form under the tight cuffs of my polyester chiffon blouse. I smear more Vicks VapoRub under my nose. Bet it's shining like a star. But Dale's starting to spoil, and I can't take it much longer. I'm praying for the red truck to get here soon.

There's nothing to see but rocks and brush, and I wonder why this place is called Red Rocks. The rocks aren't red. Every shade of orange and pink—some almost purple, but no red. Should be called Tequila Sunrise, or maybe Barbie's Deathtrap.

The small fuzz of a dirt cloud in the distance is getting taller, getting closer. I'm hoping it's that red truck, and I'm praying it's closer than it looks. I need to get this van moving—get the windows down and the wind over my face. Push this stink into the back, where it belongs. It was bad enough when it was the deer and piles of rabbits and armadillos—but, now, Dale . . . He reeks.

~

In the East, they call them monsters. In the South, it's devils. In the West, they all just assume it's people from Portland. But here in the Southwest, it's always aliens. In the microcosm of my van, they're all a bit of this and a bit of that, stitched together. An armature of deer bone supporting a motley of beaver and bear; snakes and squirrel; alligator; coyote and rabbit. Dale. Whatever has been (or can be) hit with a van. But I know this is what he would have wanted. I know the man's wants—know them every which way. And that makes it easier, the knowing.

~

The dirt billowing off the back tires of whatever's coming this way hangs in the air. If I listen, I can almost hear an engine. I'm hoping

17

it's not a crazy desert person. Praying it's not the police. That would give the game away.

More Vicks.

I start the van. Maybe, if it's not the red truck, I can outrun them. I check the mirror, and have to crank it to see past the deer strapped into the back seat, its legs folded in like a spider's, past Dale's head that bobs with the chug of the struggling engine. He's wrapped in a white motel sheet that isn't quite white anymore.

No cars behind. Just that cloud up ahead. In the sparkle rising off the hot pavement, a smear of red. And I thank God.

I fumble with my camera case. Hands are shaking—Dale always did the talking. I slip the strap over my neck just as the red truck pulls alongside my van.

The ranchero leaves it running—right there in the middle of the dirt road—and walks over to my window. Oh no.

I pop the door, jump out, and slam it quick behind me. He gets a whiff. I can tell. His salt-and-pepper mustache does a dance under his nose, and he brings his thumb up and swipes it across his nostrils. Then he pinches the brim of his hat.

"Miss Ricky?"

I exhale and put on my best Miss Georgia pageant smile. "Mister Valez?" I hold out my hand—all sea-foam chiffon and powder-pink nails. He wipes his hand on his jeans and shakes mine. His hand is the texture of an armadillo shell, and just as dusty.

"I hope you brought a fast camera, Miss Ricky. No one ever seen 'em more than a blink. Got a good trigger-finger for that thing?" He nods at the bulky camera hanging from my neck. The weight of it is pinching my curls.

"Only the best in the country. But you know that already, or you wouldn't have called, right?" Pageant smile again, throw a shoulder forward, Marilyn laugh.

But he's looking at my nose, not my tits.

Shit, the Vicks.

I scoop away the slimy layer. "Oh, sorry. Hit a fox or something a few miles back—something smelly, anyway. Could hardly stand it!"

He smiles, then. Teeth bright in his dark face. Handsome. Too bad he's the kind of nut-job who'd answer my ad.

"Follow me, Miss Ricky. The turnoff is hard to find. It's why I had you meet me here." He climbs back into his truck, and I slip back into the van.

We drive toward a dip in the pink desert rock. Bluffs rise all around us. In a low hollow there's a splash of green, neat rows of alfalfa surrounded by wild sage scrub. Barbie's Oasis.

A stir of black cows crowds one end of the ranch. They've cleared the scrub around them, but they're clinging to the fence—half a field away from a tower of fresh hay, nearly climbing over each other's backs. There's a heap of black at the base of the haystack.

"They got another last night," Valez says, climbing down from his pinging truck.

I'm hoping the sweat from my hands isn't going to damage my camera. Praying Valez doesn't see me sweat.

His stare turns icy. It cancels out the heat of the sun. "I'll give you five thou for a picture of what's doing this to my cows."

We walk over to the heap, and I start snapping pictures. The poor creature is desiccated—shriveled and twisted, its insides on the outside, but all dry. Paler than the inside of a cow ought to be. There's a smell of char and ozone.

"Have you had autopsies done?" I can't help but wonder what a vet would think of the pile of organ jerky.

"Course, yeah. Unknown cause of death, apart from being in pieces."

"It looks—and smells—like it might have been struck by lightning. Have you had any electrical storms?"

The ranchero frowns.

I feel the heat again. "I'm sorry—it's my job to investigate. Sometimes that means—" bat the eyelashes, lean a bit forward— "playing the devil."

He nods, and looks down at the cow husk. "No storm. And no sign of lightning on the ground here."

He's not wrong about that. I snap a few more pictures and tuck my camera away.

"I'll need to get these developed and do some research on the area. I'll be back the day after tomorrow to start trying for that picture. You've definitely got something going on out here, and Out of this World Photography is prepared to document it for you. I've

19

got a week before I'm due at my next assignment. I'm sure I can get something for you." We shake again. That rough hand drives the rest of the spiel right out of my head.

"Can you find your way back to town?" he asks.

You drive forever on that one road, then turn right on that only other road and drive another forever . . . "Yeah—thanks."

As I drive away, he's standing over that cow, the dirt blowing up from my tires shrouding him in grit.

~

The two-hour drive back to town takes six on account of all the snakes. Too many to pass up—too handy—and I pluck them off the side of the road, peel them up where they've gone flat under tires. It should always be this easy.

I'm sweaty, covered in dirt, and starting to smell like the inside of the van by the time I pull in to the lot full of storage garages.

The attendant stares at my van parked in a double-space garage. He side-eyes me. "I'm not saying you're allowed to—'cause I can't say that—but if you're planning on sleeping here, for the love of God, keep the engine off in the garage. For my sake." He squeezes his eyes shut, and his shoulders shiver. The man's seen things.

Marilyn smile, all my teeth showing. "Oh, I'm not sleeping here. I'm just running late for an art show. Need some space to work on my sculpture, then I'm back on the road." Pull my shoulders back, tilt my head. My curls—all limp from sweat and dry heat—tumble over my shoulder.

The attendant just shrugs and hands me the key. Good enough.

Once the door is pulled down, the only light comes from a naked bulb with a rusty chain swinging from its base. It's going to be hard to see my stitches. Dale usually took care of this part.

The old tarp—only barely blue anymore—sticks to itself as I try and spread it over the concrete. I weigh it down at the corners with hammer, saw, wrench, and sewing basket.

I unload my bag of snakes. The deer comes out in pieces, but that's just as well. Saves me the trouble. My chiffon is destroyed, though. And before long, so is my manicure.

But the snakes are all skinned—the best bits laid out. The deer is deboned, and its long limbs are stripped and ready.

Ready for Dale. Dear Dale.

I can feel the sponginess of him through the motel sheet. The heat's done him in. But he'll be perfect. He'll be a star.

I cut away a lot of what's gone bad. How strange that what goes bad gets sweet . . . and I toss it into the muck bucket.

I sew the snakeskins over the stringy layer left behind—elongate his limbs with deer bone. Cloven feet. Snake spines for long fingers and an armadillo shell skull. All covered in rustling rattlesnake diamonds. I fill his mouth with snake fangs. No trace, now, of that sweet sideways smile he always had, even when kissing.

Shaping the brow and the space around the eyes—Dale always said that's where the art is. I get it, though. Use a bit of muck from the bucket to fill it out. It's all about the expression, really brings it all to life. Sells pictures.

I stand back, look him over. Can't suppress a shiver. That'll do. Dale wouldn't say it, but I will: It's better than the Giant Devil Bat of Baltimore we made entirely from squirrels.

~

I've got to drive with the lights off—stupid, in a place like this—but there's nothing for miles but ranchers looking for lights. Valez can't know I'm back early; can't know that the photo I'll sell him will be sitting in my van the whole time I'm looking for his aliens.

I find the perfect spot, just off the far side of the bluff. The terrain will match, and he'll never see my camera flash.

The night is damn cold—a shock, after the heat of the day—but the air is all sweet sage, and I can finally smell something other than Dale. Or Dalien, as I've called him since his transformation. He'd appreciate that.

I drag Dalien from the van and pull him into a boulder-strewn patch of tall grass. I drape a sandbag over the board at his feet and tug his arms up—wrench at the heavy-gauge wire wrapped round the bone inside—till he's posed, snake spine claws up and fanged jaw gaping. The sealant that coats him is still tacky—still a slick shine. It reflects the moonlight beautifully. Makes him look wet, like nothing in this rocky world. He's perfect. He'd be so happy.

I kiss him one more time. Run my dry tongue over the stitches in his lips.

Rocks and weeds catch at my heels as I stumble through the dark. I have to get a good distance. The shot can't be perfect. It can never be perfect, or it will give the game away.

I turn and take a few shots. He looks good, but they aren't quite right. More distance, more climbing over rocks—hoping I won't fall, praying I won't meet any live snakes. I finally find the perfect spot. A nice flat rock, still a bit warm from the sun. Just where I'd sit to watch for aliens, if I was looking for a monster.

I settle in, and point my camera back at Dalien. But I can't find him. All the dark and tall grass—I zoom in and sweep the landscape, searching the side of the bluff. Nothing. Goddamn.

The temperature is creeping up, though it's hours from dawn. A bit of wind, too, like a storm is coming. Must have gone too far.

I crawl back over the rocks to the grassy spot—I'm sure it's the same spot—and there's no sign of Dale.

I'm starting to sweat. The smell of the van is leaking out of my pores. If someone found him and reports it . . .

I scan the field. The cows around the bluff are making a racket, stomping and bellowing. The air smells like ozone and charcoal. There's a crack overhead. Lightning.

But then a crescent of lights flashes over the bluff, and there's Dalien—suspended, caught in the glow.

My shutter finger flutters as the glowing ring of lights reaches an intensity like Dale's old blowtorch and my eyes are squeezed shut and my finger just clicks and clicks the button till another crack sounds and the sky goes dark. Darker than it's ever been. And every time I blink, I see that crescent of lights like it's burned into me.

The cows are screaming, but the air is back to calm, back to cold. I hear Valez shouting. I sink into the tall grass. The dry blades prick at my knees. I'm thumbing through the pictures on the camera, hot breaths coming so fast they're fogging the screen. Valez has gone quiet. The phone in my pocket starts to buzz—but I can hardly feel it. I'm numb.

Dale always said we might get lucky. He said, in the meantime, we'd make our own luck. Make our monsters until we caught one.

Dale, you always said you'd take care of me—and you have. You have.

My prices have just tripled.

DEAD MAN'S CURVE

THE FIRST THING we did was dig up the dead coyote. In the deep freeze of winter, the only earth that moves is earth that's been moved before. So when you need to move a pile of dirt, it's going to be one on top of a coyote. They're the only road kill that gets buried. Anything smaller dries up or gets scavenged in a day, and anything bigger—you take it home and eat off it awhile.

And they're always jumping in front of cars.

The thing hadn't been buried deep, but it would have to do. It stuck to the frozen hole and came away in pieces, brittle bones punching through parchment skin and fur dust. We crumbled it into a cluster of sagebrush and set it all on fire. Gave it a quick salute. Just in case.

We rolled the limp driver into the second-hand hole. Had to fold him up a bit—knees up by his ears—but he just fit, and we covered him with crumbling, frozen slag, more rock than dirt.

"Well," Ed said, rubbing at the spot where his prosthetic chafed his thigh, "'bout all we can do 'bout that."

"Did you check his cards?" I tossed the spade into the back of our squad patrol truck, burying it in a layer of empty cans.

Ed quit rubbing his leg and pulled a ratty Tyvek wallet from his pocket. He cupped a hand over the radio mic on his shoulder, rubbed his thumb over the switch to make sure it was off.

"Benjamin Macey. 34. Iowa. No picture of kids or nothing. No one will miss him."

"How far you think we are from the last one?" I asked.

"Not five miles," he said.

I spat in the dust. It froze to the stones. I dragged the heavy-gauge chain from behind the truck cab and hitched it to the back. The metal stung my hands.

The car was beaten in on the driver's side, broken and twisted. Dry pieces of prairie grass stuck in every seam.

"Taking this one to the usual place?" Ed asked.

"Same as the others."

Ed limped over and helped ratchet the chain around the twisted axle. The POS rattled like a bone cage as we dragged it up the side of the bluff, whipping it around the switchbacks to Dead Man's Curve. We disengaged the chain and gave the car a good shove. It knocked itself to pieces all the way down the mountain, spraying bits of metal off into the trees. It flipped at the bottom and landed in the front seat of the red minivan from last month—we dug up a lot of old holes that day. Big holes and little holes. No one left to miss them.

At least a dozen vehicles cluttered the gorge, the mountainside glittering with their leavings. Ed and me, we put every one of them there. Got to put them somewhere. Can't leave the prairie ditches lined with old metal, with hood-ornament headstones, with evidence. At least people drive these switchbacks a little slower these days. All those steel carcasses, better than a posted sign. But it's not the switchbacks they should be worried about.

Ed nudged me. A trail of dust rose behind a vehicle along the road out on the open plain below. The dust cloud churned with a tangle of black birds—crows, oil-slick rainbow feathers flashing through the dirt like a back-alley burlesque.

"Was a pretty shallow hole this time," Ed said.

We watched as the speck—that old Winnebago—slowed past the site of the accident. The cloud of crows dropped, clawing at the loose dirt over Benjamin Macy 34 Iowa.

The speck peeled out, spraying dust over the inky pack. It tore off across the plain and disappeared behind a bluff.

"Was him, all right."

I slapped the binoculars from Ed's hands. They jerked on the end of the nylon cord around his neck. "Course it fuckin' was."

The crows raised their own cloud of dust. Single birds lifted, having had their fill of Mr. Macey, and trailed off around the bluff where the old Winnebago had vanished. Back on his tail.

"Better radio in another abandoned wreck at Dead Man's Curve," I said. "Where'd you get that?"

"It was in his glove box." Ed spun the barrel of a large revolver.

"Well, be careful, or you'll blow off another foot, or worse."

"Be fair, Cap, that weren't an accident." He slid the cylinder open and counted bullets.

"There's no anti-venom in lead, Ed."

"Worked, though. Blew that rattler and his venom into the next county." He spat and thrust the barrel though his belt. "We gonna chase him?"

I shook my head. "Waste of time."

"You could let me drive. Should be able to catch a ratty old camper."

"You saying I can't drive?"

"No. I'm saying you always drive and we never caught him."

"And we're never going to catch him—not chasing after. Just like them damn birds never have."

"He has to stop sometime." Ed rubbed his leg.

"Closest I've seen him to stopped is when he slows to shake those birds off onto his kills. He's trying to outrun them. Hoping the fresh kill will give him time to get away. Scavenge or be scavenged." I climbed into the driver's seat.

"So you're saying what?"

"We have to wait for him out front of where we know he's going to be."

"He's all over these roads. How we going to know where he's going to be next?"

"Well, idiot, he'll be wherever the next body is buried."

~

Problem was, the next body run off the road by the mad Winnebago was buried in a fluffy pile of airbags, powdered like a baby's bottom—and crying like a baby, too, when we pulled him from his mangled Prius.

"What do we do now?" Ed asked, fingering the revolver in his belt.

"Shut up, Ed. Sir, if you can walk all right, I'm going to need your license and registration."

The heaving man hauled himself upright and stumbled back to his car, the back of his tweed trousers clinging, dark and wet.

"Think the birds will eat him anyway?" Ed stood on his good toes, whispering in my ear.

"No, Ed, I don't."

The powdered man returned with his papers. Ed paced around the wreck while I read over his stats. "Portland? You a hippie?"

The man raised his hand to his head. "No—other Portland—other coast. Lobsters, not whales."

"Wales? Ain't that another country?"

"I said shuttup, Ed!"

Ed fished through the cans in the back of the truck and pulled out the shovel.

The lobster man raised his eyebrows. A goose egg had started swelling above his eye.

"Looks like you hit your head pretty hard, Mr. . . . . Brooke."

He prodded his forehead with his fingertips, swaying on his feet.

"You're not drunk, are you, Mr. Brooke?"

"No! I'm not. I'm just on my way to look at a house in Arizona. I never even saw him till he was right on top of me."

"You get a look at the driver?"

"No. He was moving too fast. I was watching the road."

"Did he have a pack of birds after him?" Ed leaned on the shovel, stirring up a pile of loose rock.

"Birds?" Mr. Brooke looked to me, touching his head again like maybe he'd hit it harder than he thought.

"That's deep enough, Ed."

"No it ain't."

"The chain, Ed."

Ed threw the shovel like a javelin and it crashed into the bed of cans.

Mr. Brooke jumped a foot in the air, shaking. He folded his knees and sat right down in the road.

"He's not going to slow down if he's got nothing to shake those birds off onto." Ed rubbed his leg like he was trying to start a fire. "You got kids, Mr. Brooke? Family?"

Mr. Brooke shook his head.

Ed put a hole in it.

"He ain't even buried, really." Ed kicked dirt over the shallow hole, trying to cover up the soiled seat of Mr. Brooke's tweed trousers.

"I don't think the birds care much, Ed." I threw dirt over Mr. Brooke, aiming for Ed's boots. "Shouldn't have shot him. You're taking this too far."

"And you don't never take things far enough. No one's coming looking for this one. He's a lone wolf—coyote. Roadkill. No one will miss him."

"The birds might have come anyway—might have been good to see if they did or not. Might have been useful information."

"You said you thought they wouldn't."

"Do I look like a goddamn expert on man-eating birds?"

"Yeah, you kinda goddamn do!" Ed kicked a clod of frozen dirt with his bum leg, sending it scattering across the road. "And I don't reckon he'd thank us if them birds ate him alive."

"Hurry. Get in the truck and haul that wreck away."

"How come you're the one gets to stay?"

"You can't catch a moving car on one leg, Ed."

"I'm not going to catch him. I'm going to shoot him."

"You've done enough of that for one day, now get up to the Curve."

"You're welcome, Cap," Ed said. He ripped the shovel from my hands and tossed it in the truck again.

He sped off toward the bluff, the battered Prius rattling behind, trailing road dust and airbag powder.

I climbed into a pile of sage in the ditch, opposite the shallow grave. The ground froze my ass, but the sun heated my head under my hat. Sweat ran down my neck and froze in my collar.

A patch of sky grew dark—the rising cloud of dust kicked up behind the tires of the Winnebago, flashing with black crows. The engine grew louder. I pulled my stiff legs under me.

I heard tires grind on the dirt road. The racket of birds made my ears ring so I almost couldn't hear the Winnebago slow. But I saw the birds drop, heard them scream, clawing at the ground. When they tore into Mr. Brooke, I smelled his blood and the contents of his bowels.

I sprang from the sagebrush onto the road, swatting at dark feathers, coughing on dust. The single glowing eye of the Winnebago's only taillight guided me through the dirt cloud. Wind blew like a cyclone.

I ran, reached, and grasped the handle of the narrow back door and pulled myself onto its flimsy doorstep.

The door bent when I pulled, but clung to the frame at the latch.

I yanked my baton from its holster and beat at the cheap aluminum lock.

He noticed me then, or seemed to, because the camper began to sway and swerve. I clung to the back of it like a bride in the bitch seat and braced my feet against the metal bars of its tilted stairs. Finally the door opened enough so I could fit both hands inside and work at the latch. Its metal folded, and it swung open.

I hung out to the side, peering in around the edge. My view was a dark tunnel, odd shapes black against the sun pouring through the windshield.

Behind me, crows blanketed the ground, swarming over the late, unlucky Mr. Brooke.

I dragged myself into the dark Winnebago.

The camper rocked like a station wagon at lovers' lane, shaking on its axles as it tore across the road. The air inside clung hot and close with that strong smell of parchment and fur dust that clings to my hands now, always.

To my left, a mattress lay mostly rotted, eaten away by a dark stain. A film of filth coated the shelves and counters, all a uniform dingy grey.

Up front, in a tattered seat, the driver pulled at the wheel, swinging it around and tossing me over, dumping me into the reeking bed, then crashing me through a particle-board tabletop.

I steadied myself as I climbed toward the back of his stringy salt-and-pepper head. He never turned to me. His mirrors were all dark, like the crows had filled them—stopped them up with their bead eyes.

I reached for him. My fingertips brushed the back of his head and dry, greasy chunks of hair peeled away, uncovering a scalp as grey and spotted as a fossil.

The Winnebago tipped up on two tires as it swung around a sharp curve in the road. It shuddered as the tires skidded against the dirt.

I fell against the back of the driver's seat, wrapping my arm around the driver's bony chest. His arms jerked. The wheel spun. The camper left the road with a jolt that threw us both to the floor, tangled in each other's raking fingers. We rolled toward the front of the cab as the Winnebago thundered down an embankment.

His rags tore like paper. His skin came away in my hands. He smelled like dry mold and feathers.

The front of the camper caved in with a roar and a rain of powdered glass and splintered metal.

~

A tumbleweed rolled across my face, snagging in my beard. Light drove like a spike through my head as I peeled my eyes open.

The Winnebago sat wedged between two aspen trees. Bits of pale, rusty paint peeked out from under layers of dust and dead leaves. Dry, dead stalks of milkweed hung from the wheel wells. Bindweed wrapped it, tying it to the copse of aspens. It had grown up though the holes in the rusted hood and coiled around itself, then frozen dry.

I patted myself down. A lump on the head and a few bruises. Probably a cracked rib or two. I cursed my way to my feet and walked over to the wreck.

Old, burnt flecks of metal curled away from its sides. They were cold to the touch. I walked the length up to the driver's window, crushing frozen weeds under my boots.

A stone-colored pile of bones sat slumped in the seat, wrapped in rags, its forehead resting against the crooked steering column. The salt and pepper hair hung in loose patches: the same hair I still gripped, wrapped around my knuckles, tangled in the same bits of rag.

"Captain!"

I hollered, nearly wet myself. I flicked my radio on. "The fuck, Ed?"

"The hell have you been? I've been driving all over the county."

"We went off the road. Guess I was out a while. Years, by the look of it." I poked at a loose plate of bone on the skull, and it fell away into the cavity.

"You get him?"

"Yeah, he's dead." I released my finger from the mic button. "Too dead," I whispered.

"Where are you, I'll come get you."

"I think we're off behind Rodger's Bluff. In a group of aspens just past the bend."

"Be there in ten."

"Did you check his cards?"

I shook my head. Felt the pressure of the blood pulse in the bruises on my forehead.

Ed reached into the cab. The skull wavered on its spine, jaw swinging, as Ed dug around the body. He pulled his hand back wrapped around a stained leather square.

"Nathan Jones," he read, "43. Nebraska."

"Kids?"

"Yeah. Three, looks like. Older boy, two girls."

"Somebody out there missing him." I tugged at the back door of the camper. It fell away from its hinges, but the weeds held it in place. "Somebody's out there looking."

"This can't be the same camper, Cap. This one ain't running, let alone running folks off the road. My guess is he ran this guy off years ago, and we just never found 'em."

I gave up on the back door and walked around to the front. "It is him, though—that's him." There was nothing left of the passenger side windshield. Bits of red cloth hung in ribbons from the edges of broken glass. "This is the same camper—I know it."

"It ain't in two places at once, Cap."

I pulled a piece of shredded cloth from the glass and felt the tightness in my chest wring those cracked ribs. "This here is a man divided from himself, Ed. He's everywhere at once."

"Let's get back on the road," Ed said, slipping the wallet into his pocket. "I'm driving, this time—least till we get your head looked at." He slid behind the wheel, propping his peg leg against the gearshift.

We headed back around Rodger's Bluff, out onto the open plain.

"Surprised we never got a call in on that old camper, 'specially for a family man," Ed said. "All those kids, missing their dad."

A family man. Thinking hurt. "How are your kids, Ed?"

Ed glanced at me, eyebrows raised. "Oh, fine. Andy—he can shoot a hole clear through a quarter at a hundred yards. Ben's so good with the horses he could talk one off a cliff, all sweet-like. May's got her first boyfriend—nice kid . . . You should get you some, Cap."

"Some what?"

"Kids. Family. Someone to miss you when you're gone."

I nodded, but it made my head spin. My vision grew cloudy. "I think I may have hit myself harder than I thought, Ed. Having trouble seeing."

"Aw shit!" Ed shouted, laying his foot on the gas.

"Jesus, Ed, it's fine."

"No, it's not—it's him and his damn dust cloud."

I spun in my seat and my head kept spinning, but I pinned my eyes down on the mangled front grill of the Winnebago. It sped up behind us, pouring dust into the sky. The glass of the windshield was dark, but I caught a flash of that salt-and-pepper behind the dash.

Ed gripped the wheel, tires sliding in the dirt. The Winnebago loomed large to the left. It felt like the very road itself tipped and dumped us onto our roof, rolling across the prairie. The siren lights shattered. The roof folded in. The shocks shook us like an angry rattlesnake as we landed back on the wheels.

I rested my forehead on the dashboard, waiting for the world to stop spinning. I heard Ed, then, panting like a thirsty coyote. Heard him grunt. There was a whine building in him that set my teeth on edge.

I opened my eyes as much as I dared—saw Ed heaving his shoulder against the caved-in driver's door. It crushed in on him like a tin can, pinning his good leg down to the seat. It didn't look so good anymore. He pounded at the door.

"Hold on, Ed, I'll get the saw from the back."

"Them damn birds are coming!" He clawed at the edge of the window, his nails folding back.

"Just a minute, buddy, I got you." I fumbled at my door handle.

"Hurry, they're coming!" His eyes rolled from me to the mirror.

"I don't think they'd eat you, Ed—though thanks to you, I can't be sure." I staggered out of the truck and leaned on it, sliding along to the tool chest in the back. The Winnebago's dust trail faded off down the road.

"I can't move my leg!" Ed flailed in the cab, shaking the truck. His voice sounded tattered, like the screams holding there had ripped his throat.

I pulled the chest open and popped the latch on the saw case. I snapped the blade in place.

A gunshot burst inside the car, then three more. What was left of the windows crumbled.

"Ed!" I slammed the tool chest closed and ran to his door.

His fists pressed against his ears, his right hand wrapped around the revolver.

"Ed, what are you doing?" I started dragging the saw across the doorframe.

"Worked last time." He slumped over in his seat, across the console.

"Ed?" I leaned on the saw.

Ed reached an arm over to the passenger door handle and heaved himself away from his seat, trailing blood and stretching sinew, skin, and muscle over the console and into the passenger seat.

I wrenched the door from the frame and tossed it into the ditch.

"You'll have to drive now. We can leave that for the crows." He pointed at his leg, still tied to his thigh with ropes of tendon and stringy cords of massacred muscle. Blood filled the bucket of the seat beneath him. His hand dropped into his lap. His eyes went limp in his grey face.

"Oh, fuck, Ed," I said, pounding the roof of the car. "That shit never works twice."

I tossed the saw back in the tool chest and pulled out the shovel. The cold wind turned the wet on my cheeks into a shell.

I paced up and down the road, sucking down breaths of frozen dust till I found a coyote grave. I opened it—a deep one. I wrapped Ed around what had been his good leg, right alongside the coyote. Gave them both a salute—just in case. I put the carbon steel leg in the tool chest. "They're going to miss you, Ed. I'm going to miss you."

Two of the tires had gone low, but the truck still drove, and I raced it back to the old Winnebago as fast as I dared go on the dirt, the dust from the dragging tires kicking up into my face through the hole where a door should be.

I backed across the field and hitched the chain to the back of the rusty wreck and dragged it from the trees. Door panels popped off into the tall grass as the camper scraped free. The skeleton shook apart as I pulled it up the embankment back to the road.

A spot of bright red shone in the dead patch of grass where the camper had rotted.

I climbed from the open driver's seat and walked over.

Another body, dark hair, splayed, in a shredded red shirt and jeans. Just a kid. The driver's boy. His skin had shrunk against his bones, smooth, untouched by crow or coyote. That old camper had shielded him—saved him from scavengers. Maybe that's why the old man was always leading them away, drawing them elsewhere. Feeding them other things. Things no one would miss.

I wrapped him in the thermal blanket from the emergency kit and set him inside the Winnebago, back in the passenger seat, where he belonged.

The old camper tires had long ago rotted dry, but I dragged it down the road, plowing a furrow through the street.

I stacked their bones in the coyote grave with Ed. I covered them over with the dust I'd carved from the road. I piled dry sage bushes over the mound and set them on fire.

I dragged that empty camper right up the side of the bluff, yanking it around the switchbacks, and I dropped the thing over Dead Man's Curve. It was a thousand dusty pieces before it ever hit the bottom, scattering itself over the cars it had chased down.

I dangled my legs over the edge and watched through Ed's binoculars at the line of dust already cutting through the plain, its hungry little stowaways flashing their feathers.

A billow of dust rose as the speck—that same old Winnebago—stopped with a jerk at the grave. It idled. The dust settled around it. Crows circled above, their screams carrying up the side of the mountain.

They dropped, then, and fell on the camper. The screech of metal and the shriek of birds echoed off the surrounding bluffs till it sounded like the earth itself had torn open and hell was pouring through.

As the sounds faded, the dust settled, the air cleared, not a bird in the sky. Not a car on the road. No sign of the Winnebago. Just a rising column of sage smoke.

I stood, pulled Ed's leg from the truck, and pressed the foot against the rear bumper, leaning on it, adding a leg of my own, shoved the truck over the edge. It rattled over, down, and settled in the scrap bowl.

I hitched Ed's leg over my shoulder and hiked down the road, around the switchbacks, and stared out across the prairie. In the winter, everything looks dead. Everything snaps, if you bend it. Everything scavenges, and nothing worth missing is left behind.

IN TONGUES

PASTOR THOMAS MINSTREL ran one hand over Miranda's bulging stomach. His other clutched a microphone. Beads of sweat ran down the microphone's shaft and trailed along its cord like dewdrops on a cobweb. Miranda watched the droplets, afraid to raise her eyes to the hissing crowd.

"Seventeen and a sinner!" Pastor Minstrel didn't need the microphone. The speakers hummed with the effort of filtering his voice. "What kind of lesson is that for our children—to see one so young follow Satan into the sins of the flesh?"

The crowd mumbled assent and raised their hands as if their palms cupped the air below the low ceiling, as if together they held it aloft.

Miranda flinched as moisture landed on her face and thought maybe the pastor had flung sweat at her, wondered if that made it holy water. Wondered if her skin would start to hiss.

She tried to swallow the hitch in her throat and bit her lip to still its tremble. It seemed the entire county had turned out to shame her. Even people she'd never seen inside the church were lifting up their hands and convulsing with the Holy Spirit.

"Repent!" Pastor Minstrel's red face had fogged his glasses. He pulled them off and licked the lenses clear. "Bring Jesus back into your heart." He stomped toward her as the crowd roared.

Miranda's hands rose to cover her belly. There was a gentle flutter under her fingertips, a deep stirring in her core that grew more frantic the louder the crowd screamed. As if the little thing inside felt the Spirit, too—as if it knew what she had tried to do. *But I didn't. Don't accuse me.* Her breath caught on the lump in her throat.

"Do you know what I found this morning?" Pastor Minstrel turned from the crowd to face Miranda. The congregation went silent. His heavy breaths rushed over the microphone, amplified through the room. Hair stuck to his damp forehead, and Miranda focused on the line where the yellow faded into grey at the roots. His suit smelled like wet wool and cologne.

Miranda shook her head.

Pastor Minstrel stomped across the stage to the altar. His footfalls caused the carpeted risers to sway. Miranda felt nauseated.

He ripped a gold-sequined cloth from over a small mound resting there.

The congregation gasped. Women shrieked, and a hundred hands raised to painted mouths. Pastor Minstrel struggled with the smile dancing in the corner of his mouth. He turned to Miranda till it was tamed into a stern frown. He spun back to the crowd.

"Mr. Allen's lost lamb. Or what's left of it. Coyotes chewed it raw and left its remains right here on the steps of this very church. A lamb! Slain! Just as your spirit has been slain by the devil!"

Miranda glanced up at the crowd and saw Jake's face—handsome, pale, but almost as sweaty as the pastor's. Dripping and terrifying, like that night in the hayloft.

Well, he knows now. Not my lonely secret anymore. She felt the baby stir against her hand. *Ready to meet your daddy?*

~

Miranda pressed the vinegar-soaked rag into the creases of a ceramic angel's robe. A wall of holy glass eyes stared down at her from her mother's mismatched row of curio cabinets: some large and doe-eyed, some tiny black pinpricks. A crowded flock of angels with golden halos and outstretched palms, all covered in a layer of dust and dirt that blew in from the dustbowl fields. *Probably dried cow shit, too. More like bullshit.* Their painted faces all smiled softly, frozen in serenity.

She glanced over her shoulder to see if her mother had seen her smirk. But Mrs. Datlan was staring deep into the bottom of a bag of Cheetos, her round feet propped up by her floral brocade recliner.

Miranda moved on to the next angel, polishing away the grime.

"That's right, you dirty girl. Wash the angels, wash your sins away." Mrs. Datlan's evangelizing was punctuated by a series of loud crunches.

Miranda stared at the expansive wall of angels. Their eyes always seemed to follow her.

"I would have washed it away. You wouldn't let me." She ground the rag deeper into the lines of a ceramic angel's face. The paint of its eyes came away against the rough cloth.

Mrs. Datlan struggled out of her chair, spilling Cheetos across the dingy carpet. "If you think any child of mine is going to murder my grandbaby with the help of some sin-spewing doctor, then all the angels in the world can't help you, girl."

Orange-powdered fingers raked across Miranda's face.

"I'd beat you bloody if I could. But you're carrying a blessing, even if it is a bastard one. Now finish up."

Miranda's hand shook as she reached for the next angel, ringing the figures against each other like small bells. "And when did I stop being your blessing, Mama? When did I become your curse?"

Mrs. Datlan crumpled the empty Cheetos bag and threw it onto the sagging, dusty corduroy chair that still occupied the center of the room, its cushion five years cold. "You're not my Miranda. My Miranda left me." Mrs. Datlan's voice broke. She slouched back to her chair.

Miranda nodded as she scraped the face from another angel. "True enough. She left with Dad."

"Dad is with the angels. You can never go there now."

"The damn angels are everywhere." Miranda let her fingers loosen, felt the figure slip, and watched it fall to pieces at her feet.

Her mother howled. The baby stirred. *That's right, little angel. They'll holler and you'll dance, just like I always did. But not anymore. I've had enough.*

Jake twisted her hair in his fist. She pressed her back against the tractor tire and tried to turn away, but he gripped her chin and wrenched her face to meet his.

"I don't get any say in this? And how do I even know it's mine, huh? You little slut."

"Jake, I didn't even want to—"

He hit her stomach and drove her breath from her. She gulped air, drew in a stuttering gasp, and his fist came again. Her scalp burned as her hair slid through his fingers. Her knees hit the ground in a cloud of dirt that rose and choked her.

"I'm. Not. Paying. No. Fucking. Child. Support." He drove each word in with a kick.

Miranda curled around her middle. She heard the soft scraping click of Jake's knife. The same one he'd used to carve their initials in the barn loft. The same one he'd used to cut a lock of her hair. She remembered how his skin smelled like sunlight and hay as she'd kissed his neck while he carved a heart around their initials.

Adrenaline hit her like a white-hot flash and she was on her feet, reaching for the tractor's ladder rungs. A sharp line of pain spread at her ankle where he slashed at her legs as she scrambled into the cab and slammed down the lock.

Jake pounded against the window. Miranda reached for her bloody sock and saw the tractor key in the ignition. A green rabbit's foot dangled from its eye.

Jake's face disappeared from the window as the tractor shook itself awake. His shouts sounded weak and distant over the rumble of the diesel engine. Miranda rolled the tractor forward. Jake followed, stabbing at the thick tires with his knife.

Miranda rubbed at the bruises spreading across her belly. Bile rose in her raw throat. Her rage swelled, heart rate pumping blood from her ankle, blood to her face, blood beneath the tight skin of her stomach. She slammed the gear into reverse and thrust her foot against the gas. The tractor shuddered and lurched backward.

Jake's bobbing head disappeared from view. His scream ripped through the hot, open air of the ranch.

Miranda squeezed her eyes shut. She shoved at the stiff gear and drove forward, then backed up again. She imagined the scream travelling forever across the vast Wyoming plain, kicking up trails of dust in the barren ground. The nearest thing for it to reach was the distant white speck of Pastor Minstrel's church, and the dust-colored cinderblock jailhouse beside it. Miranda shivered and pressed the gas again. The screaming pitched, then stopped. *Angel, if your blood could stop the crops, maybe his will water them back to life. Maybe we just need the right blood to end this.*

She sat in silence and rested her forehead against the window, watching the line of dust rise behind Officer Barnes' car as he sped over the fallow fields, chasing the fading scream toward the idling tractor.

Maybe they'll think it was an accident. Another farm boy fallen, caught under the grinding weight of his father's living, of his future. She pressed at the lumps rising across her belly and wiggled her toes in the shoe that was filling with blood. Pain shot up her leg. She couldn't run. Not far, anyway. Not fast enough. Her lower back ached. The pain wrapped around her as if embracing her from behind. She shut off the tractor and squeezed the green rabbit's foot in her fist.

Her foot slid off the ladder rung and she fell into the blood-soaked dust. Shreds of Jake's white t-shirt, stained the oxblood color of gore and fallow dirt, were scattered around her. His mangled hat, bristled with torn hair, rolled in the wind.

Miranda crawled over the shallow dunes of the field toward the oncoming police car. Dry stalks of long-dead crops pierced her palms. The pain in her middle grew into an insistent pressure. Her thighs and arms shook and she fell into the dirt. Her tongue felt as dry as the grit against her cheek. She waited for Officer Barnes, prayed he'd get to her quickly.

Sorry, baby. I know a girl needs a daddy, but a daddy has no need of a girl, and anyway, I'd have found you a better one if I'd known you were coming. Oh God, you're coming.

~

Miranda sat in the jailhouse, kneeling by her steel cot, and pressed her palms against her ears to shut out the amplified sound of Pastor Minstrel's gibberish that streamed from the speakers next door. Her lip curled and bile rose in her throat like a scream. She heaved until blood ran down her chin and her stomach clenched in spasm. The bruises from Jake's fists and feet had darkened to burgundy, deepening every hour as if they ate through her like acid. Pain wrapped around her lower back, and when it squeezed her, the little flutter inside her would still. When the pain eased, the baby would stretch, fighting back against the tightening of its space.

Waves of contractions washed over her, each one building off the ebb of the one before. She caught her breath and screamed. *Too soon. I'm not ready. She's not ready.*

"Sheriff! Officer Barnes! Help!" The squeeze cut off her cry. A flush of warm water slid out from between her legs and washed into the pool of bloody vomit.

No one came. The whole county was crowded into Pastor Minstrel's church, praying for Jake Griffith's soul. The shrieking of their holy delirium rattled the thin glass of the jailhouse windows.

Miranda pulled herself up onto the steel cot, rolled onto her back, and gripped her knees. The world spun around the slickness between her thighs.

～

Pastor Minstrel had built the Pentecostal Church of Our Lord exactly so that at 8:17 in the morning—or, as he called it, 7:77—the shadow of the cross atop the pointed steeple would fall across the squat grey jail next door.

"They will hear us sing!" he'd shouted that day five years ago, as he cut the ribbon stretched across the new church door. He wielded the scissors like a sword. "They will hear us praise Him! Oh del hoo laloay mala koole hale!" His tongues rattled the speakers and startled sleeping moths from the eaves along the western side of the exterior walls, bathing the jailhouse with his voice. A halo of dust had risen in the fields, concussed by a tide of sound waves.

～

"Life is sacred," Pastor Minstrel said to the crowd assembled in the small yard between the church and the jail. Miranda's baby girl slept, limp and tiny, cradled in the crook of the pastor's arm. "New life is a gift from God."

The sun beat down on the pastor's silver-yellow hair, and onto the baby's pink face.

Did they put sunscreen on her? Miranda shuffled her feet. The shackles around her ankles dragged like a chain plough in the dry grass.

"Here, in the sight of God, we name this child. What is her name?"

"Rebecc—" Miranda started.

"Tiffany! Her name is Tiffany." Mrs. Datlan stepped forward. Her fists were clenched in front of her holey Tweety Bird t-shirt, her lips orange and twisted into a grimace.

Miranda dropped her head. Her vision spun, the edges of her sight darkening and brightening in waves that threatened to buckle her knees, wash her down to the dirt.

"Tiffany!" the pastor shouted. The speakers rattled, and the baby's name echoed off the jailhouse wall behind Miranda's back.

"We will raise this child in the light of God. We will guide her soul away from her mother's sin." Pastor Minstrel paced. The microphone cord slithered through the grass like a snake.

Miranda tilted her head back and rested it against the rough grey cinderblocks of the jailhouse wall. Tears dripped off her jaw. She squinted down her nose at the crowd. Mrs. Datlan wove through the congregation, pausing at each member, dropping a bulging Walmart bag at their feet.

"This young lady has brought the wrathful eye of God to our town. She has invited Satan into our community. Do you know that she wanted to end the life of this child? To shut out the spark of God's life—a gift granted to her in her darkest hour, and she shunned it." He stalked in front of his audience, driving his feet into the dry powder of the earth. Baby Tiffany's head bobbed, unsupported. *Open your eyes little angel. Just once, so I can see.*

Pastor Minstrel sauntered to Miranda and bent down to her face. "And then she took from us one of our own. She took from this child a loving father. She has no place among godly people."

Miranda squeezed her eyes shut against the sun. Her knees trembled.

"As her sin bloomed, our fields grew fallow. As her spirit withered, so did our crops. And we did nothing. But our God is a forgiving God. Repent and pray with me." He dropped to his knees.

The crowd raised their open palms to the sky. Their mouths gaped, and from their throats rose a guttural cry. Their tongues wagged over their teeth.

"Kaholy nabida kala haveel lalakohlay!" The pastor screamed into the microphone. The metal speakers shook dust from the church eaves. The baby began to wail, its tiny face screwed up in outrage.

The crowd's fervor swelled. Miranda's mother dropped to the grass, convulsing, orange drool running down her neck and staining the collar of her shirt.

"Let the Holy Spirit take you all! Sing in the Spirit with me!" One of the mounted speakers shook free of a bolt and hung at an angle, rattling against the dry wood siding.

The crowd swayed, shaking their hands at the sky and singing in the language of angels.

"It is our duty, as agents of the Lord, to show the unsaved the value of the life taken from us! Show her what we think of her shunning the gifts of God! Show her what we think of her pact with Satan!" The speaker shook itself free from its remaining bolt and tumbled into the grass.

As one, the crowd dropped their hands and reached for the plastic bags at their feet. Out came handfuls of dirty ceramic angels. Dusty again, and faceless.

Miranda pressed herself against the wall. Her chin trembled. She looked to Pastor Minstrel and shook her head. *No, not like this.*

He smiled and licked his teeth. His eyes slid to Mrs. Datlan. She nodded, weeping, eyes still rolling in spiritual reverie. "All the angels in the world can't save you, not now, and I brought 'em all."

Pastor Minstrel's microphone shook. "Show her what the Lord thinks of those who would snuff out the spark of God's light!"

The angels flew at her. Their wings shattered against the cinderblocks around her. They broke against her forehead and her teeth. They cut into her stomach, still swollen from birth, still red. They tore at her arms, her legs, and caught in her hair. She tasted the dirt of them, felt their grit in the blood that filled her mouth. And as she sank to the grass, she smelled smoke, and saw, through a red haze, the speaker—smoldering in the dry grass, small flames licking up the side of the church wall as Pastor Minstrel held her baby aloft and hollered nonsense to the sky from a vortex of faceless angels.

THE EYES OF
SALTON SEA

WE NEVER EXPECTED anyone to come back. Tourists won't eat fish that might have eaten other tourists, nor bathe on beaches where the sand is bone and the water dark. They don't sip drinks on a shore that comes and goes, rises and falls in floods and droughts, and every time it leaves behind a fresh blanket of dead fish. But the scavengers came. First, birds—for the fish. Then, men—for the wrecks that poked out of the fishbone sand like grave markers.

From the presidential suite of the abandoned resort, our balcony was a crow's nest where we watched for the treasure hunters and filmmakers who came in investors' SUVs, towing rented boats. They brought their cameras and robots, their hired divers and diggers, and enough money for the few of us who had stayed behind to make a living. It was a new kind of tourist. Not rich, but wild. Dreamers, like Alden, all after gold and tragic stories. The Salton Sea had both.

We housed them on the first floor of the resort, and I'd cook the fish they didn't think twice about—sometimes fish they'd bring in themselves, their grins big—addicted to finding things, if only dinner.

And they'd ask Alden questions—interview him with their wide cameras. He'd show them his gold and pearl crucifix. But he never spoke of the ship in the inlet.

It was the sort of secret we didn't even tell each other. Because someday the water might clear again, or recede even further, and all that would be left is gold and pearls. A treasure beach. When the shore shifts again.

I didn't like the big cameras or the questions or the way they stepped across the dry fish bones as if it was any other dirt beneath their feet. I encouraged the sunflowers and yucca claiming the old golf course, read the books left forgotten in the bedside drawers. Sewed the ballroom linens into new sundresses. I fed stale crumbs of ice cream cones to the swarms of birds who seemed to be the only ones who understood what it meant to belong here.

The treasure hunters asked Alden to guide them and he'd decline, on account of his feet—and they'd think he meant that it hurt, or that he wasn't a strong hiker or swimmer. But I knew he was afraid that the curse would take another piece of him. Like it was waiting for the rest of him.

~

When we were young, the water was clear and fresh. My brother and I would swim in the shallows, where a rainbow of polished round stones shone up at us like a thousand eyes. We'd watch the yachts bob across the sparkling water and listen to the music carrying over the waves. Alden celebrated the popularization of the bikini while I cupped my hands in the water, knowing that somewhere along the shore, the Beach Boys were swimming. While our mother cleaned resort rooms, we spent our days in an endless vacation.

We thought the sea was clear because it was young—unmarked by the wear of anxiety that had weathered our mother's face. We thought it was beautiful. But a young sea has a childlike temper, and one night it swallowed the towns and the desert around it. It had rained for a week straight and the swollen farm canals flushed their *agua negra* into the Salton Sea and the sea heaved. Some tourists ran for the boats, and some ran for the surrounding hills. Alden and I perched on the roof of the resort. Mother stayed below, going from room to room—cleaning, as if in competition with the scouring wave.

When the water withdrew back into its bed—then lower and lower still, till it shrank back to a fraction of its former self—the people withdrew as well, each drifting further from the other till nothing was left but the broken bits of resort towns and those of us willing to stay, and those who had died in the water. Like mother, her apron a shroud, a duster bouquet of wet feathers in her stiff fingers. The receding water had pulled her from the hotel, as if calling her to the beach to play. Her hair had caught on the wrought iron fence and tied her there. I spent hours untying those dark, wet knots. I wouldn't let Alden cut them.

When the tourists left, the workers followed—their white service jackets the same no matter where they went. And then the fishermen left—back to the ocean coast, to happier shores where the fish didn't tie your gut in knots. To ancient oceans with mature tides, not the fickle temper of this inland sea.

The town was nearly deserted. The big hotels sat like empty seashells, still stinking of the life that used to be there, pieces beginning to break off around the edges. The news declared that the pleasure towns had turned to ghost towns. We supposed, then, that we were ghosts. And we haunted our old resort, stretching across luxury linens in the presidential suite. We needed that familiar shore, needed to be near the cluster of concrete crosses set back from the water in the tall, dry grass. Near where mother lay safe under the desert. I dug my roots deep into the rocks.

The beach, now extending hundreds of meters from the resort doorway, shone white with crushed fish bones. Their desiccated bodies plated the bone sand like scaled armor. The sharp jaws and jagged ribs of wrecked yachts poked out of the slick mud.

As everything dried, baked under the desert sun, the toxins that had stripped that water to glass clarity concentrated in the remaining sea, so that at high noon the water was the color of a sunset and a chalky residue clung to anything that had been wet.

When the wind blew, that powdered bone carried the poisons right between our teeth, into the corners of our eyes. It flavored the back of our throats like a bitter pill. If you squinted and held your nose, it was paradise.

We turned to the beach looking for whatever might be left of our lives—or anything we might use to forge new ones. We ran past the old shoreline out onto the mud flat that had once been seabed and across the rainbow eye stones that had watched as our world fell apart.

The new shoreline rose and fell as if the earth beneath it rocked. It carved out twisting inlets and hidden lagoons. We followed it, hiking the topography of old seafloor, near the hills where the stones betrayed an ancient high-water mark that promised a future of nothing but sea. We came to a stretch of choppy shallow water surrounding the battered hull of a ship. It was larger than the yachts of rich musicians that had dotted the water before the flood. It had a round hull and two tall masts that trailed tattered sails like funnel webs. A third mast lay beside it, half-buried in sand. The wood was crusted with an armor of sprawling arthropods.

Alden waded out into the water toward the wreck. He crawled around the hull in search of gold and silver, but instead we found bodies—staring up out of the water, eyes like a thousand polished stones.

I stepped lightly into the water. I was scared to see my brother splashing, leaving a foaming wake that disturbed the surface. He bent and dragged his fingers through the rocks, looking for coins. I nervously filled my sundress pockets with pretty stones, my own small treasures. I paced the shallows and sat in the stones and twisted my hair, tasting that new chemical tang that hung suspended in the still air on the back of my tongue.

The way the water nudged the bodies, they looked as if they slept, and might wake and grab my ankle. Small brown birds with feathers as fine as hair bobbed their heads in the water and nibbled at the corners of their mouths.

Alden pulled his hands from the water, cupping them below his face and smiling for the first time since the flood. His fingers—wrinkled and stinking from the water—clutched a gold and pearl crucifix.

He wanted to stay and find more. He wanted to move the bodies, comb the wreckage, pick it all apart like a bird on a fish. But the sky was growing dark, threatening rain. I backed away from the water, afraid of the fickle shore and storm-fed tides. Alden was forced to follow. He held his hands to the sky and marked the spot in his memory, tracing the old shoreline pattern on the hill above.

As we walked back to the resort, the bright white beach began to snap under our feet. The water turned red as rust, and the rainbow of stones was buried under stiff dried fish.

He tried to go back the next day, but the skin of his feet had turned the color of the dry tilapia shore, the whites of his eyes the color of the rusted-out campers in the surrounding desert. Whether it was poison from the toxic water, a corpse virus, or a ghost ship curse, he didn't care. He limped, feet dragging through the fish, till the fever slowed him, then stopped him, and he knelt in the crackling granules of beach.

"Bones," Alden said, running his hands through the splinters. "Some are fish, some are birds, bet some are from the yachts we never found."

I knew he said it to scare me.
It worked.

The scavengers paid for their rooms at the resort, sometimes in food, sometimes in doubloons, or, when Alden wasn't looking, with pretty stones or sea glass. They tied their boats at the water's edge—a long walk, now, from the resort's door, and getting longer every year. They hiked across the bone beach, inspecting destroyed structures, tiptoeing around the bulbs and fins of unexploded dummy bombs from the naval base on the north shore. They followed old train tracks that lead straight into the water, and tied rags around their faces to keep from breathing in the dust cloud of evaporated pesticides and fertilizers. They dug in the sand and trawled from their boats, and—if they were brave or foolish enough—dove in the water.

They found artifacts of the Salton Sea's heyday. Speed boat parts, depression glass shards, even a flask engraved with F.S. that the diver swore was Sinatra's.

Some would ask about the lost Spanish galleon. Others would laugh, and the night would be spent telling tall tales of tall ships.

The diver with pale brown eyes the color of sand drying in the sun was the first to ever ask about a curse. He'd met a fisherman, now working far from here, who spoke of his old seaside town and its flood wrecks and the riches no local would touch, and which no diver could find.

Alden just laughed and shook his head. *Don't scare away the business* is the motto of every haunted shore. Stories sell, but paradise sells better.

"I'm going to find that wreck," the golden-eyed diver promised.

Every season there's at least one treasure hunter who wants to buy more than room and board from me. If I feel like it, I say yes. If he has nice eyes.

The golden-eyed diver had scars like he'd been at war with the sea. The snaking lightning of jellyfish whips. The dotted crescent of a small shark's appetite. The starburst of a rogue harpoon.

I traced them with my fingertips and gathered his stories. And then he asked for mine.

"I can tell you know about the wreck," he said, smiling with half his face, scolding with the other half.

"It's just an old wives' tale," I said.

"Tell me anyway. What do the wives say?"

"There's a ship, somewhere out there. Too big and too old for the Salton Sea, and no one remembers it. There are bodies aboard—rich people with nice jewelry. Gold. Pearls. They must have gone down in a flood, or when the water receded."

"But no one has ever been there, to see what's left?"

"The water changes. Sometimes it's sea, sometimes it's sand. Bone. It might have been re-submerged in toxic water, or buried in a sandstorm. There are people who say they've seen it, but no one has ever seen it twice."

"Ah. Well, not much point then. How far have you been out onto the sea bed?"

His probing fingertips and thick red wine made me sleepy, dizzy. I wanted to lay my head on his sun-hot chest and sleep.

"A half day, no more. I could never sleep on those bones."

~

In the morning, he was gone, as adventurers often are—but this was the first time I felt sad for it. Alden noticed.

"You wanted that one to stay?"

"Wouldn't have minded. Best he left, though. He only wanted the wreck."

"They all want the wreck, even the ones who don't know it. You didn't tell him where, did you?"

"No. Told him it was probably long buried. Or never existed." I toyed with the stones in my pocket.

Alden nodded approval and handed me coffee. "Maybe he'll come back for you after he's made his fortune."

"Ass."

Some did come back, but not for me. They came for treasure.

I licked my lips, tasting him still. "I hope he does come back, though. He had good stories."

I stretched my sore back and made the climb to the roof to clean the day's fish. The birds had learned to catch the strings of offal I threw over the side. I named them by the way their pinions pivoted on the wind—after fish, the way they dove for each scrap. Marlin was the largest. He'd eat till the breeze couldn't carry him; then he'd drift into the sunflowers below.

The rooftop was a mess of fish guts and bird shit, awaiting a long-overdue rain. The horizon promised a storm. Black clouds bubbled up above the dark strip of distant water studded with the bright jewels of treasure divers' boats. The rain would come and the shore would creep closer. The water would get deeper and bury her secrets.

Far to the north of the gathered boats, closer to the brewing storm and the distant hills, the water seemed rougher. The white gauze of chopped waves laced its surface.

A red boat bobbed on the inlet.

I dropped the pail of fish. Heard the frantic beat of descending wings behind me as I raced back down the concrete stairs, around and around, back to the lobby.

"Alden! Alden, he's at the inlet! He's in the water!"

Alden paled. "I don't know what to do about that."

"You have to stop him. We have to save him!"

"How? Dive in after him? Set a net? Bait a hook with your pussy?"

"Fuck you, Alden! We have to go."

"Go to the beach. I'll meet you there." He limped out from behind the desk.

I didn't wait to ask his plan. I ran.

My feet found their way across the bone beach, each footstep snapping down, sinking beneath the small skulls, their empty sockets folding shut under my toes, raising a fine dust of chemical calcium. I dodged bubbling mud pools and slid over polished eye stones. I grazed my shins on young yucca growing up from the new beach, until my knees hit the bone grit of the hidden inlet. The water was deeper than it had been years ago. Only the tip of a mast was visible above the water, its scrap of sail like a grey flag.

The red boat rocked offshore, anchor dropped into the dark water, her deck bare, her winch line taut.

I advanced as far as I dared, my toes right up against where the sand turned wet.

"Robb!"

I knew he couldn't hear me. There was no one else on the boat.

SARAH READ

His whole life was strung on that winch line. I twisted my hair into fisherman's knots. The sky had begun to growl.

Alden came stumbling up behind me, a large package under his arm, his pack slung over his shoulder. He let it fall to the sand and pulled the ripcord, and a small inflatable raft expanded at our feet.

"Is it safe?" I stared at the dark water and the thin rubber bottom of the raft.

"No. Doesn't matter—we have to do this."

We dragged the raft to the chopping waves. I flinched as the water brushed my feet. Alden didn't touch the water. He hopped over the side and pulled me in after.

We cast off and paddled to the idling boat. I climbed over the rail and ran to the winch, slammed the lever, and anxiously watched as the line coiled slowly around the bobbin.

Alden tied the raft to the boat and stumbled to my side, pulling a pair of loppers from his pack. He reached out and clipped the line.

The sprung end whipped across my face. I cried out and fell back against the railing.

"Alden!" I cupped a hand over my bleeding cheek as my vision cleared. "What are you doing?"

He had moved to the side, where he sawed at the anchor line.

"He knows where the wreck is. He'll lead a hundred other divers here. They won't wait for another quake wave or a drought to clear this dark water. They'll have it stripped clean in a day. And everything we've waited for will be gone."

"I wasn't waiting for anything. Is this the only reason you stayed?"

"We'll power the boat out of the inlet and set it adrift."

"What about Robb? He could die down there. Without his line—"

"Just another diving accident."

"You heartless fuck."

"Happens all the time. You think this is the first time a diver's found the wreck? I ought to throw you in, too. Blabbing secrets to a scavenger."

"*You're* a scavenger. No better than them. Worse. How many divers have you left down there? How many?"

Alden threw the boat in gear and angled it toward open water. He steered against the tide as we wound toward the broad horizon, our raft bouncing along the side.

54

I watched the black water behind us. It had gone perfectly still. Even the wake of the boat calmed too quickly. There was no sign of the diver.

~

The other divers noticed Robb's absence. Their competitive nature didn't follow them ashore. They assumed he'd run out of funding, or hope—or that he'd hit a honey spot and camped out. No one would think the worst for hours. Maybe not till his boat was found. If it was found.

I tried to remember how many times I'd heard this conversation. How many divers had been reported lost. I wondered how many I never even knew about.

Alden laughed with the crews, his twisted feet twitching under the table.

They were still gathered in the lobby, increasingly drunk, riding out the storm with an endless supply of stories on their tongues, when the report came in that Robb's boat had been found drifting. Al at the West Shore Casino had spotted it. The police were on their way—a courtesy call.

Alden took the phone from my hand. "No. We haven't seen him since last night. Or was it this morning? Sis, was he there when you got up?" The divers stared into their drinks, cheeks red and ears straining.

I scowled back as the report continued. The boat's line had been cut. Anchor gone. They suspected something—foul play, perhaps by another diver. But they could prove nothing. Gulls make bad witnesses. So do the eyes under the water.

The divers drank more—to Robb, and all the others that came before, to all the souls claimed by the sea.

The ones they would plunder.

Come morning, the divers were strewn about the lobby as if they themselves had been wrecked there, tossed around as if by the storm. Outside, rain hammered the corrugated steel that patched our roof. Steady dripping echoed through the resort halls. The sea had crept closer. Boats that had been anchored to shore now bobbed a hundred meters out. Our raft had been tossed halfway up the shore.

I put rum in the orange juice. Extra grease for the eggs. I knew they'd dive anyway.

I had just set the steaming pots of black coffee on the table when I felt the weight of eyes on my neck and a hand on my waist.

I turned and met a pair of golden eyes, bright like beach agates, shining round like ancient coins.

"Robb!" I threw my arms around his neck. His wet hair dripped cold water over my arms. His neck against my lips tasted like oil and aspirin.

The divers began to groan and pull themselves upright. They rose scowling at the sound of my shriek, but soon switched to cheering as they saw Robb, whole and hale, in my arms.

The commotion brought Alden out of the office. His smile split his face, but his eyes stayed cold.

Breakfast ran long as Robb recounted his survival story—his voice rough, throat salt-water chapped.

He'd felt his line snap. Watched it sink around him in coils, tugged by swift currents. Instead of surfacing, he said, he'd followed the line, followed the current, hoping he might find a treasure trove—a deposit of flotsam.

"Did you?"

"What did you find?"

"The ship," he said.

Every mug slowly lowered. Full forks sunk back to plates.

"Did you go in?"

Robb smiled. He reached into a bag at his wetsuit belt and pulled out a fistful of treasure. Some gold, some silver, some black with oxidization, some glittered with cut stones, bright with pearls.

Nervous laughter circled the table.

"You didn't . . . You wouldn't disturb the remains, though. Must have just been . . . Maybe a box of treasure, right?"

Robb's grin widened. His eyes weren't dilating, but remained fixed discs of gold. "Must have been a chest," he said. "Big pile of goods all in one place."

The nervous laugh circled again. Alden's smile had slipped.

"You register your find yet?" a diver asked.

The hangovers were gone. Sobered with gold lust. Filled up with need.

Robb's round eyes bored into the man who'd asked. "'Course. Sorry if I kept you waiting. Made you worry. But when I saw my boat was gone, I swam to one of yours. Radioed it in while you were down."

No laughter, then.

"Now, about my boat . . . " He slipped the treasure back into his bag, precious metal rattling like chains.

"I'll give you a share in mine till your insurance—"

"You're welcome to come with—"

"I can draw up a contract right now—"

Robb held up his hands for silence. "I only want one partner in this, and it's the man who knows these waters best."

Every diver smiled, sure Robb meant them. Alden looked ill. Robb looked at Alden.

"It's not your feet that stop you from diving. It's what's down there. That ends now. I know you've been waiting a long time. Suit up." Robb tossed a mask at Alden and rose from his chair. He kissed me and took my hand, leading me back to his room.

The divers sat silent behind us like a flock of greedy birds.

~

"You shouldn't have gone into that water," I said. "You shouldn't have taken that gold." I twisted my hair as he buzzed around the room packing his bags.

"I didn't."

"What?"

"I was never in the water. Not there."

My heart dropped like a cut anchor. "But, your boat—"

"I was watching from the shore. By the hill."

I sat on the bed, my hands shaking. Every secret I had now lay naked under his bright eyes, like exposed seafloor under a hot sun.

He knelt before me, ran his fingers over the scab on my cheek. "I saw what he did. I saw you try to stop him." He squeezed my hands between his and leaned in to kiss me again. I pulled back.

"But those coins?"

"From older dives, other shores. I keep them in a jar on my dash, as a reminder."

"Of what?"

"Time. Death. That the sea controls both." He let go of my hands and zipped up his duffel bag.

"Where are you going? What are you going to do?"

"I'm going to put your brother in the water."

My gut heaved and I felt the sea at the back of my throat. "Robb, no. That beach . . . I know you don't believe the stories. Yes, there are bodies under there. And yes, probably treasure, too, but it's not worth it . . . "

"You're right, it's not. Not to me. But it is to your brother—worth lying for, worth killing for. Worth hanging around this ghost town. Must be worth dying for, right?"

"Please, Robb. He did an awful thing. But please don't hurt him."

"I'm not going to. He's going to hurt himself."

I shook my head. "It'll be harder than you think to get him in that water."

"No, it won't."

Most of the boats waited near the shore, hoping Robb would come to them, waiting for him to pass so they could follow. Other boats swept up and down the water line, looking for him. None had seen him lead Alden north, darting from ruin to ruin, across the bone beach to the deep inlet.

Robb had warned me to stay at the hotel. I watched from the roof, from the center of a cloud of birds angry that I hadn't brought fish. I twisted my hair till the ends broke off in my fists.

I waited till they appeared on the far side of the mud flats before I followed.

Robb had no need of a boat, not in the calm black water that followed the storm. He used the same inflatable raft we'd used to sneak onto his boat. The water didn't ripple under their paddles.

They moved toward the spot where the grey flag had been as I crept across the round stones. I watched as Alden slipped a snorkel over his face. Not even a tank. He was still shaking his head, still reluctant. But Robb held out something shiny in his hand. Alden froze.

The gold? A gun? It didn't seem to matter which. Alden slid his legs over the rounded side of the raft. His withered feet dipped into the dark water and his back arched. He dropped into the sea.

The water rippled away from him, the circles widening, growing—till they were a ring of waves cresting back toward open water and shooting up onto the beach, tossing limp tilapia at my feet. I danced away as the water chased me and sheltered in a mound of yucca and cactus at the base of the hill. Over and over, each ring curled into another wave, like a wild tide climbing the shore as if to make the resort waterfront property again.

Robb steered the raft over the unnatural swells, surfing their crests back toward the beach. A wave slid the raft over the sand and deposited it on a pile of drying fish.

There was no sign of Alden.

Robb climbed from the raft and pulled me from my hiding spot, leading me back across the beach toward the resort as tendrils of water spilled across the mud behind us.

"We need to go back for him, Robb." I pulled against his grasp, wanting to turn around. "He'll drown in that tide. Christ, you didn't even give him a tank."

"Would have been a waste of a tank. The thing is done."

"What are you talking about?"

"They have the gold back. Their treasure is returned and they've caught their thief. The curse is broken."

"There's no goddam curse! We need to get him out of the water—he can't swim—"

"He can swim fine. He knows what the water wanted; knew what it would cost him. He didn't steal that gold, he bought it. Now he's paid for it."

He pulled me off the bone beach and into a copse of tall sunflowers.

Behind me came the sound of lapping water. Of music. The Beach Boys playing from a yacht that cruised past the resort. The arcing waves dragged at the beach, pulling dried fish back into the water, leaving fine white powder sand in their wake. I squeezed my eyes shut and swore I could hear laughter, the buzz of neon. The smell of fish frying, not baking on the shore.

I looked out at the sea, waiting to see if the water foamed with hunger, if it would surge right through the front doors and fill the rooms with bones and the dead. But the water had stopped, just kissing the beach. The music continued. Robb hummed along. The people on the yacht danced and waved.

"They can't stop here now—there's nowhere nice enough to stay. But they'll be back. A whole fleet of them. Crowds." Robb reached down and pulled up a fistful of weeds, the small beginnings of my sunflowers. "Better get to work. Let's get this place ready. Clear out the trash and trailers, fill the pool. Clean the rooms."

"What are you doing?" I grabbed the seedling flowers from him and pressed them back into the dirt.

"Treasure hunting." He shook the sticky soil from his hand.

I shook my head. The birds above us, circling, made me even dizzier. Robb placed his scarred hands on my shoulders. They felt like anchors, like heavy stones pressing me in place.

"I'm not the guy who takes treasure out of the sea," he said. "I'm the guy who puts it back. But if I found a billion dollars in treasure, I'd use it to live in a beachfront palace with a beautiful woman. So I don't much see the need to sail off again. I'm staying."

I tore myself out of his grip, spat in his golden eyes, and ran back to the beach, north across the powdered bone to the edge of the water, as close to the hill as I could get.

The water was clear. Fresh as a young sea with a temper. I could see straight to the bottom. There was no Alden. No wreck. There were a thousand smooth stones, round and bright as eyes.

UNDERWATER THING

NOTHING IN THE sea stays still for long. The weights strapped to Mandy's wrists and ankles and the brick tied around her swollen middle wouldn't keep her down there forever. Chains are only as strong as their oxidizer, and even the tightest twist of rope unravels as its proteins do. With time and science, she'd be let go, and Tyler knew it.

Tyler hoped those ties would outlast her flesh and bone, outlast the thin flesh and soft bones of the creature growing inside her. That whatever was left would be scattered, evidence washed up on disparate shores.

He was certain the thing would have been born a monster. It would have been contorted, as twisted as his face had been when he shot his seed into her young body. Her disgust for him would have brined the baby in poison, tainted any creature born of that union. *Girls like her make monsters out of men like me. Breed monsters from us.*

When he'd moved into Karen's home, the whole house smelled of Mandy. Her room was only feet from the one he shared with his new wife. The couch would be warm where she'd been sitting. Her wet towel hung on the bathroom door. Her underwear was in the dryer when he washed his clothes.

He wasn't made of stone.

~

I'm an underwater thing.
Make me a harpy now
Make me a hydra
Make me
Make me Mother
Father
A part of you.
Let the water cut me free.

Tyler lay on his bed, half-watching the news as Karen dressed for a night with her friends.

"Make sure Mandy studies. She has exams tomorrow. And she needs to be in bed by ten." Karen threw her bag over her arm and straightened her jacket.

"Yep. I know, she knows—we're good. She's already in her room studying." Tyler smiled and waved at Karen. She'd be back late, giggling, cabernet on her breath. She'd fall into bed, sleep deeply, wake late, and leave for work hungover in the morning. It was her night-out tradition.

She repeated her instructions at Mandy's door. Tyler heard Mandy's quiet, agreeable response. She was a quiet, agreeable girl. They blew kisses and Karen left.

The news droned on. The ticker hadn't changed for ten minutes as talking heads repeated the same points, rephrased, with increasing drama.

At ten, Tyler listened as Mandy brushed her teeth. He heard her gargle and gag, counted out the quiet minute while she braided her hair. He heard the bathroom doorknob turn and saw the rectangle of light spread across the hallway floor, till the switch was flicked and it went dark.

"Night, Tyler," she said from the hall.

"Night, Mandy," he said.

The news faded into a sitcom, then an infomercial; then he went to her room.

Karen kept her hand over her eyes in the morning, flinching from the light, so she didn't see the pale shock of her daughter's face. She didn't notice the tangled hair, lack of makeup, and glazed eyes. Eyes that moved too quickly, that jumped to every movement or sound. She didn't notice Mandy's raw bottom lip, or the way Tyler couldn't stop staring at it, couldn't sit still.

But the school noticed. They called by lunchtime—said Mandy wasn't feeling well, that she had failed all her exams, wouldn't eat.

"Didn't she study last night?" Karen asked, rubbing her face with both palms.

"I saw her in her room, at her desk. I assumed she was studying." Tyler unfolded a newspaper, spread it open in front of his face.

"Well, next time, check."

"She probably just has a cold. Maybe they'll let her retake the tests when she's feeling better." The newsprint stuck to his damp fingers as he tried to turn the page.

"Maybe the nice teachers will." There was a tone to her voice that Tyler didn't like.

"I would have let her."

"You must have been a nice teacher." This tone was better. Friendly, attentive.

"Some thought so. Some didn't."

"Sounds fair. Do you miss your students?"

"I used to." He lowered the paper and smiled. "I like being here." *I've found a replacement.*

"I wish I could stay here with you." She groaned as she got up from her chair and her knee joints popped. "I've got a long afternoon on my feet ahead of me. Wedding season approaches, and everyone wants to try six different styles."

"Not me, I like the one I've got."

She laughed and kissed his bald head. "Call me when Mandy gets home; let me know how she's doing."

"Yes, dear," he said.

She kissed him again, then left for the salon.

Tyler set down the paper, his sweaty handprints staining its edges.

He went to Mandy's room and pulled the sheets off her bed, reeling when the scent of her ballooned off the fabric and surrounded him. He'd had no idea she was a virgin. At sixteen, the way kids acted these days, she was probably the only one in her school. How many of his school staff meetings had been concerning strategies for keeping kids from copulating in every corner of the building? The librarian had been at her wits' end, stumbling over amorous students in the stacks. She'd never stumbled over him, though. He'd been careful. Even then, none of his girls had been virgins.

He dragged the basket of bedding into the basement and stuffed the sheets and mattress cover into the washer. He added the sheets from his and Karen's bed as well. It was sheet-washing day. That was all. A routine chore.

He started the washer and watched it spin, the rough concrete floor digging into his knees. He pulled himself up and headed to the corner of the basement, where he'd set up some office space for himself—a salvaged chem lab table, a few plank shelves, and a chair that would only swivel to the right. Tyler brushed away a veil of cobweb and pulled down his old copy of *Chemistry for Teachers*. The center pages had been removed, re-bound with a section of blank pages. He let it fall open. Names and dates scrolled down the left page and partway down the right. The last date was over two years ago. He pulled a pen from the coffee-molecule mug on the desk and wrote:

Mandy Thurs 9/10/09 Home, Mandy's room.

He traced his finger over the old list of names, felt the indentations where his pen had pressed the ink into the paper, and remembered.

The buzz of the wash cycle startled him. He stood stiffly from his chair and moved the sheets to the dryer.

~

Friday linen laundry became a tradition as he filled the page in his book with dates and ditto ticks.

Mandy's Friday face had become a nightmare mask as she failed quiz after quiz, and all her exams. And the more she failed, the more Karen kept her home, with Tyler.

"What's wrong with her?" Karen had asked one night as they got ready for bed.

"Hormones, maybe," Tyler had said. He'd deliberately forgotten the milk at the market that day, hoping Karen would run out to the store and give him a moment alone with Mandy, but she'd shrugged and said she'd stop the next day.

"You don't think it's drugs, do you?"

"If it is, she's getting them at school. She doesn't go anywhere else."

Karen huffed. "That school. I wish she could just homeschool here with you."

"I wish that, too." He hardened at the thought, and had to tuck himself back.

Karen stalked off to the bathroom to brush her teeth, and Tyler focused his thoughts. Maybe he needed to slow down. Back off. If the change was too noticeable, he could be caught.

He heard Karen yelp, and she came running back into the room gripping a fistful of toilet paper. "*Tyler,*" she shrieked.

"What? What's wrong?"

She held the clump of paper out to him. In the center was a pink plastic stick. A blue plus sign showed in the round window on its side.

"Tyler, she's pregnant. That's what's wrong. Oh my God. Tyler, what do we do?"

Icy sweat spread across his forehead and back. *Fuck.*

"Pull her out of that school. I'll take care of her here."

Karen blamed a boy from school. She even called his poor parents, screaming at them. Tyler listened from the living room, staring at the dark staircase that led to the bedrooms.

"What have you done?" Karen demanded of Mandy.

Mandy shook her head, crying.

Tyler slipped her a bottle of pills that should have done the trick, but they just made her ill. He pushed her down the stairs, but her little sin outlived her sprained wrist.

Karen's rage grew in proportion to Mandy's belly, and soon the shame of their family was front and center for all to see, though they didn't see the half of it. Karen vowed to learn the identity of the father, insisting that she had the right to look into the face of the boy who had made her only child a whore.

Karen's Thursday night drinking turned into every night. She'd hit the bars after her shift and not be home for hours. Tyler ran out of the blank pages in his book, but he was also running out of time, and out of ideas.

The search for Mandy was quiet, lackluster. The police, upon hearing the sordid tale of her pregnancy and her mother's reaction, assumed she was a runaway. They said they'd keep an eye out, assured Karen and Tyler that she'd show up.

But Karen still pored over every paper in the county, searching for anything that might be a clue. She'd burst into a panic of tears at every Jane Doe she saw in the news, call the detective and make him check.

"We're already checking, ma'am," he'd say, and Karen would dry her eyes with the newsprint, smearing dark ink across her face.

Tyler enjoyed the first few weeks after Mandy's disappearance. Free from her seduction, he remembered why it was he'd fallen in love with his wife. She was a good woman, after all, and she needed him so much in her time of crisis. She cried on his shoulder. She was so vulnerable, almost like a child. He was needed—he could take her in his arms and show her that there was more to life than her absent, delinquent daughter. He could stroke her hair and reassure her that she hadn't chased Mandy away. Well, not completely. He couldn't assuage all of her guilt. As long as she carried the blame, she wouldn't look for it elsewhere.

Every morning, their stoop was covered in newspapers. He helped her read through them, looking for any suspicious reports. His anxiety was genuine, and she loved him for it.

My bones are heavy
But they float.
As long as there is water enough
I can taste the air.

The baby should have come October 15th. Or close to that, from the last time Tyler remembered Mandy bleeding. It was the day she would have become the mother of his child. He started drinking early, and didn't do as much to comfort Karen as he should have.

"I should be with her now," she said, over and over. Halfway through the afternoon, Tyler was willing to oblige her. Her pacing rubbed his nerves raw.

Dinner that night didn't happen—at least, not in the way he had gotten used to. He sat in his armchair, swirling whisky in his glass, listening to his wife pacing and mumbling in their bedroom upstairs.

When the doorbell rang, he was prepared to ignore it. Karen came tearing down the stairs and through the house to answer it.

"Ignore it," he said. "We don't need any more newspapers."

"It could be *her*," Karen said, clinging to the landing banister as her feet fumbled over the edge of each stair.

Of course, he thought. *She could still be alive, bringing her baby home. Must remember.*

The door hinge squeaked. Karen wailed.

He pushed himself out of his chair and staggered to the doorway.

Mandy. Her skin the color of bleached coral, eyes dark, iridescent Tahitian pearls. Stomach as flat as the deck of the boat where he'd strangled her.

Karen's look of shock quickly contorted into rage. "Where have you been? Why didn't you call? What have you done—*where is the baby*?"

Tyler couldn't speak. He didn't move, except to sway slightly as if his whisky had undone him.

The girl stepped over the threshold, face a blank mask, enduring the barrage of questions. She didn't answer.

Karen repeated her questions as Mandy sat on the couch and stared out the window. Finally, she turned her head and looked at her mother. "Water," she said. Her voice sounded like pebbles scraping each other smooth in the surf.

The ice in Tyler's glass rang as his hand shook. He knew the girl couldn't actually be Mandy. He knew, and he was the only one who knew, and he must remember that.

"Answer your mother, Mandy," he said. Her name chafed his mouth.

Her eyes snapped to him, and he felt the impact of that dark, glossy gaze as if it were a fist on his heart.

"Water," she croaked again. Raindrops dribbled from her hairline and crossed her face.

Tyler backed away. "I'll . . . I'll go get her some water," he said, and hurried to the kitchen.

He leaned against the counter and panted, felt his gut flip.

Karen was screaming in the living room again, her voice rising in shrill octaves that set his teeth on edge. "What have you been taking?! What's done this to you? *Where is the baby?!*"

"At the bottom of the sea," Tyler said—whispered, to his own white knuckles that gripped the countertop. "With her mother." Saying it out loud calmed him. No, this wasn't Mandy. This was some stray that looked like her, trying to manipulate them. Trying to claim a vacant spot in their warm home—some con artist.

Or, his gut flipped again, *a spy*. An undercover agent. Someone sent to feel him out?

He needed to calm down. To think. He squeezed his eyes shut and tried to focus past the fuzzy drunkenness of his thoughts. *Play along. Pretend it's her. Act the fool.*

He took another deep breath and filled a water glass. Then he went back to the living room.

He handed the girl the glass of water. She lifted it awkwardly to her mouth, as if her hand didn't know quite where her face was. She sucked the water down. He could hear it rush through her throat and gurgle as it hit her stomach.

When she'd finished the water, Mandy got up and walked to the kitchen, jerking her legs and swaying. She'd left a puddle on the couch where she'd sat, brackish water collected in the seams of the leather.

Karen looked to Tyler, hopelessness etched in her features. The sound of shattering glass made them both jump. Karen ran to the kitchen.

Tyler walked to the couch and dipped his finger in the icy water there. He felt more water soak though his socks where her feet had touched the floor. He pulled the curtain back and glanced out the window. No rain. Everything had been dry all week. A chill rolled up his spine.

This isn't possible. That can't be her. She wasn't breathing anymore; I felt her heart stop; I watched her sink.

He shivered under a thick slime of perspiration. It wasn't her. Mandy's eyes were blue and clear; this girl's eyes were dark, opaque. Someone was playing a trick. A mean, sick trick. *But why would they? Do they know?*

Bile rose in his throat. Someone out there must know, or they never would have staged this. They were trying to lure the truth out of him, frighten him into confessing—this was the mousetrap, but he wouldn't take the bait. He'd play along. Act as though nothing had happened. He was the relieved stepfather, happy to have her home and angry at how she had worried her poor mother. He mustn't ask too many questions. Act ignorant. And, most importantly, he mustn't touch her.

~

Tyler leaned into the cloud of smoke, breathed deeply, and relaxed. He stirred the poker in the steel barrel, pushing his record book further into the burning pile of leaves. He was sad to see his records go, but it had been risky to keep them in the first place. If someone suspected him now, this book could be the death of him, so he watched it burn. He didn't really need the list, anyway. He had the memories. He had to watch himself now. Flip the switch in his head and stifle his needs until suspicion moved on.

"Toasting marshmallows?"

Tyler spun around, whipping the iron poker into the shoulder of Phil, his neighbor, who had sneaked up behind him. Phil yelled and clutched his shoulder.

"Phil! Oh God, sorry! You scared the piss out of me!"

Phil was bent, panting in pain. "I guess I deserved that. My fault; I wasn't thinking."

Tyler let him regain composure in silence.

"What are you burning this time of night?"

"Oh, bills. Insurance papers. Stuff I don't want in the trash. I meant to get to it earlier today, but . . . " His voice trailed away. *Was this the person who suspected him?*

Phil was silent, waiting for him to finish.

"Mandy came home."

"Wow. Is she okay? Did she have the baby?" The whole town knew the scandal. Part of it.

"No. I mean, I don't know. She's not talking. She didn't bring a baby."

"Did she say where she was?"

"No. She's only said a few words. From her voice, it sounds like she's been into some heavy drugs." He dropped his head, the picture of an ashamed parent. He silently thanked Karen for fleshing out his story with her paranoia. "Wherever she was, maybe it would be better if we never found out."

"How's Karen?"

"Crazy. More than usual. I hope she settles down soon. It's like she's gone over the edge." He let his voice waver and catch. *Perfect.*

"Jesus, Ty. Well, let me know if there's anything I can do. Or Susan. I'll let her know what's going on; I'm sure she'd do anything to help Karen."

"Thanks, Phil. See ya later."

"Night."

Not bad. Vulnerable and overwhelmed.

He stirred the fire again, watching the flames grow, breathing in the ashes of his list, imagining they tasted like hair spray, lip gloss, and chewing gum.

The house was quiet the next morning. When Tyler walked down the stairs and into the kitchen, he found Karen sitting by herself, drinking wine. She stared at the stack of the day's newspapers. They were damp with dew and untouched. No need for scanning blotters and obituaries.

Tyler prepared his coffee and cereal in silence. He sat down with his breakfast and reached across the table, taking Karen's hand. "You okay?" he asked.

She turned to look at him, her eyes shadowed, frantic with nerves. She started to cry.

He got up and walked around the table. He rested his hands on her shoulders and pressed his thumbs into the tight muscles of her back. Her shoulders relaxed a little and she took a shuddering breath.

"She never went to bed last night," she said. "I was watching her."

"What do you mean?"

"She just stood there beside her bed, staring at it. She never got in it—she never even moved. I don't even know if she knew I was watching her. She hasn't even spoken a single word to me."

Tyler stopped rubbing his wife's shoulders, tightening his grip.

"I'll go check on her," he said.

He took his hands off her shoulders and watched her head sink to the tabletop, where she resumed weeping.

He stepped up the stairs quietly, his throat so tight the ascent winded him.

The only light in the upstairs hallway came from the window, through the leaves of the plant Karen had bought for Mandy's first Christmas. Mandy had cared for it, and it had refused to die in the neglect of her absence. Instead it had become feral, growing to fill the window and wrapping itself around the curtain rod.

Tyler stared into what light shone through the leaves as he rested his hand on the doorknob of Mandy's room. The door wasn't latched. He pushed it open and poked his head through the opening, breathing as quietly as he could.

She stood on the far side of the bed, facing the doorway. She stared down at the bed, her hair curtaining her face and twisting over her shoulders, like the plant in the window. Her shoulders hunched and her arms hung limp at her sides. Her stance was rigid, tense and alert. A pool of water spread at her feet, creeping under the bed and across the room.

Tyler pushed the door open and stepped over the threshold. "Mandy?"

Her head snapped up; her neck cracked. She stared at him.

He swallowed. If this girl was an informant, he had to act natural. "Honey, do you want some breakfast?"

She didn't move or answer. She stared at him, and water dripped from her hair.

Tyler backed out of the room and shut the door. He wiped his brow with the back of his sleeve, leaving a stippled stain of sweat. He walked down to the living room and sat on the couch to compose himself before Karen saw him. He breathed deeply and counted to thirty, then got up and walked into the kitchen.

"I think she's asleep," he said.

"Oh, good," Karen said, covering her face with her hands. "She needs the rest. God, she looks awful. Half dead. What do you think she's been taking?" She began to cry again. "Should we take her to the hospital? Does she need rehab or a psychiatrist? What am I supposed to do?"

"Let's just give her a few days," he said, rubbing his hands up and down Karen's folded arms. "She's obviously been through a lot and had a bad shock. We'll know better what she needs when she's rested and well-fed."

Karen nodded, and rested her head on his shoulder, pressing her face into his neck. He could feel the dampness of her tears creep down the collar of his shirt. He wanted a shower.

"Why don't you go get some rest, too? I'll wait for Mandy and get you when she's awake, okay?"

"Thank you. I don't know what I would have done these last few months without you, Ty. I don't know how you can even stand to stay here. Most people would have run away."

He pulled her closer. "I'm not most people, love. Now go get some sleep."

He followed Karen out to the living room and watched her shuffle up the stairs. He heard the bedroom door close.

He went back to the kitchen. He dumped his uneaten breakfast in the sink and went to the pile of newspapers. He tore into them, looking for any reports of bodies found in the bay, of missing people being found. He read chaotically and inefficiently, switching between papers and sections and articles, strewing newsprint across the kitchen.

It was an hour before his feverish concentration broke and he looked up to see his stepdaughter staring at him from the doorway.

He froze.

No, not his stepdaughter. A spy.

"Good morning," he croaked, choking on his dry throat. "Can I get you some breakfast?"

"Water," she said, in her burned-out voice.

He rose from the chair and backed toward the cupboard to get a glass. His hands fumbled for the faucet dial, wetting his sleeve in the stream of water. The glass filled, overflowed, wet his knuckles. He walked toward her, leaning out from a distance to hand her the glass. He backed away.

She tilted her head back and poured the water over her face. It rushed through her hair, ran off her shoulders and down her other arm, down her chest and legs, soaking her nightgown and the newspapers at her feet, as if she'd upended a rain barrel.

The wet nightgown clung to her, accentuating the flatness of her stomach and revealing the rungs of her ribcage. Her nipples looked blue, pressed up against the damp whiteness of the fabric.

Tyler tore his gaze from her torso and looked into her wet face, her hair washed back from her features, her eyes now wide open, dark pearls that held him frozen.

"More water," she said, and extended her arm, elbow snapping, holding out the glass.

He inched forward, his body unwilling, fighting his progress. He took the glass, filled it again, and handed it back.

Again she poured it over herself, further soaking her hair and clothes, the puddle below her spreading into more sheets of newsprint, running the black ink in streams between the floor tiles. The water revived her. She looked more alert, her movements becoming quicker and more precise. She extended the glass again and said, "More."

He brought her more.

After the fifth glass, he could hear her breathing; see her shoulders rise and fall. She blinked, and her eyes looked clearer, her skin more opaque, hiding the unnerving network of veins.

She raised her hand and pressed it against her chest, between her breasts. Her brow furrowed for a moment, and then she smiled and looked up at him.

Her teeth were too sharp, and the skin of her mouth was too dark, like the ink-stained water at her feet.

The water on the floor rippled out from him in waves, to the rhythm of his trembling. He stared and held his breath.

"Thank you." She turned, and walked out of the room.

Tyler watched her go, her nightgown clinging, her long wet hair reflecting green in the sunlight from the window, trailing down her back. He watched her turn the corner into the living room, leaving inky black footprints in the carpet.

He stood, trying to pull air into his lungs. He felt his heart pounding erratically, fluttering and pausing. He choked, moaned, and leaned onto the table, clutching at wet newspapers, crumpling them in his hands. Calmness returned slowly, in the form of exhaustion.

He gathered the newspapers and hurled them out the back door. He pulled towels from the closet and mopped up the inky water. He sponged Mandy's *not Mandy's* dark footprints from the carpet, soaking up the damp trail that led through the house and back to her bedroom.

He took the towels to the basement and put them in the washer before stumbling to his desk and sinking into his chair. His hands still trembled. He sat, rubbing his face until the adrenaline faded. He lowered his forehead to his arm on the desk and fell asleep.

The doorbell woke him. He gasped as he sat up, choking on the saliva collected in his mouth. He massaged his chest, climbing the stairs as the bell rang again, followed by a firm knock.

He reached the door and pulled it open. Two police officers stood on the porch. The younger of the two looked down at a file in his hands, eyes scanning the page. The older officer removed his hat.

"Mr. Stear, may we come in?"

No choice.

"Sure. Yes, of course, come in."

They walked past him to the living room. Tyler followed them and invited them to sit.

"Is your wife home?"

"No. Well, yes—she is, but she's sleeping and really needs it. Is there something I can help you with?"

The officers sighed in unison, glancing at each other. "We've found a body, Mr. Stear. A fisherman found it, in a tide pool on the beach about fifty miles north of here. The body fits the description of your runaway, Mandy." He paused. "There isn't much left to identify—I'm sorry, Mr. Stear—but she's of the right age and build, and our medical examiner says she shows signs of having delivered a baby shortly before her death."

Tyler gaped at them. "That can't be her," he said.

"Well, we can't be certain yet, of course. There's some work that must be done. Would you please donate a DNA sample?"

What? "No!" He stood.

"Excuse me?"

Here's the trap. His heart raced. He covered his face and forced himself to sit.

"I mean. Sorry. It won't help. I'm her stepfather. She's not mine.

But that's not her, it can't be her. She came home last night. We haven't had a chance to call yet . . . She's resting, too. It's been a long night."

The officers' eyes widened. "She's home? Well. That's great. You'll need to bring her by the station. We'll need you to sign some forms. Thank you for your time, Mr. Stear." They stood, and each shook his trembling hand. He couldn't meet their eyes. There was a hardness to their stare that turned his blood cold.

He followed them out, half-focused on the small talk, and shut the door behind them, turning the lock and the bolt, resting his forehead against the smooth panel of wood, listening to the squawk of the police radio from the driveway.

What are they doing? If they sent this girl to trap me, why were they so surprised to hear she was here? Did they find Mandy's body? Then who is that upstairs?

It was time to go. He'd pack a bag. Leave a note. Say he needed distance from this broken family.

He felt a splash of water against the back of his neck. He turned and saw her there, at the top of the stars, hands flung forward. Water spilled over the edge of the step where she stood.

"More water," she said.

His heart hammered. His head spun. He'd have to walk past her to get to his room. To his suitcase and wallet and keys.

He edged around her. Her neck cracked as her head rotated, locking him in her dark gaze. He backed into the hallway.

"If you're feeling dry," he said, his socks soaking through from the wet carpet, "maybe you'd feel better after a bath. I'll get it started for you, if you like . . . "

She smiled. The dark skin inside her lips cracked.

He reached the linen closet, pulled out the last towel, and handed it to her. The fabric darkened at her touch.

He turned and hurried down the hall to the bathroom. He heard her wet, sucking footsteps behind him. He sat on the edge of the tub and turned on the hot water, holding his hand under the stream of comforting heat. As she entered the doorway, the phone rang. He stood to go answer it, but the ring cut short. Karen must have picked it up in the bedroom. He sat back down. The girl stared at him.

Karen flew down the hallway.

The girl didn't turn, didn't blink, her unmoving eyes locked to Tyler's.

"Ty, I've got to go down to the station." She was pulling her coat on. "They said they found something—some evidence. I told them she's here, but they said . . . Never mind. I'll be right back, I'll call you." She spun and raced down the stairs. The front door slammed.

Tyler stared at the girl. "You're not Mandy."

She lifted her dripping nightgown and pulled it off over her head. She dropped it on the floor, in the puddle at her feet.

Her naked skin was blanched, a lacework of blue veins showing through the damp translucence. Her breasts were tipped with blue bruises, hanging over the prominent ladder of her ribs. Her sex was hairless, the color of India ink. Dark blood oozed from an open wound at her navel, where a stump of chewed cord dangled.

Her palm pressed against his chest, soaking her handprint through his shirt.

"I'm your daughter," she gurgled, and pushed him back into the steaming bath water.

She climbed on top of him, straddling him, pinning his arms to his sides with her knees. Her limbs grated his, coral-hard and heavy as rock. She sealed her cracked lips around his, her hips thrust against him as her muscles rippled in peristalses that arched her back.

Water poured from her mouth, into him, filling him. He felt his stomach swell, straining to burst at the tide rushing in. His lungs filled and convulsed against the current, trying to push back the weight of so much water. She heaved again, and the water filled his throat, pouring out of his nose. Salt burned his eyes. Her hair hung around them, clinging to his face and then falling into the water around him, crumbling into sand as more water poured into him.

As the spasms in his lungs grew weaker and his vision darkened, her skin hardened, scraping him, crumbling away.

With one final thrust, a rupture seared deep within his gut, bursting against the flood, tearing him open.

She shattered, a million sparkling grains of broken shell raining around him, filling the water that filled him, burying him in silt and dark, foaming water.

UNDERWATER THING

Sleep with a current in your mouth
Eyes like glass
Tumbled to sandpaper clouds.

TALL GRASS, SHALLOW WATER

MOTHERS SAY "Stay clear of the water." At least the good ones do. The kids say "Dip a toe in and Genny will grab you."

Maybe some Gennies grab. Maybe some Gennies have to. But my Genny never did. All her daughters were gifts. All her girls were given.

The other mothers say nothing; they put their daughters in the water.

Mother wrapped me in a long piece of linen and laid me in water not deep enough to be dark, but deep enough. The sky was low and worried, and the tall grasses wove their shadows over me like a blanket. It was Genny that found me and took me for her own—raised me up in a world of weeds and wet and swamp rot.

When I was old enough to follow directions, but still young enough to follow directions, she named me Laura Leigh and sent me back to Mother.

"Bring me meat," she said, and tied a tangled fish line around my ankle. "Girls have to eat, and mothers should feed their daughters. It's the way of things. Bring her to me, and she shall feed you, as she always should have done. Bring Mother to the water and you shall have meat."

But the memory of Mother's face was rippled with green water.

"Any weeping mother will do, if the tears are ripe," Genny said.

When Genny laughed, her teeth rattled like bone dice in a horn cup. She softens the sound with slick packs of algae pressed into the dark spaces of her mouth. It roots there, multiplies like weeds in a garden.

"Hurry, girl. Bring me gristle to clean my mouth."

She said it shouldn't take long. "All mothers weep," she said. "That's their secret. Find one whose secret is dark like the center of the water. Find one with eyes like a river. Dark meat—stringy meat—that will clean my teeth."

The line around my ankle is tight enough to squeeze, but not to cut. It whispers through the tall grass behind me.

The kids hear it drag across the ground, but the mothers don't. The kids call me Laura Leigh Hiss on account of it. None of their mothers weep. Their meat is too soft for Genny's teeth.

Every day I spend away from the water, the line on my ankle pulls a little deeper.

"We don't see you in school, Hiss," the boy called Andrew says. His voice is not unkind.

"I don't go to school," I say.

"You have to go to school—it's the law. Or your parents get in trouble." He kicks a trench in the sand under the swing. The deep sand is wet, the way anything deep is always wet.

"I don't have parents," I tell him, and he stops his swing mid-kick.

"Oh," he says. He digs deeper, to even wetter sand. "Do you want to see how high I can go?"

I say yes and he soars over his damp sand pit, hair straight back and bare knees kissing the sky.

Andrew's mother hardly ever weeps. Her meat is soft as snails.

Three days in, and my foot below the fish line has turned the color of deep water. I lie in a trench of cool sand under the swings, wiggling my fingers into the earth, seeking moisture, seeking home.

Andrew comes over, kicking sand up behind his heels. His cheeks are pink from the sun. He slips his legs over the swing and kicks away from the ground.

His dry-eyed mother stands in the shade of a tree, tapping at a phone.

"Do you really not have parents, Hiss?" Andrew's voice whips across me as he swings past.

"Well, I did once, I guess. Not now, though. I'm looking for a mom. But she has to be a sad one."

"Why sad?"

"Genny says they're stronger."

"Who's Genny?"

"You ask a lot of questions."

"You sound like my mom." He leaps from the swing as it arcs forward and lands in a splash of sand. I squeeze my eyes shut as the grains rain down on me.

He looks to his mother, grinning, but she's still staring at the phone, the glowing screen broadcasted in the reflection on her glasses. Some brightly colored game.

"Do you live here at the park?" He bends to re-tie his shoe.

"No. Maybe, for now."

"Is it cold?"

"Not as cold as the water." I pull the long linen strip around my neck closer, tuck it into my collar.

"Ya know, Kyle's mother is sad."

I lift my chin from the stained linen wrap and pull my fingers from the sand. "You know a sad mom?"

"I guess she's not a mom anymore."

"You can't ever be not a mom anymore. No matter how hard you try. That's what Genny says."

"Well, she cries a lot."

I rise from the sand and walk to Andrew. The line at my ankle tugs. Andrew backs up a step. Leaves his shoe undone.

"Where is she?"

"The red house. On 5th. The one with the new tire swing out front."

"Which way is that?"

Andrew points past his mother, out across an overgrown soccer field.

"Tire's still got all the white paint on it. Never been used. Mom won't let me on it."

"You should ride it anyway," I say.

Andrew's mother looks up at me as I pass her. Could be she hears the hiss of Genny's line. Maybe she smells the fen. But her phone beeps and she turns back to it. Lights are seductive, in the bog and in the hand.

Kyle's mother's house is only mostly red, and partly the grey of old wood where red used to be. The swing hangs from the tree, limp as Spanish moss. Wasps hover around it, darting in and out of the dark hollow of the tube.

The door knocker hangs from one hinge, the other fallen loose as if someone had knocked too hard—and then no one had. I pinch the narrow bar and tap it against the metal plate, and wait.

The whole house seems to creak as movement comes alive inside. Filaments of spiders' webs fall away as Kyle's mom opens the door.

Her eyes are wide and brown, with golden sclera and heavy red lids. Her dark hair wraps her ears in wild wisps. She drops her gaze to mine and thin lips pinch shut over yellow teeth. She pulls a heavy sweater close against the late August heat.

"Yes?" Her eyes rise over my head and scan the street.

"Are you Kyle's mom?"

Her eyes shoot back to me. The bottom lids tremble and fill.

"Yeah," she says, "I'm Shannon. Were you a friend of Kyle's?" Her eyes spill over and her voice hitches. "I don't remember you. I'm sorry. Kyle's gone." Her hands rise to cover the collapse of her face.

My ankle throbs. I step up to the weeping woman and raise my arms to her. She pulls her wet hands from her face and wraps her arms around my shoulders.

And Genny pulls.

Kyle's mother screams.

And Genny reels us in.

~

I smell the rot of tall grass in shallow water. The water parts against my back and washes the sting of daylight from my skin. The squint of my eyes relaxes as the sun disappears behind the wall of deepening green.

Kyle's mother's scream turns to foam against my neck.

We settle in a cloud of silt at the bottom of Genny's bog. Genny anchors us with long reeds as soft as leather.

"Welcome home, Laura Leigh. And what meat have you brought for me and your sisters?" Feathers of algae wave in the current of her words.

I look to Kyle's mother. The tangle of her hair rivals Genny's, and through the blue of the water her teeth look almost green. Her eyes, though, look darker, deeper even than the water where we stand, and wetter.

Genny bends her long neck and leans in close to the mother. The woman flinches back from the soft touch of the weeds flowing from Genny's mouth.

Genny's long tongue, dark as bog wood and rough as stone, emerges from the soft green center and presses against the woman's eyes. The stream of bubbles from her mouth wreathes Genny's face.

Genny runs her tongue across the mother's eyes, lingering at the corners, probing the lids. She pulls back and turns to me.

"This meat won't do." Dark slime rises around her as she advances on me; tattered bits of weed fall from her mouth as her angry words shred them. "You brought me the wrong kind, girl." Her hand, slick and firm as driftwood, grips my jaw. "What sort of mother is this?"

The water around me grows colder, darker, and my thoughts slip back to the warm sand of the playground. "She wept. I saw her. I have her tears, here, on my neck."

The hole in Genny's face where a nose would be presses against my collar. The net of her hair wraps my face. Her cold lips clamp against my skin, her slick teeth raking me, scraping at the fine brine of the mother's tears. The pull of her mouth hurts as ice creeps into my fingers and toes.

She pulls back with a pop; water spins like a drain between us.

"Yes. She wept. But they were the wrong tears, girl." Genny turns back to the woman. "You never thought to bring him to me—that it might be better for both of you?"

The mother's brow lowers over her dark eyes, and her lips pull back from her teeth—definitely green, under the water. "What are you saying? I should have drowned my son?"

Genny waves her long fingers, sending small currents off into dark water. "You could have ended his pain. And wouldn't it have been a relief for you? You destroyed yourself caring for him—and for what?" Genny sucks a strand of algae through her lips and chews.

The mother's fists release into claws. She moves slowly against the heavy water toward Genny, kicking up clouds of black mud in her wake. "I loved my son. I loved every last moment we had together."

I can almost feel the heat of her face warming the freezing water around us.

Genny spits out the chewed string of algae. The pieces drift around the mother, landing in her hair.

Genny turns to me. "You see, Laura Leigh? She weeps for her son, not for herself. She weeps for the mother she wanted to be, not the mother she is. She would never have brought me a son—even when she should have. Her meat is old wood. It would pull my teeth straight from my face."

"I'm sorry, Genny." I dig my toes into the cool mud. "Send us back. I'll find another."

"I'll send you back, yes. Find us a mother more like your own."

She turns back to the mother and pushes her long fingers into the woman's hair. "I can't send her back. She's been here too long. She's full of water now." Genny lowers her mouth to the mother's. Strings of algae shoot into the woman's mouth. Her throat bulges with it. A fountain of bubbles flows up from Genny's kiss, and when she pulls back, Kyle's mother's mouth is a gaping O. The green-tinted whites of her eyes are stretched with red. She floats, rocking in the soft current of Genny's laugh.

~

My ears pop and fill and pop again as I ascend. Tiny fish with barbed mouths follow me, drinking from the red that flows from my ankle.

The sun is down, so the surface catches me by surprise—a shock of cold air, then a thousand knives of starlight.

I kick toward the shallows, reaching, till my toes brush the thick slime of the bottom. I grasp at tall reeds and pull myself to land.

I lie there—the long grass bent under my back like feather knives. I hear a hiss.

I open my eyes wide and round as a fish's, drink in the moonlight, and search the shallows.

It's Kyle's mother. Her hair wraps dry reeds, pulling them with the lap of the tide. Her lips are the color of the sky.

I pull her hair off the weeds and tuck it around her face. "Is it better now?"

"Yes," she says, though it could be a frog croaking.

"You're not meat," I say to her red eyes. "You could almost be a Genny. You could almost be a mother for us all."

She laughs, or it might be a night bird.

I smile. "You're too tough. Too tough for meat, and too tough to be a Genny, I guess." I pinch the heavy eyelids shut.

"My son," she says. And it must be her. I peel her eyes back open.

"Your son is gone."

"My son."

"You need a son. If you had a son again, could you be a Genny? A Genny that still knows how to weep? Could you be my Genny?" I don't wait for an answer—can't still the tide in my ears or the waves in my heart. "I can get you a son."

There are tires in the bog—ones full of fish spawn and snails. A perfect shelter—dark like the black mud and tucked away from the current. If you hold your ear close, you can almost hear the life teeming inside.

The hum of wings is much louder. I can hear it from the street. Small black bodies drift around the tire, each on its own subtle current of air.

Their sting is less sharp than Genny's barbed fingers.

I scrape the papery nest from inside the rubber tube. The wasps stab at me, wriggling against my skin, driving their venom deeper. It feels like heat, like life. Like the burn of sand baked in the sun.

I'm careful not to scratch the paint. "Goodyear," it says in perfect white letters. But it hasn't been a good year. Not for this swing, and not for this street.

I roll it ahead of me, chasing it as it bounces to the playground. I have to push it through the sand. Even the smallest dune knocks it over.

My hands are swollen with wasp venom and black with hot rubber. They smell like oil and summer.

The tire falls to its side in the trench under the swing set. I wait.

It isn't until the next afternoon that Andrew comes skipping across the sand, his shoelaces trailing behind him like my fishing line.

"Hey, Hiss," he says, as he dives stomach-down across a swing. He sees the tire in the sand and stops himself mid-swing. "You got Kyle's swing!"

"Yeah. This is it."

"His mom just gave it to you?"

"Sort of, yeah."

"So is she your mom now?"

"Almost. She will be, soon."

Andrew grins. "Great. That's good for both of you, then, isn't it? You get a mom again and she gets a kid." He reaches and pats himself on the back.

"Yeah, it's good. It's almost great. She wants a son, still."

Andrew nods as though he understands, and resumes his stomach swing, arms outstretched. "Where are you going to put that swing? Shoulda left it on the tree."

"It was full of wasps."

"Oh, that's gross. Can I see?"

"I scraped them out. I think I'll take it to the pond. Set it up over the water."

Andrew's face lights up. "That's the best idea, Hiss! You can jump off it right into the water." He leaps backward off the swing and lands on his behind.

"You want a ride on it?"

His face is pained, though not from the fall. "Can't."

"It's my swing, now. You can tell your mom it's okay."

"Naw, it's not that. Can't swim. I'm not allowed at the pond."

I reach down and take his hand, pull him up from the ground.

"That's silly," I say, "the water's shallow."

"My mom says it only takes a few inches, if you don't know what you're doing."

"Yeah. True." I can almost see her face—just a few inches of water between me and Mother. "But I know what I'm doing. You'll be with me."

"I dunno."

"Kyle's mom will be there. Look—the paint's still fresh. It still has all the little rubber hairs on the tread."

His face splits into a smile. Two teeth are missing. "That'll probably be fine, then." He turns and shouts over his shoulder. "Mom! Can I go visit Kyle's mom?"

She turns from the group of blonde mothers and nods, hardly making eye contact before turning back to her friends and their conversation.

I feel a tug in my heart, not unlike the one at my ankle. "Go give her a hug."

"Why?"

"Because she's your mom."

He shrugs and jogs across the sand, into the grass and shade where the moms gather like driftwood. He circles her neck with his arms, and she smiles, kisses his hair.

Andrew helps me lift the tire from the sand.

"Heavy," he says. "Aren't these supposed to float?"

"They don't," I say. "They go straight to the bottom."

~

"Hiss, no way that's gonna hold."

I'm wrapping my tangled fish line around a tree branch. "It's made to catch river monsters. It can handle you." The tire swings from the other end of the line.

"Monsters?"

"Like really big fish."

"Oh, I caught one of those." He waves his hand, bats away a few flies. His shoes are tied together by the laces and tossed over his shoulder. His jeans are rolled to the knee, but already starting to slip. Brackish water wicks up the fabric, creeping up his legs.

I can see, from up the tree, the flash of Kyle's mother's sweater hidden in the reeds of the shallows. Andrew doesn't see her. He only has eyes for the swing.

He splashes through the shallow water and steadies the swaying swing. "You're right about the water. Not too deep at all."

"Genny says it's hardly even a pond."

"What is it, then?"

"She says it's a drain." I hadn't understood her when I was younger. I do now.

Andrew shakes his head. "Naw, it's a puddle."

"Puddles dry up. And you can't lose things in a puddle."

"You lost something, Hiss?" He bends down and peers into the water. "My dad says I can find anything."

"Not me, no. Some have, though." The knot is tight enough. I pull on it, testing the line. It slides sharp across my palms.

"What did they lose?"

"Everything." I leap from the branch into the water.

The splash soaks Andrew. He spits out brown water.

"Hiss, gross!"

"What's the matter?"

"Fish pee in this water!"

"There are worse things in this water." He's staring at my face, and I realize I'm smiling.

"Your teeth are green," he says.

I cup a hand over my mouth.

"Don't you brush?"

I shrug. "Got no one to make me."

He nods and resumes picking at the rubber of the tire.

"Are you ready?" With my ankle free of the line, I can feel the blood rushing back into it. My toes almost feel warm.

"Been ready all summer!" He starts to climb into the tire ring.

"Let me go first. Then you aim for where I land. That way we're in the same spot and I can grab you if I need to."

He nods. "Your swing, your rules."

Rings of ripples spread across the water. Something in the shallows is moving.

I slide my legs into the center of the tire.

"You're doing it wrong, Hiss," Andrew says. He's shaking his head; his mop of sandy hair sways across his brow.

"How, then?"

"You'd have to let me show you. I'd have to go first."

"Fine, you go." I slide out of the swing. The ripples on the water have passed the center of the pond—the dark middle where the shallows drop away into Genny's pit.

Andrew stands in the O of the swing, his toes curled over the edge of the tube, the fish line gripped in his fists. "You have to be standing to get the best jump." His toenails are too long, and dirty. He leans his narrow shoulders back and kicks his feet forward. The tire swings, brushing the tips of tall reeds.

He pushes it higher—farther out over the rippling water. Closer to the pit.

The branch above is bending and swaying with the momentum. Leaves fall around us, raining into the water. They float along the surface before getting snagged in dams in the forest of reeds.

"Watch me, Hiss!" The swing arcs forward and Andrew releases it. He soars over the water. His gold hair blows back from his face—a mask of rapture. He thrusts his arms forward like Superman.

The water below him is churning, a soup pot beginning to foam.

Just as Andrew reaches his apex and tips toward the dark water, pale hands and sodden arms stretch up from the center of a widening whirlpool. Andrew's arms clutch at the air, his legs kicking, as he lands in Kyle's mother's arms.

Her hands fold over him like reeds in the wind, and they disappear below the surface. The water stills.

I stare at the dark mirror of water. *I should have gone first. I should be with them.*

The swing arcs back and knocks Andrew's shoes from my hand. They splash into the shallows. The sound breaks my stupor.

I drop into the water and slither, gliding like a water snake to the center, and I dive.

The water at the bottom of the pit is clouded with black silt. Currents race across each other as if a dozen storms rage overhead.

At the center of the swirling curtain of sand is Kyle's mother. She holds Andrew close, his head pressed against her neck. His eyes roll toward me slowly, his lids half-mast. Bits of algae and torn reed circle them.

As I approach, the woman pulls Andrew closer and turns away from me.

My throat is tight. I loosen the strip of linen around my neck. I reach out for the woman, and she hisses over her shoulder. Her teeth are green—greener than when I last saw them.

I draw my hand back. "But you said—"

"I promised nothing." She sets Andrew down in the mud, and stands in front of him.

"But I brought him to you. I brought you a son, like you asked."

She smiles. "You did. He's beautiful."

Andrew's head hangs, chin to his chest, hair drifting over his eyes.

"But you love kids." I want to take Andrew's hand. I want to lead him to the playground, let him get warm again on the hot sand.

"I do."

"And you took a child. You're a Genny now. You should be my Genny. I helped you!"

"I didn't take him."

"You did! You pulled him under!"

"He was a gift."

The cold of the water hits me all at once. I shake, and the floating silt trembles away from me.

My Genny steps through the curtain of reed and silt. Long ribbons of algae twist around her face. She laughs, and small fish startle from the bramble of her mouth.

"Cherish him, Shannon. They grow so quickly," Genny says.

The woman nods and wraps her arm around Andrew's shoulders.

"But do it elsewhere," Genny says. "This drain is clogged."

Shannon lifts Andrew and walks away, out of sight past the tumbling detritus in the currents.

I'm frozen everywhere but my eyes, which burn as though the sand were salt. "She loved her son so much. I thought she'd love me, too, if I were hers."

"I loved my daughter, too," Genny said. "But you are not she." Genny's face is hidden by the mass of weeds, but her voice sounds choked with sorrow.

"My mother didn't want me. Kyle's mother didn't want me. Why wouldn't she take me?"

"Because she can't."

"Because I'm yours?"

"You aren't mine anymore."

The dark mud of the fen bottom slides between my fingers as I drop to the ground. The floating silt scrapes my throat as I howl—a twisting cyclone of bubbles reaching for the sky.

Genny's barbed fingers press against the underside of my chin and raise my face to hers. Somewhere, through all that green, I sense her coal eyes.

"Laura Leigh, you are your own now. You have grown. You are a Genny."

The current strips the words from my trembling lips. Genny pulls me to my feet.

"You took a child. You drove him into the water to calm the rage of your own loss. You are a Genny now."

"But it didn't work. The rage is still there. The loss. It didn't work."

"It never does. But you'll never give up."

My hands are still clutching fistfuls of mud. Genny wraps her driftwood fingers around my wrists and squeezes until I release the grains into the churning water.

"But you must go elsewhere, too. This pond is mine. This is where the mothers know to bring my gifts. Find a bog, find a river, find a sea—find your family."

Genny tucks a strand of algae behind my ear and turns away. I watch her vanish into the dark water—the closest thing to a mother I've ever known. Closer than the woman who wrapped me up and drowned me. Closer than the moment where Kyle's mother held me and wept against my neck.

The water no longer feels cold. It feels empty. The currents echo.

I pull my linen strip tight around my throat and push myself forward through the water.

There's a river in the woods. There's an old mill there. A tree that drips vines over the gurgling water. The stepping stones are slick. When it rains, the water roars.

They say not all Gennies grab, and mine never did. But some have to. Sometimes, it's the only way.

Not all children are gifts.

INTERSECT

WHEN I'M LYING awake, I like to think about how, in a parallel universe, my daughter lives. That there she has chestnut hair, forget-me-not eyes, and lips like a snapdragon. How—there—we laugh and raid the raspberry patch, stain those lips red. At three in the morning, when the wine wears off, I think of how those lips will part when I squeeze her cheeks. Somewhere out there, it's happening, I like to think.

But not here. In this universe—the one I'm too scared to leave despite all it has done to me—in this one I left her at the bottom of a toilet bowl.

I suppose somewhere out there, if what they say is true, she has chestnut eyes and forget-me-not hair. Here, we'll never know.

When I give up on sleep, I get up, pee on a test stick and leave it, like always, on the cistern for Jason to read, and I go out to water the garden.

In a parallel universe, Jason gets up an hour later and reads the test—maybe runs outside to show me. Or maybe just drops it in the trash, buries it, saying nothing.

In a thousand parallel universes, if what they say is true, Jason probably stayed.

Here, though, in this one, I have the garden. There is that. Somewhere out there, I'm probably clutching my blue-haired daughter as we weep over wilted irises. Here, my hands cup blooms so big they drag their stems to the ground.

Somewhere I have it all.

The garden takes till noon, and I suppose somewhere I'm layering a sandwich for a hungry mouth at the table, swinging her feet and smacking her petal lips.

Here, the layers are bills on the table and I'm dragging my feet, wrapping my lips around handfuls of dry cereal.

After lunch, in another world where I probably had quiche, I cut a fistful of garden blossoms and drive them, in a car I own, to Jason's small plot at the cemetery. Poor Jason, who, in a world somewhere, shot himself over the guilt of leaving me alone in my grief. Somewhere out there, he must have felt guilt.

In another place, far from there, I shot him—in the back, as he turned away. In a thousand somewheres, I'm in a different prison altogether.

Here, it's when I remember that I haven't yet brushed my teeth. Or checked the test. It's negative, of course, because—here—it takes two.

I bet somewhere it doesn't.

I bet somewhere I'm squinting at that strip, and cupping a hand over my mouth as tears of joy well up in my eyes. I can almost feel it, across all this distance. Or maybe that's a memory from long ago. Maybe it hasn't been that long. I bet somewhere it was only yesterday, and I'm about to live those four golden months—before it all splits again. Fragments of worlds flying out of my mouth with every scream, taking root like grafted roses, in the dark corners of space—growing there, into other possibilities. Other fragments split, again and again, like a zygote dividing—one that keeps going. One that doesn't fail.

Maybe in one of those probability shards is a girl with hair the color of roses. Lips like lavender.

By the time I put the strip down, the afternoon sun will have dried the garden, and I can sit there and gently squeeze the snapdragons. Somewhere, we sing a duet—me and the flower.

Somewhere, before dinner, she sings as she sets the table, as I stir the sauce, Jason kissing me on the cheek as he loosens his tie.

Here, I skip dinner.

It's probable that somewhere we cry diamonds. If anything and all things are possible, somewhere we cry daughters. Spread a towel over your lap, pour out your heart, and fill your life with children. Maybe ones with lavender hair and eyes like roses, and lips the tender green of aphids.

Here, tears change the flavor of the wine. Make it taste like the back of your throat. Like the fur on your teeth that you forgot to brush again.

I bet somewhere wine tastes like bleach, like rat poison, like drain cleaner.

There are places, I'm sure, where I never have to sleep. Where the sun is always out, and I can stay in the garden with my wildflower girl. Here, the wine pulls me under, but maybe to somewhere else. Somewhere close, where we intersect.

GRAVE
MOTHER

THE GRASS GROWS thick and green on both sides of this rail fence, each field fed with the early dead. On the right, stone lambs sleep beneath sentinel angels that weep over piles of wilted roses. On the left, granite sheets coated in lichen sink into the dirt, names worn shallow in the stone. And my face, here on the rail, an eroded marker—marble made grey with age. Here lies Margaret— Meg, to those who knew her—which was no one, not even me.

Outside the fence, the stone-toothed hill slopes down into the woods. Trees push back up onto the hill, roots lifting the desecrated stones, wreaking unseen havoc on the small, unconsecrated heads resting below. Roots thread through soft fontanelles.

The fence presses into my tailbone where I straddle the rail. Rose stems prick my right foot, thistle weeds jab my left. Margaret stabs my left, buried deep in her fallopian tomb. I bathe the rail in blood.

I saw her heart beat for a moment—three quick flashes of a fluttering valve on a black screen. But altogether in the wrong place, to the left. I signed the papers on a Thursday, to end her and save me.

When it rains, old roses wash under the fence and down the hill, where they tangle and make a dry bramble arching over the leaning stones. Their seeds dry to husks before they ever take root.

On the right, dates stretch the stones wide, from weeks to years. On the left, a single day, maybe three. On my face, the lines carve a lifetime, counting backward from the day that should have been Margaret's day. They soaked her in poison on a Friday. They said if I didn't, I'd die.

I saw her tangle of bones, a compressed nest all in the wrong place. They said some would pass through me and some would become me, but some stayed, and turned to stone. And I mark her, everywhere.

The babes deep inside the high hill rest till rapture, while Margaret and I—we waited for rupture, and now it's come.

I swing my right leg over the fence, sink my feet into the weeds to the left, turn my back on the rows of angels. The warm coat of blood running down my legs soothes the nettle sting and thistle prick of the bramble by the woods.

I find us a place in the tangle of roots, like the tangle of her stone bones, and I lay us down. Here lie Mother and Margaret, and as I fade into the earth, she'll remain, watching over me, my own stone angel, my sleeping lamb. And I, the ground for Margaret, all in the wrong place.

THORN
TONGUE

HEATHER DREW THE long thorns out of her wrist and palm. Her skin swelled around their venom, sealing the pinprick holes shut so no blood flowed. She rubbed at the sore nodules and felt the sting of the poison spread. Pinching the long barbs between her fingers, she pressed the wide ends of the thorns into the spaces where her teeth had been—tasted the copper tang of blood and the earthy dust of the vine, felt a cold wetness flow down her chin and knew it ran red. She'd need fangs to get Estella back.

She reached deep into the bramble and caressed the vines, collecting the barbs in her arm, drawing them out and filling her mouth with them till her tongue bristled and the vines hung bare.

With her swollen arm, she pushed past the seeping ropes. The milk of their broken fibers soothed her punctures. As the swelling eased, the trapped droplets of blood sprang free and dried in hard beads, like studded armor.

The sweating flower fumed sweetness at the center of the bramble.

Heather knelt at the tongue of one petal and ran her finger through its amber juices. She rubbed the nectar over her eyelids. Numbness spread through her face.

She waited.

When the air above the flower danced with heat and its perfume drove the breath from her lungs, a wet rattle sounded from the flower's center. The stamen wavered, scattering a red cloud.

Heather leapt onto the flower and thrust her hands deep into its sticky core. She hauled out her catch, pulling free a writhing pink form which she clamped in her jaw, trapping it in her nest of thorny teeth.

It stilled.

"Never in all of its blooming has this flower been reaped. Tell me, Thorn-Tongue, why do you pull me from my home?"

Heather clenched her jaw.

"I can't help you if you won't answer my questions, girl."

Heather growled, but did not release her bite.

"I see," said the creature. "But speaking of—how are your eyes?" He waved a hand with gnarled knuckles through a floating cloud of pollen. He twisted in her grip, peering back at her over her nose.

His face was pinched. A tangle of brow hedges hung over yellow eyes that sat deep along a hooked nose. "Just fine, I see, and shining with my honey." He relaxed and hung slack in her mouth.

Heather lapped at the oily, sweet blood that coated her tongue and ran in rivulets through the thorns.

"I suppose we wait. Do you mind if I sing to pass the hours?"

Heather's heart quickened. She did not know the creature would sing. She did not know this trick, or its counter. Her rapid breath stirred the bristles over the creature's laughing eyes.

"I will sing an ode to your breath that you bathe me in, fair Thorn-Tongue." And he began to sing—a foul limerick laden with suggestions for better uses for her tongue. "Stop your ears, lest I offend you, child-mother. Or shall I sing of your sweet girl? And the joy she brings my queen?"

Heather glowered down her nose at the creature. Her jaw ached.

The light filtering through the hanging vines grew soft, and then dim.

"That's it, then, Thorn-Tongue. The day is over. Release me, and I will tell you where to find your once-unwanted daughter."

Heather's jaw trembled, but held.

"You must be Shadow's girl, to know my tricks so well. It won't be long now. I wonder—did he tell you this is the easy part? The part where you could still turn and run, like the last of Shadow's child-mothers? A changed mind can turn and change again, can it not? You did not want her at all—and now you do—enough to walk this path?"

Heather ground her jaw and felt a warm burst of oil over her tongue. The creature yelped.

"I hope you kept your teeth in your pocket, child-mother. You're going to need them."

As the vine shadows grew long, the petals of the flower curled and pulled inward, sealing in the poison red cloud and the bobbing stamen.

The amber honey hardened to a dark shellac and the pod began to sink into the earth, drawing its forest of vines behind it, until nothing but a dark cave lay at Heather's feet—a gaping hole in the wasteland she had crossed as she pulled her teeth and wet her rough tongue with blood.

The creature's rattling snores travelled through the thorn roots and tickled her mouth.

Heather reached up and pinched the end of his nose and the tip of his tail, then stretched her tired jaw and drew the thorns out of his middle.

Yellow eyes shot open and dripped honey at her through the darkness.

"This has never worked for anyone, you know," he said. "Even Shadow's own bride—in the days before his many girls—never returned from the wood beyond the tunnel, and most turn back before they ever reach it. It's much easier, you see, to turn a circle than to hold it at the half. But by all means, carry on. The farther you go, the sweeter your little one sings." Mud-colored lips pulled back from green teeth as the creature grinned up at her.

"First question?"

Heather wrapped her mouth around the long thorns. "How do I get to Estella?" The bristles clattered as she spoke. Blood ran down her chin.

The creature's hedge of brow rose. "The child has a name now? Well, that's new. She's not 'the baby'?"

"Answer my question."

"What was the question again?"

"That was my first question—I will not ask it a second time."

The creature smiled. "Such a clever girl. Well-coached. Shadow must want you to succeed. Does he want the child as well?"

Heather bared her thorns and hissed.

"You get to Estella by following the path, of course. Second question?"

"Where does the path begin?"

"At the bottom of your feet. Last question."

"What is your name?"

Yellow eyes narrowed. "That is not Shadow's last question."

"That is my last question. Answer me."

"Krandall."

"Thank you, Krandall."

"You won't, before the end."

Heather crawled around the bleeding creature and sat with her legs dangling into the hole where the flower had vanished.

Krandall curled in the dust behind her. "At dawn, sunlight calls my flower back to bloom, girl. And you'll be pulp for my roots."

She turned and stared into the little man's eyes. "Your flower is out of season." Heather pushed with her palms and slid into the hole.

In black dark, the tunnel threaded through the dirt at worming angles. Heather slid around its curves, felt her skin give way to the relentless grind of stone and dirt till her flesh sang raw.

When she crumpled, landing at the bottom of the pit, she heard her impact echo around her.

The flesh of her mouth hung in ribbons where she'd clenched her jaw in the fall. The raw skin of her thighs glowed with pain as she stood.

Heather stepped backward, toe-to-heel, until her back brushed against the cavern wall.

She pulled a thorn from her mouth and placed it by her heel.

Her fingers brushed small stones from the embankment as she circled the room, counting her paces till her damp thorn on the floor pierced the sole of her foot.

She had passed three openings in her circle of the room.

Ella favored my left side. She rubbed at the scar that swelled along her waist.

Heather entered the passage to her left, leaving another thorn at its entrance. She pulled two teeth from her pocket and slid the long roots into place, where her thorns had been. She felt the loose teeth quake in her mouth as she hurried, soothing her tongue against the smooth enamel.

A steady buzz rattled dust from the cavern walls as she pressed on through the darkness. She wiped mud from her watering eyes.

Daylight punctured the tunnel. Shafts of it shot through the shadows to the floor.

She saw a stirring ahead—the buzzing now loud enough to tickle the hollow of her throat.

An army of mud wasps swarmed through the bars of light—as large as herself—spreading sticky mud over small chambers writhing with larvae.

Heather pressed down on the peeling flakes of the flower's honey that crumbled from her brow and hung in her eyelashes.

A wasp settled on the tunnel floor in front of her, watching her with his myriad eyes. A bolt of sunlight sparkled over his hairy abdomen. The buzzing stilled.

"A sweet surprise!" The wasp flicked forward and landed at Heather's feet. He rose up on spindle legs to probe her face with his long, bristled mouth. "Yes, you taste just like her. Sweet as nectar. But you are too late. Your little pupa has grown wings and flown the hive. We finished her for you. Gave her wings, and poison."

Heather swallowed the pounding of her heart that rose in a scream from her gut. "How late?"

The wasp rubbed two pronged feet together and slicked them over a protruding stinger that jabbed out from between its legs. "Nearly a day. She'll have finished her ballad by now, I daresay, and then . . . "

"Then?"

"Sweet as nectar, you are. You both are." He slid the stinger down the side of her raw thigh.

Heather lowered her honeyed eyelids. She reached, lightning-quick, and grasped the stinger, wrenching it around so that the wasp writhed on its back. Acid peppered her face as she pulled.

His wings buzzed, scraping at the dirt of the tunnel floor.

Heather twisted. The swarm swept toward her in a hissing cloud.

Hairy chitin fractured, splintered the stinger from the twitching abdomen. She waved the stinger, sweeping it across the beams of light, and the swarm scattered. The wasp curled on the floor, rolling into a knot of legs. Heather wrapped her lips around the base of the stinger, sinking her thorn-teeth into it, sucking the sour acid from it like a straw. She hissed around the shaft. Poison glistened at its tip. She rushed and the wasps fell away, crawling into hollows whittled in the muddy walls.

Heather leapt from beam of light to darkness, leaving tattered wings in her wake, and ran through the tunnel.

Ahead, light shone—warm and golden like the flower honey, and she rushed into it, and into the ropey web stretched across its glow.

The web twisted with her, snapped and wrapped where she strained, then it trembled with her, as she lay back—exhausted. She felt the fibers stretched across her quiver, saw the low-slung bulb of the spider descend, the abdomen shining with a thousand sticky globes. Rough, scaled legs brushed over her. "You taste of insect and earth, of flower's honey and of mother's blood. What thing are you?"

Heather eyed the sticky globes, and saw soft stirring inside each. She flicked her tongue and pressed the stinger into one cheek.

"I am a mother," she said.

The spider lowered, and grasped Heather's face in her mandibles, sucked at her mouth.

"You are a child."

"But a mother . . ."

"In name only. You are a once-mother."

Heather felt her throat constrict, and the tight web clenched to fill the slack against her heaving chest.

"How old is your web, widow?" Heather asked.

"I wove it before the sun this morning, and drank the dew."

"Have you built here before?"

"Always. I love the taste of wasp, and honey. Of mothers." The spider inched forward.

"What of daughters?" Heather turned her head and sawed at the web with the stinger. Threads tightened as the spider grew near.

"A delicacy, and only for the queen. I will have my own daughters soon. If you would seek daughters, mother, I would give you mine. Nest them in you till they grow strong enough to feed from you. Would you nurse my daughters well?"

Heather wrenched at the trimmed web and fell free, rolling to the grass. She sprang to her feet and pulled the stinger from her cheek. She forced it through the palm of her hand, sliding it between her narrow bones, and waved it in front of her. "My daughter came through here. Did you see her?"

The spider lifted its front legs, rearing up large, mandibles grasping at the air. "I will trade you an answer for just a small taste."

Heather breathed. She held out her arm, the stinger protruding from the end. "Tell me which way my daughter flew."

The spider lunged and gripped her arm, driving its fangs into the stinger.

Heather dodged the crimping legs, and fell to the side, the stinger slipping free into the spider's crushing jaw. The spider hissed.

"Empty. Are you a dead thing, then, or a liar?"

"Both." Heather crouched, ready for the spider's advance.

The spider studied her, jaws clacking. "Such a sweet mother, with such sweet breath, and such a foul flavor. A shame about your daughter. East. She flew east, into the shadow of the sunset past."

～

Roots roped over the dew-soaked grass and climbed up into a dark canopy. Vines hung from the shadows, twining around the knots of wood jutting from the earth and forming thick, sinewy columns.

Heather climbed through them, chasing the high note of music— the tiny voice lost in the trees. She tore through the thick blue grass that grabbed at the rough skin of her knees and elbows, rubbing them raw. Slats of bark ripped at her hair, pulling it free and wrapping it into the tall columns.

She sucked juice from the sockets around her loose teeth and spat against the pale wood, marking her path in blood. Damp thorns littered the ground behind her.

For the way home, she thought. *If not for me, then for her.*

The root columns grew dense. Heather pressed through them, leaving pieces of herself in the gnarled burls that dotted the wood.

The columns ended abruptly, forming a near-solid wall around an open clearing. The grass stretched across into darkness, filled with more trees and hanging vines.

In the center of the clearing stood a tall woman, her skin the color of sage. Her eyes seeped golden light that lingered around her in a fragrant cloud. Moss hung in sheets from her angled shoulders, cloaking her in velvet. She smiled at Heather.

"You want her back, do you? But you never had her. She was never *yours*, not really."

"She was. She is." Heather placed her vine-arm across her

scarred abdomen, tracing the rippled flesh. Purple flowers bloomed along her wooded skin. "She belongs here."

"Ah. I see. You don't just want her back—you wish to undo what was done—uncut the cord. Well. My little nightingale is your. Little. Rosebud." The tall lady pulled a wet lily from her mouth, the petals uncurling in the light from her eyes. She dipped a finger in the center, trailing it in circles through the sticky dew. "Which would *you* rather be? A nightingale or a rosebud? Make flight and music? Or wither, tethered?"

Heather felt her lips grow dry and rough. "Don't forget bloom."

"Oh yes, there is bloom. Such a magnificent . . . few hours."

Heather's throat grew stiff and fibrous. "I am here. I made it to your grove. It is no longer your decision." Her vocal cords twined together, sprouting offshoots that curled her voice away into hidden parts of her mouth.

"It never was my decision—it was always yours, and you made it for me. You betray yourself. Usually one so uncertain does not make it this far. It's been so long since this old growth has seen a sapling."

Heather's fingertips sank and spiraled into the earth, roots plunging in search of water. "Put her back!" she screamed. Loam shot from her tongue.

"She cannot live in you. You know this. You knew it from the beginning. If I put her back, you will both die, as you would have done before Shadow sharpened his knife."

"She is mine."

"She never should have been." The dark woman crossed the clearing and spread the sticky flower sap across Heather's eyes and lips.

Heather felt it burn through the folds of bark that coated her face, felt them slough away, and her raw skin stung against the cool air. Small flowers tumbled from her hair, blanketing the grass around her.

The dark lady turned back to the trees. "Come, sweet child. Your mother is here."

A breeze stirred the blossoms in the grass. Estella stepped out from between two pillars of vine. Bright wings bristled from her half-formed back that twisted like the tree roots.

"Shall I fold her into a fist of bone? Punch her into the small spaces of your insides till you bleed and your heart fades, and carries her away with its silence?"

Heather clenched her hands and felt the soft, empty fingertips crush against her palm. "We're meant to be together. We were meant to *go* together."

"Shadow didn't think so."

"Shadow should not have spoken."

"It is his child. *You* are his child."

"No! She and I are *mine*. I never signed his paper. He *took her from me*."

"I agree, of course. None of you are ever his, and all of you, before long, fight your way to my grove. Or try to. And most become my trees. My grove of child-mothers, audience to nightingales. In the end, you are all mine. In the end, Shadow will be, too. He'll come after one of you, one day. Or, maybe, after me."

"He won't. He can't."

"In time."

"Never. I took his teeth and his eyes. I took his fingertips and his feet. There is no path that he can follow now, no trail he can trace." Heather spat thick honey, veined in blood, into the moss at her feet.

The dark lady smiled. "Vengeful little sapling. I wonder if you're even fit for my forest."

"He took her from me. And so did you. Now give her back, or your grove will burn." Heather's eyes heated. The air in front of her ignited in a blaze.

The dark lady retreated, then tossed her head back and laughed. "Of course! Krandall warned me you were different. I should have known. You are Laura's girl. Or the girl I left for Laura when her girl came to me. You *are* mine, my dear—you are *my* daughter, and Shadow's. I thought you came to give me new growth for my grove, and here you bring me a legacy." She spun, and darkness extinguished the light in front of Heather's face.

"Three generations, here in my wood. You were meant to die in your cradle, little changeling, not grow and bear fruit of your own."

The trees around them creaked and bent, stirring the air with wandering leaves. Estella curled in the fallen blossoms, and lay sleeping at the dark lady's feet. The tall woman cast the light of her eyes down to the sleeping child. "Let her stay. Please. You stay, too.

I do not mean to stir your wrath. It is lonely in my wood, and I have always wanted children."

Heather swallowed the taste of honey rising in her throat. "What sort of mother would you be to her?"

"More than you were." The light came up, sharply, into Heather's eyes.

"More than you were to me?"

"Yes. Yes, of course."

"Where are your other precious nightingales?"

"In the trees. Asleep, in their mothers' arms. I am not a monster, you know."

Heather listened to the gentle rattle of loose teeth in her face. "I am."

"I made you that way."

"And you can unmake this?" Heather ran her hands over her eyes.

"I would make you bloom, here in my grove."

"A magnificent few hours."

Light poured from the dark lady's eyes and ran down her face, pooling at the hollow of her throat.

"Root me where I can hear her sing. Where she will sleep in my branches."

"Take your place here, in the center, daughter. You will fill the clearing, and be my thorn-tree, my child-mother. You will shade the light of my eyes."

Heather walked into the open space. She knelt at Estella's side and whispered into the curling blossom of her daughter's ear, "Dream now as I will dream of you, always."

Tall grass clung to the soles of her feet as she took her place in the center of the clearing. She tipped her head back, and felt the bark cleave to her, felt her limbs stretch and twine. New sprouts grew from her in bright flashes and filled the space of the clearing, stole the sky of the grove.

Estella sang. Thorn-Heather's leaves trembled.

THROUGH
GRAVEL

W E TWISTED OUR bent backs and held our flowers up through the fine-grit gravel and soggy cigarette filters— up through the gaps and the spaces where things didn't fit together anymore, and we waited.

Beth came to us that spring in her red cardigan, reaching down for the buttercup sprouting from the crack in the sidewalk. She pinched the stem, as delicate as her own little fingers, and she was gone before her guardian could turn to see why she had stopped. She slipped through the cracks of the busy world above, and was ours. The first child of the new spring. The first child in more than eight years.

In the dark of the understreets, by the light of the grates and drains overhead, she smiled nervously as we marveled at her small digits, at how the dimples in her knuckles were fading into lily-slim fingers, at how straight her spine had grown without the weight of the city pressing down from above. At the gap in her smile.

Many of us had gaps in our smiles that year, but none so fresh as hers. Our arthritic fingers grasped at her shining hair. Youth was a balm to eyes even as weak as ours.

We huddled in excited half-formed factions for the meeting where one of us would be blessed with her guardianship. When the hour came and the name was drawn—and it was mine, Aemon—I confess, I wept.

I had never dreamed that when I stooped to my own small flower in the pavement years ago, I would be given a new life, one far from the paths of those I'd lost aboveground.

A new child. My heart filled with love for her—filled the holes in the spaces where things didn't fit together.

I stumbled through the custom of her adoption. It had been so long since I'd seen it done. I wrapped her in my parka and handed her a tarp, freshly patched, washed and folded. It would become her room, and annex to my home—our home. I gave her a trowel—my better one, with the smooth handle and less rust. I sprinkled her brow with water from the Last Drain.

Though it was Chev that had drawn my name, he was the one to protest. As soon as the ritual was complete, he stood, his reverence for the old customs the only thing that had kept him in his seat till then.

"Are you sure you're up to this, Aemon? You are old in years but young to our kind. Perhaps the child should be placed with someone younger and with more experience in our ways." He meant himself, of course. He'd been here since he was a tiny thing, born to the understreets to a Kindred mother long since washed away. But he still had youth in him. His hair still grew the color of shadows.

"I am no stranger to raising children, Chev."

"Yes. I recall. I believe it is relevant for us to inquire as to the nature of your daughter's death?"

Gasps echoed off the high stone walls of the meeting chamber. Chev raised his hands. "This is a rare moment where I feel a discussion of his life before coming to us as Kindred is not only prudent but necessary."

I thought of not answering. This was a violation of my rights. As far as the Kindred are concerned, no one has a life before their life underground. Our lives start with the appreciation of small flowers, from the time we notice a spot of brightness and pause to take it in. When the city forgets us and we slip through the cracks. We are born again beneath the streets.

But Beth looked scared. Her cheeks, rosy with chill a moment before, had gone white. I couldn't have that. For her sake, I let the fight fall from my shoulders.

"It was a car accident. My wife and daughter were driving home from the ballet. A drunk driver struck them. They both died."

I felt Beth's small hand then, inside my own. It was already taking on the cold of the underground, but it warmed me better than any sun that I remembered.

Chev's gambit had worked against him, and the Kindred shot him troubled glances as they crept away into their tunnels, to their tarp homes to cultivate their small patches of flowers, in hope of catching a Beth of their own.

Beth clutched her tarp to her chest, her red sweater darkening in the damp air of the tunnels.

"I'm sorry about your daughter." Her pupils stretched wide in the darkness, searching for scraps of light. Soon they would learn to fix open into the black stare of the Kindred, able to pull in the light from a storm drain three tunnels down.

I squeezed her small hand. "You're my daughter now, and the only one in all the understreets."

She was silent, then. I thought it was out of shyness. But knowing her now, I believe she was thinking. Planning.

"Why doesn't anyone else have children?" Beth crumbled compost over the delicate buttercup sprouts that lined the old brick wall.

"Most of us are very old. Only the very old and the very young stop for small flowers anymore. And the young these days are older than the young that used to be. There are too many cares on their shoulders to bother with a small bit of brightness underfoot." I looked at how her arms bent to her task, willowy and lean. "And you are very old, or very young, for a newborn."

I could hear her thinking in the way that she breathed. Slow and shallow, like a rush of fresh air might interrupt her train of thought, though the air isn't fresh. Not down here, and not up there.

"Do you miss your mother, Beth?" I shouldn't have asked it. I should have done as Kindred do and pretended she'd never had one. That the canal through which she was born was a drain—her caul the tender leaves of sidewalk weeds.

"I never knew her. I don't miss the nuns. They never let us play in the dirt." She ran her fingers through the black soil at the base of an unfurling sprout.

It's not uncommon for a Kindred. It's easier to slip through the cracks when no one is looking.

"Are you bored, Beth? Are you lonely?"

"No." She plucked at a mushroom sprouting from ancient grout and popped it in her mouth. "But maybe a little. Or maybe just worried."

I paused in my digging. "Worry isn't for the Kindred." I fixed my black eyes on her. "Worry leaves no room for small flowers." It's what Belle had told me once, when I was newborn to the understreets, before the sun had faded from my skin and my collar sprouted lichen.

"But I'm worried *about* the Kindred, Aemon."

"No need for that, child. We left our worries aboveground."

"But if there are no other children, who will there be when the elders are gone?"

"No one, love."

"But who will tend the flowers?"

"No one. Might be that's an end for small flowers in the city above. Or might be that they never needed tending. Might be that the tunnels will fill with streams of wild buttercups."

She smiled through the dark, and I saw her eyes were as black as mine. But then her smile wilted and her pupils shrank to pinpricks—her eyes wide discs of blue.

"I'll be alone, then. When all of you are gone. That can't happen," she said, and jabbed her trowel into the offal piled under a drain.

~

Toes tapped like the incessant drip of water, echoed through the meeting chamber as we waited. Beth balanced along an old train rail, dragging her toes through the grit, oblivious to the empty seat that held the elders rapt.

Roz never came.

The agenda was cast aside in favor of organizing a search. Chev knew where her tarp was, but none knew her fishing spot—her crack in the sidewalk where she held her flower, hopes high.

"Her knees have ague," Dane said. "It won't be far from her tarp."

No maps are allowed in the understreets, but any Kindred worth his muck can follow the glowing fissures in the street overhead. It's the branching vascular system of our world.

Dane found Roz in a bright beam of light pouring from the hole where a slab of sidewalk had fallen in and crushed her. Her fragile frame curled in at jointed angles, like a dry spider. She held a fistful of buttercups—one still pinched in her outstretched fingers. The flowers drank in the light and glowed with it.

We squeezed our eyes against the glare, wrapped strips of black cloth across them, and felt our way toward her. She had to be moved before the sunwalkers found her—before their light-kissed faces peered curiously through the hole, now a window to our world.

There was a rustling and crunch of gravel.

"Aemon, what should we do with her flowers?" A small voice echoed from somewhere in front of me. I peered at her from beneath my cloth. She stared at Roz's fallen form, her face pinched in a familiar kind of pain. Her childhood had faded from her in that moment—her shoulders squared and fists clenched.

"Beth, get away from there! The street here isn't stable. Put your blindfold on and stand back."

"I don't need a blindfold, Aemon, the light doesn't hurt after a minute or two." She kneeled and took Roz's hand in her own.

Chev's deep voice came from the left. "Obey your father, child. If you would be Kindred, your eyes must be attuned to the dark. Light poisons them. Shun it."

"The light isn't poison. Our flowers need it, so we need it. We need *more* of it," Beth said.

Heavy footfalls fell beside me. I ripped off my blindfold.

Chev had removed his as well, and he sprinted to Beth, grabbed her ear, and dragged her from Roz's sunbeam. My eyes burned in the light. Chev swung her by the ear into my arms. He narrowed his black eyes to see, and glowered. "Your duty is to raise her as Kindred. If you fail in this duty, you will be banished. I'll raise her myself. Properly."

Beth clutched at the redness of her ear peeking from between her curls.

Dane stood from where he'd cleared the concrete from Roz's crushed form. Raw pinkness bubbled up from where she had folded. "You can't banish a Kindred, Chev. And even if you could, you shouldn't. We need every Kindred who comes to us."

"If you could see her eyes right now, Dane, you'd know she isn't one of us."

Beth's eyes were as wide and blue as the sky. Sunlight danced across their shining surfaces. My own eyes had stopped burning, and I stared in wonder at the way the concrete dust sparkled in the beam of light.

"Change takes time," Dane said. He hefted Roz into his arms. "I only hope we've got *enough* time." He walked into the tunnel, heading for the Last Drain, the final resting spot of all Kindred.

Beth handed me a bouquet of Roz's buttercups. She grinned. Light glinted off her snaggletooth smile. "Your eyes are green," she said.

Roz's tarp was patched, washed and folded, and handed to Chev at the next meeting, ready to be given to the next child, whenever one might come to us.

Beth sat in Roz's empty chair. Chev overlooked it, though his brow lowered at the breach in decorum. There were now more chairs than elders.

Chev stood with his fists clenched in his coat pockets. "We are here to discuss new openings found to the street above. Has anyone witnessed promising new fishing grounds?"

No one answered. Beth toyed with a strand of yarn that had unraveled from the cuff of her cardigan. Her black eyes roved over the circle of elders. "Have you checked at the new museum?" She flinched as all eyes turned to her. I reached for her hand.

"What museum, child?" Belle asked.

"There's a new children's learning center, up on Wilson Stree—"

"We do not name streets here," Chev bellowed, his voice frothing into a white cloud in front of his mouth.

Beth stared at him. The soft lines of her face hardened. "In the far west sector, there is a new children's museum. They have a large parking lot, and a playground. The concrete is fresh. It may crack when it settles."

Dane stood. "I have no new fissures to report in the far west sector. But I will check there often in the next few weeks." He nodded his thanks to Beth.

"Have you tried—" Beth's voice trailed off as Chev hissed at her further interruption. She lowered her eyes.

I squeezed her small, cold hand.

Belle stood. "I would like to hear what the child has to say."

Beth slid off the end of her chair, shoes tapping against the damp brick. "Have you tried making a crack?" she asked. "Splitting a small hole in a spot where you know our flowers might be seen?"

Chev made a sound like a drain. "If finding small flowers were so easy, those that found them would not be Kindred," he said. "The Kindred are drawn to them because they are looking for something—and only in that moment understand that they have found it. It is a rare person who stops for small flowers."

"But what if it isn't? What if Kindred aren't rare at all? What if they're just in the wrong place?"

Chev's voice rose and echoed through the tunnels. "A Kindred still looking for their flower is not yet ready for the understreets. This meeting is over." He stalked from the chamber, vanishing into the tunnel that led to his tarp.

The other elders remained in their seats, looking at Beth.

"We don't have many tools," Dane said.

Beth held her trowel out, small fingers curled around the worn handle; its blade flashing in light so faint that even our gaping pupils strained.

Beth slipped the edge of her trowel into the seam where the rough under-grit of road met the smooth sidewalk near a drain, where the road had been opened before and worked soft. She twisted and pushed, digging away at loosened slag until a small seam of light opened and grew across her knuckles. She pushed the metal in farther. The plane of pavement shifted.

Beth's dark hair was showered with grey dust that sparkled in the light from the new fissure. She turned to me and smiled. I traded a flower for her trowel, and she raised it into the daylight. We breathed the fine dust that hung in the air.

Laughter and joyful shouting spilled through the beam of light. Within moments, the flower was pinched. The world blurred, as it always did at the birth of a Kindred. A deep scrape, as if all the streets of the city above were sliding over the tunnels, sounded in my ears. Like the world pulling apart and then falling back together.

Beth tumbled to the tunnel floor, a fair young boy in her arms. His hair was so bright it stung my eyes. He smiled at Beth, and wrapped his chubby arms around her neck.

Trowels chimed like small bells against the rough rock overhead. All through the tunnels, they made music, and seams of light opened across the understreets. So much light that new flowers bloomed— ones we hadn't seen since our sunwalker days. Our faces pinched, adjusting to the new brightness in our world. Our black eyes began to shrink back into a multitude of color.

"I wonder what color Chev's eyes are?" Beth dug at a sooty spot overhead. A small rush of dirt dusted her hair. She coughed and scrambled back as a chunk of concrete fell at her feet and shattered. The sounds of a busy street tumbled down through the new hole.

"I don't think we'll ever know, darling. I don't think he's coming back. And if he does—be kind to him. He doesn't even remember the sun." I collected the fistful of flowers that the bright boy—Beth had named him Bracken—harvested from our small patch.

He never spoke a word, but smiled and followed Beth everywhere. His feet were bare and unflinching against the cold tunnel floor, and his golden hair soon took on the texture of seaweed.

In Chev's absence, the Kindred's gapped smiles twinkled in falling bars of sunlight. The old adoption rituals were abandoned. Every elder now had a child—some two—and laughter sounded in the underground for the first time in living memory. There were now more children than tarps. The future of our line was secure.

~

A sound like a siren wailed through the tunnels. Kindred crawled from under tarps, blinking in the light. As the sound fell and then rose again, I realized it was a child, crying. I raced around corners, down tunnels, now unfamiliar in their sunlit map, until I found the source of the cries.

Belle held a young girl in her arms, fresh from the streets above. The girl pushed at Belle's face, her eyes wide with fear.

Belle looked to me, bewildered, her brows raised, raining concrete dust across her cheek. "What do I do? Why is it crying?"

Chev stepped out of the tunnel behind her. His face had grown gaunter, his eyes even blacker than before, as if he'd sheltered someplace deep, away from our growing light. "Because it isn't Kindred. That's a sunwalker child you've pulled down. Your greedy opening of the streets is contaminating our world."

Belle looked in horror at the child, and dropped it. It scrambled away from her, backed to the wall, and reached up for the light from the hole Belle had dug. A woman was screaming in the street above, and the child screamed in answer.

Beth ran up behind me, her face pale, her hand clamped around Bracken's fist.

"Go home, you two," I said. "Let us handle this."

The commotion aboveground intensified. The roaring screech of power tools sounded from the drain grate nearby. The understreets concussed with the assault of a jackhammer.

"They're coming," Chev said. "Leave the child and run. Its kind will claim it soon. Hide—or you're finished. We all are."

Beth lifted Bracken's feet from the ground and clutched him to her chest as she splashed down the tunnel. I limped after them.

"Pack the tarps," I called to the disappearing bob of her curls.

The Kindred packed their homes on their backs and vanished into the network of tunnels as the sunwalkers broke through to reclaim their stolen child. Dust rained all along the cracks we'd made—our unnatural breaches widened under the stress of the city's machines.

Beth, Bracken, Chev, Belle, and I huddled in an enclave, listening to their frantic mission. A loud crack echoed from the tunnel. It traveled, ripping along the underground network. The air filled with dust. A roar like a wrecking train followed. And then all went black with soot, then as bright as day.

The stone all around us seemed to roar, the bricks at our backs throbbing with the vibrations of the world coming undone. Tides of dust rolled past our enclave, chased by light strong enough to throw our shadows against the walls.

The city had fallen. The understreets were now the settling ground for the rubble of that which had rested above our heads. Small tracts of tunnel remained, clogged with debris.

Chev rubbed at his eyes and gasped as the pure sunlight raked at his pale face. Beth reached up and took his face in her hands. His breathing slowed. His eyelids split and peeled back to reveal nothing but a field of white shot through with bulging red capillaries. The red spread through the sclera like a stain. His pupils had contracted to nothing, sealed, shut off from the light forever. Beth's hands flinched back.

"You see what you've done, child? That's an end to us all. The sun has risen on the understreets, and the time of the Kindred is over."

I pulled Beth and Bracken behind me. Belle reached out and stroked Chev's cheek. "What do we do now?" she asked.

Chev choked on another wave of dirt blowing through our small section of tunnel. He grasped Belle's hands to his cheeks and a tremor slipped into his voice. "We do what we have always done. We follow the tunnels. Whatever is left of them."

"But where?" Belle asked. In the light, her bulging white knuckles writhed like compost grubs.

"To the only place left—the last place, the Last Drain."

~

Chev shoved Beth in the small of her back. She stumbled through the knee-deep water toward the metal grate. "You're the expert with a shovel, child. Now dig."

I grasped Chev's wrist and squeezed till he let out a grunt. "Touch her again, and I'll send the rest of you where your pupils have gone." Rage made me young again. But Chev pulled away from me and spat into the reeking water.

Belle held Bracken out of the water and stroked his damp curls. "Enough, the both of you. You wear my nerves worse than the sirens."

The crooning alarms hadn't quit since the dust had settled. The city above had rushed to the aid of its fallen streets. Crumbled houses wedged like barricades along our ancient pathways. Dane's tunnel was gone. He and his three children were somewhere beneath the ruin of a home that had had green curtains and white walls.

Chev flinched with every strike as Beth's trowel chimed against the cement that encased the bars blocking the opening of the Last Drain. Her brow furrowed in concentration. "I don't understand . . ."

"Don't understand what, love?" I watched as her breathing turned slow and shallow again.

"If this is where you take the Kindred when they die, why isn't there space already? How do they get through?"

Belle looked to me and shook her head.

Chev nodded to the grate. "You'll find out soon enough, child. Sooner, the faster you dig."

With the bar pulled free, we squeezed through the gap, the water at our feet flowing in a current that pulled us toward the space beyond.

"There," Chev said. "We have passed through the Drain. All the Kindred are dead, now."

Beth's fingers scuttled up the side of my coat, gripping their way to my elbow. "Aemon?" She swept her foot across the unseen floor of the drain tunnel. "What are we standing on?"

The floor rolled beneath us, shifting like a landslide.

"Your ancestors," Chev said. "Or my ancestors." He reached into the dark and pulled a skull from the slick water. "I'm not certain they'd accept you as their own. Not after what you've done." He held the stone face up to Beth's. "Look into their black eyes and apologize, girl, so they may let us pass safely over their graves."

"Enough, Chev!" Belle took the skull from him. She kissed its brow and lowered it back into the water. "What do they care anymore?"

We stumbled over the rolling bones of our ancestors till the drain's pull grew heavy and its current pressed us against another grate. Beth hammered at the concrete while Bracken pulled, leveraging his tiny weight against the bars. When their arms grew tired, Belle and I took over. And when we wearied, Chev took the trowel from us and drove it into the crumbling rock.

"It seems there are drains beyond the Last Drain," Beth said, rubbing the ache in her elbow.

Chev paused, running his fingers through the water.

"There are whole worlds outside of what you know, aren't there?" she pressed. "This isn't the end at all."

The water beyond the grate ran clearer, the floor smooth brick interrupted with rusted train tracks. Numbered doors dotted the walls at intervals. Chev eyed them suspiciously, as if they would burst open and pour forth an army of angry sunwalkers.

The water grew lower and lower, disappearing through invisible cracks, till it ran in isolated rivulets. Beth's cardigan trailed loose strings into it like trolling lines from a hungry vessel. The tunnel echoed with gurgling—the sound of water falling. Belle had begun to squint, and I realized that the tunnel was growing lighter.

The floor sloped to a low dip where the last water trickled into a grated drain. Chev stopped.

He crouched over the drain and pressed his face against its darkness. "Here is our path," he said.

No one responded.

"Give me the trowel." He held a gnarled hand out to Beth. She handed him the tool and stepped back.

"Daylight bathes the understreets. We must go under again. Under-under. The Kindred belong beneath it all, where *rare* flowers grow—where they're appreciated and not taken for granted." He threw himself against the bricks, driving the trowel between them.

"Or maybe . . . " Beth looked over her shoulder at the growing glow at the end of the tunnel. Her eyes flashed a small sliver of blue. "Maybe we should keep going."

Chev tossed a loose brick over his shoulder into the shrinking puddle behind us.

"We could teach them, up above. Show them. We don't love small flowers any less for being in the light. *That's* what makes us Kindred." Beth moved toward Chev.

Chev panted and heaved at another brick. The edge of the grate showed through the old grout like an exposed ribcage. He laughed with what little air he could draw, but his smile faltered.

"Maybe you're right, child," he said.

Belle and I looked to each other. She pulled Bracken close.

"You were right about the Last Drain, after all." The fight had gone out of his voice.

"What about it?" Beth took a step closer to Chev, her toes edging up to where he lifted the groaning metal from the stones.

"That wasn't the Last Drain." He swung his legs into the dark hole. He handed the trowel back to Beth. "This is."

He vanished into the dark, falling with the water that spilled over its edge, its droplets glowing like bright eyes in the rising glow from the end of the tunnel. We never heard him land.

At the end of the tunnel, the metal of Beth's trowel flashed like fire against the crumbling rock. When she paused, we saw our faces in it, pale and veined, pinched against the sting of pure daylight. Bracken reached through the bars and grasped at the tall grasses that grew up against the opening. I lay my palm against the bricks, the end of the understreets, and said a quiet goodbye to my home.

When we broke through into the stiff grass, we sank into it, burying our faces from the sun, and slept.

We woke as the sun dipped behind a distant hill, relieving our eyes from its sting. We were curled in a ditch—our tunnel set into the side of a hill that overlooked the fallen city. Clouds of dust rose from its ruin, glowing in places where flames shot from tears rent in gas lines and electric hubs. Between us and its endless light, the hill stretched, full of flowers. Blue, like Beth's eyes. Curling leaves green, like mine.

Bracken ran into the field, hopping over and around the flowering clusters, lowering his face to the bright blooms.

We waded onto the hillside. Perfume rose around us and masked the dank funk of the compost and tunnel water.

"Can we live here? Can we make a living like this?" Belle clutched her hands to her chest. Tears traced pale tracks across her dusty face.

"I suppose we'll try." I reached for her hands and pulled them away from her heart, folding them into my own.

Beth called after Bracken. He danced away down the hill toward a tall rose. He cartwheeled around it, a breathless singsong of joy tumbling up the hill back to us. Beth ran toward him. "Bracken—" Her voice strained, the last syllable of his name a wail.

He righted himself and reached for the tall stem. The peach bloom bobbed, orange in the light from the setting sun. He wrapped his small fist around the barbed stem and cried out from the sting of its thorns. The hill seemed to roll beneath our feet as if the earth had turned to water. Bracken vanished.

Beth screamed.

Belle and I ran to her, long grasses catching at our feet. Beth had fallen, sobbing into a patch of blue flowers. I pushed her hair back from her face, cupped her cheeks in my hands.

"Shh, Beth, shh."

She wailed like a sunwalker.

Belle wrapped Beth in her shawl. "That boy goes where he's meant to. He's a new kind of Kindred. He knows tunnels, and cities, and fields. He pulled at the tallest flower—and someone, somewhere, knows that makes him special. Might be it's Chev, in the under-under, building a new world. And when we're ready, he'll hold a flower for us, child. Don't cry."

Beth rolled out of her embrace and ran her fingers through the grass, pinching each flower she came to, pulling at it, ripping it from the ground and moving on to the next. She carved a barren path in the hillside.

Belle and I sat in the blue flowers and watched her trail lengthen in the stretching dark.

"She won't find it that way." Belle brushed torn petals from her shawl and wrapped it back around her shoulders.

"She'll realize that soon."

"But will she realize it before she pulls out all the roots?"

"No. Not her." My heart ached for her, but I smiled. "That one breaks worlds."

"Then how will we find the lad?"

"He'll be at the other end of whatever flowers are strong enough to grow back."

STILL LIFE WITH NATALIE

ITS NOT A GRAVEYARD, it's an ecosystem. I mean, yeah, there are graves, all tilting across a ragged lawn, and that's all most people see—death, stones like rows of dry teeth. And in some graveyards, that's all they want you to see—marble stark against a blank slate of manicured grass. And yeah, the light's better in that sort of place, where the trees are tamed into shape and let the sun through. But the flowers are better here.

To paint flowers, you need an old cemetery. A century of mourners' offerings gone to seed, taken root. The best kind of garden gone feral. And wild, native things carried on the wind that feed on all the richness under the soil.

It's impossible to get my easel level on the lumpy ground. All my paintings are askew, slanted—I like it that way, now. It's a whole new perspective—a new way to look at graves, at flowers.

We don't have cemeteries like this back home. The water table is too high. All the bodies get stacked in stone huts, or burned and stored in a field that's paved like a parking lot of corpses. And nothing grows but infernal moss. You know how to paint moss? It's a wash of green. It takes less skill than finger-painting.

I add a bit of blue to the petal of a tiny violet.

At home, all that heat and wet makes the lifecycle swift. Accelerated decomposition. Sprouts splitting their seed cases right in front of your eyes. Plants die in layers, black and sticky, each generation insulating the last.

It's cold here. Things move slow. It's only September, but the tips of my fingers ache. The cold soaks in and everything smells like ice weeks before the snow arrives. The light has changed, and I realize I've been here for hours, only a few small blossoms finished. My models will shrink overnight, close up, maybe get nipped with frost.

I swish my brushes in my canteen, toss them in a stained wood box. I lay the wet canvas carefully in the trunk, nestled between the easel and spare tire.

I look back at the wild violets peeking out of the shadow of the stone. Their heads are already lowered, as if praying over the grave. A few of these blossoms will live forever, though, on canvas.

The picture will never be finished now. None of them ever are. Life moves too fast in the graveyard—the light shifts, and death comes too soon.

"You're going to fail that class, Colin. Are you going to tell your mother? Or shall I?" My mother's cousin, her doppelganger running twenty years behind, thumbs threateningly at her cell phone, scrolling through the texted chronicle of reports she's made on my progress.

"I paint better than the professor."

"Not if you count finished pieces." Natalie stretches across the couch like she wants me to paint her. I've told her I don't do portraits. I do still life. "Still Alives"—the flowers of the dead. They're the memories—the last remaining thoughts of those that feed the roots. Clear minds grow pretty things. Dark thoughts grow weeds and poisons. I'm not just painting flowers, I'm painting echoes—the last stories the dead have to tell.

I can see in Natalie's eyes that her grave would grow thistle and nightshade. I've warned her to see to her thoughts, lest she sleep eternal in a weed patch. But I think she likes it. I think she'd finger-paint dandelions.

"So what are you going to do for your first New England winter? What are you going to paint?" She cracks her back and folds an arm behind her head.

"I took some photos. I guess I'll paint from them." She must see me shudder. Knows I hate the thought. Knows it's not the same.

"Are you still going to call them 'still alives' if the flowers are dead under three feet of snow?"

My teeth hurt. My whole face does. It must be the cold.

They call the largest model a conservatory. It has a heavy-duty composite frame and panels made to withstand heavy snowfall. Best of all, they're opaque, and the light inside is milky, ambient. Deep troughs of rich earth line the long walls. The aisle is just wide enough for my easel.

Natalie squeezes a lump of dirt in her hand, crumbling it. "What are you going to plant?"

I'll need a lock for the door. "Nothing. Just going to see what grows."

She furrows her brow as best she can against the stiffening effects of Botox. "Things don't just grow, Colin, you need seeds."

"There are seeds in there already. I just don't know what. Violets, probably. Definitely roses, lilies, carnations. Dandelions, probably. Weeds."

Natalie's face falls. She shakes her head and scrubs her dirty palm against her pants. "Colin, you didn't."

"I can't give up my theme, Natalie, that's half the beauty of the painting."

"You took the grave dirt?"

"Just the top layer. I put the sod back down. No one ever goes there. No one will ever know."

The conservatory door slams. Fiberglass panels rattle like dull drums. She'll be calling my mother. Condensation dribbles down the frosted fiberglass. Sweat runs down my back. The heat—the dampness—it feels like home. But the grave soil is pure New England. It smells of promise. Of stolen summer. Of art.

"You're grinding your teeth."

"What?"

"That's why your jaw hurts." Natalie pulls my hand from my jaw and wipes at the mess my fingers have left behind. Dirt. No paint. There hasn't been paint for weeks.

"It's not worth the stress, Colin. Just drop the class. Take an incomplete and register again in the spring, when the flowers are back."

"I can't fail, Natalie. That's not an option."

"Waiting for the right time isn't failing. Your theme is important to you. Great. Your professor will understand. But you're not going to get daffodils in October, Colin. Not here. Not unless you plant them yourself. That's not how nature works."

She's right. Her words are skunk cabbage and nettle, but they aren't wrong. I said it myself—it's an ecosystem. You need the whole cycle to make life.

I miss my classes. I tell the professor I need the time to work—need the light. It's not a lie. I head back to the graveyard, where the flower stalks have turned to dry sticks and the grass stabs at my knees and palms like little sabers—like an army guarding the treasure under the soil.

The New England winter earth is hard—hoarfrost crackles under my spade as I pry at the layers of dirt. A lattice of ice, holding everything together.

I lay the lumpy bag carefully in the trunk, nestled between the shovel and spare tire. Haul my harvest back to the long conservatory.

Finger bones rattle in terra cotta pots like dice in a cup, casting my fortunes. I drop fistfuls of rich earth over them—the same dirt they've known for thirty years. Long leg bones stretch along the flowerbeds. The oil at their core no longer shines, but it's still there—a matte stain on dry meat. I can smell the life left there through the dust, like iron and old fruit. I seed my ground with these forgotten dreams, and see what grows. Pleasure or poison—it's all art, either way.

I'm tired, and my back aches too much to bend over my canvas. And I need time. Patience, while the roots find their source.

I never thought I'd be so glad to see moss. I wash green across the canvas, feel the texture of the woven fibers against my roughened fingertips, calluses grating, my skin cells becoming a part of the piece. The smell of it comes in waves as intoxicating as the color—chlorophyll sweat clinging to my face like dew. My breath comes so quick it dries the paint in front of me before I've finished spreading it. I dip my hand back in the paint and smear it across the canvas. A few more days of warm wet and filtered winter sunlight, and there will be flowers. Flowers always follow the green, and the green always comes first.

The stalks all bend under the weight of shrinking blooms. Petals drop to the dirt without ever growing vibrant. The paintings all look as if they are viewed through smoke. I dab more brown along the edge of a leaf.

"Are you ever coming inside?" Natalie only speaks in oily ivy now. She casts so much darkness that I swear the plants are starved for light.

"I need to turn something in tomorrow. At least show some progress." I rub my arm along my upper lip, wiping away the drops shaken loose by speech. Her glasses are fogged, but I feel her look. Like my mother peering out of her eyes.

"It doesn't look like the flowers are doing very well." She touches the tip of a finger to a limp petal and it falls.

"God damn it, Natalie!"

She turns on me, leans into her shout. "They're not 'still alives,' Colin. They're dead. You're letting them die. Flowers need to be nurtured." She turns away so fast that the breeze in her wake knocks another petal free.

She's right, though. About the nurturing. Flowers need to be fed. Not just once, but over and over. I need to complete the ecosystem. I'm going to miss class again.

~

All my nails are split and my palms are a mess of blisters, but I can hold a brush.

I never noticed how many colors there are in dirt. It isn't just brown. It's a thousand browns, gold, green, even blue like Natalie's hard eyes.

And ants aren't just black, but are mahogany anywhere the light shines off their beaded bodies.

Spiders the color of dirty glass—inside a dark rainbow of organs.

Worms the color of salmon and skin, and worms the color of bone.

The dirt is alive. Still alive. Long after the flowers die. Long before new seedlings split their casing and take root, punch tendrils through the earth to the richness waiting there.

Nothing grows in dirt that isn't moving, churning, recycling itself in the long throat of worms.

Life comes from life, or what life leaves behind, hidden in the dark center of bones. And hollow bones hold only echoes.

The liquid pooling in the sunken eyes is mustard-seed yellow, almost ochre, but a color I've never mixed before. My hand shakes as I dip the brush, gather pigment from around brittle lashes, and spread it along the edge of a daffodil. The perfect color for where the shadow of a headstone falls across the buttery petal.

There are flowers now. It's early spring in my little garden. But there aren't enough blooms to fill a gallery.

I lower the head of Albert Vernon 1926–1999 into the pot at my feet. Scalp slides from bone and teeth tumble from leathery lips as his cheekbone comes to rest against the pottery.

"Show me a pretty story, Albert," I whisper to him. The smell of him sticks to my tongue, stink turning to flavor, and it's ochre, too. "Your wife was all wild morning glory and bluebells. I bet she covered you with roses."

I pour dirt over him. Gather water from the condensation troughs and saturate the soil. I need more blossoms, and fast. I still haven't finished a painting.

~

Natalie brings me a package. She walks right into the greenhouse. Doesn't knock. I need a lock.

The package is wrapped in red paper, green ribbon tied around it. Already? I'm running out of time.

I don't want to set my brush down, but I do it. Get it over with. If she argues, I'll just be distracted longer.

"Merry early Christmas. I thought you could use this now. Didn't want to make you wait." She smiles. It's a nice smile. It's a shame I don't do portraits.

Then her face wrinkles. "Ugh! It stinks in here."

I scan the beds. Everything planted, nothing visible except the flowers. Little pops of color bobbing over buried secrets.

"I got a weird fungus. Can't get the stink out." I smile back, take the package, snap the ribbon, rip the paper. Inside the box, resting on a pillow of tissue, is a pair of wool fingerless gloves. The stitches are strained in places, loose in others.

"A lady at work showed me how to knit them. I thought they might help you paint outside in the winter."

She'd sewn roughly-cut suede patches to the palms.

"And maybe your hands won't get so beat up gardening."

Her thoughts are all buttercups and forget-me-nots, morning glory vines twisting around my heart.

"Thank you," I say. I've forgotten how to say anything else.

She smiles. Sunflowers—black-eyed Susans. Colors I haven't seen for months. Hues that have gone dry in my paint box. Colors I need.

The composition of her thoughts is stretched across the canvas of her face, and it's more than I can resist.

The secret of Still Alives is that they're portraits. Not of faces, but of minds—a moment of heart frozen in time, like a bulb wintering in the cold earth before the right gardener calls it up from the soil. Not everyone gets a portrait of their best moment. Only kings and queens, and Natalie.

The earth in my flowerbed dances with life. And from its shifting soil, a thousand blossoms unfurl. It reminds me of home.

GOLDEN
AVERY

A VERY HELD THE panties at arm's length and stretched them wide. "Whose are *these*?" she asked. And every face turned to her, just like they always did. Her strawberry-gold hair and cold blue eyes turned every head at camp, including mine, and when I turned this time, I saw my underwear pinched in her fingers in not at all the way I had dreamed it.

The elastic strained between her fists. Her gloss-slick lip curled, then slid into a smile as stifled laughter echoed around the room.

It was a stupid question. Everyone knew they were mine. But stupid questions were just another tool in her makeup kit.

I stomped over to her, feet splashing on the tiles, my face as red as my sunburned shoulders, and I gripped the elastic waistband in my fist and pulled.

She pulled harder. "Keep stretching, they'll fit in no time!"

If my ears hadn't been full of lake water, the laughter might have ruptured them. A small miracle, I guess.

She let go and I fell back into a rank puddle on the locker room floor.

Avery steadied herself as if the ground shook. Girls laughed and ran out of the tiled shack.

The clammy water soaked the back of my skirt. The fabric clung to my ass as I hiked up the hill to the cabins. I was running out of clothes to change into—I hadn't figured I'd need three outfits every day. I'd have to check in at the office and rent more uniforms. They had plenty more, in the largest size.

Avery and her groupies were already at the activity tent, so I changed in peace instead of trying to squeeze into the shadowed alcove between the bunk beds and the desk. There were no fingers pinching my rolled waist, no snapping of bra straps. I rubbed my hip where I'd landed, wondered if I'd get an ugly bruise—a target for their bony fingertips.

A wolf spider skittered from behind the trashcan. I scooped her up and slipped her between Avery's sheets.

The activity tent was quiet—rows of plucked brows drawn down in concentration as teens scraped pocket knives across the bark of long branches.

"Carve a walking stick for tomorrow's hike," instructed the paper placed at each setting. Atop the paper sat a thin Swiss army knife. Leaning against each chair, a rough branch.

There were no counselors in sight. There often weren't. Still, arming fifty fifteen-year-olds with knives and sharp sticks seemed like poor planning. But they were all intent on their task, and hardly anyone noticed when I walked in and took my seat.

If I had carved more quickly, I might have made it out without ever having been seen—but the scrape of the knife on the wood, the smell of the fresh pulp—it was so hypnotic I remained still much longer than I should have.

"We could hunt pigs with these spears," Avery said, her voice like fairy bells and river music. Every face spun to her, then to me. "Want to practice, piggy?" She snorted through her upturned, freckled nose and thrust the stick at me.

It jabbed me in the shoulder. I yelled and my knife slipped, sinking into the palm of my hand.

I leapt from my chair and ran at her, around the table, trailing blood—chasing her across the tent.

She danced out of reach. I panted after her, reaching for the flapping hem of her skirt. She spun in the air, hair spreading in a rose-gold arch around the vortex of her laughter.

Her eyes sparkled when she laughed.

That was Avery, then.

Avery *now* struggles a bit with her boyfriend, her college classes, her share of our rent. Her weight.

Mostly she struggles with the fact that, while she played beer pong, I nibbled celery, and now I'm the one turning heads.

But I love her. Always have. Small miracle.

And she loves me, and has loved me since I sucked the venom from her spider bite. Never mind that the spider wasn't venomous and no amount of sucking could draw all the poison out of Avery. I know, I tried—sucked long and hard.

I give her my expensive fat jeans as I shrink out of them and slip into something slimmer.

She'll pretend like she likes it—says it's good to have curves—but the tall stack of fad diet books at her bedside is as straight as a column.

Six months ago, she brought home a sack of expensive creams. I rubbed them over her till I couldn't tell where the cream ended and her soft skin began. I cupped the puckered speck of her spider-bite scar in the pale crescent knife scar on my palm.

Still, her thighs dimpled. I like them that way, but she cried an ugly cry, face twisted, and reached under my skirt and pinched me—hard—on my smooth, firm thigh.

It bruised, but it was lovely.

Three months ago, I handed her an old dress. She held me and wept and asked for help.

I taught her how to sit down to a healthy meal. How to then excuse herself discreetly. And how to bring it all back up—every crumb and calorie in accelerated reverse.

I taught her she could have her cake and eat it too. Guys love a girl with a healthy appetite. If she's thin.

She took to it rough at first—the godawful mess she made—but I told her it gets more dainty with practice. Ladylike.

She shed a few pounds, but not many. She tried to steal my jeans but put them back, with the ass cut out, when they didn't fit her.

I told her she'd have to stop drinking her red wine—empty calories—if she wanted to turn heads again.

"Besides," I said, "it isn't healthy."

She said she needed the buzz.

So I brought her some speed.

Three weeks of that and we had progress, and her eyes lit up just like I like them. But she couldn't fit into her birthday present—that pretty camp-girl uniform—the polo and pleated skirt I'd taken from her trunk and saved, for a special occasion.

Two weeks ago, her boyfriend left her. He said it was because she was acting crazy, but we know better. We know what *they* like.

She said she'd try anything.

You can get anything online these days. To any company, a sale is a sale, and medical equipment is no different. Hell, we even got free two-day shipping.

The curved injectors and cannulas arrived last Friday. My ex hooked us up with a cocktail of painkillers and antibiotics. I stayed up all night on YouTube, becoming an expert.

On Saturday, I told her to get naked and lie down in the bathtub.

The drugs made her eyes dull and she puked in her hair, but she didn't seem to feel the small incision. Or the narrow wand sliding in beneath her creamy skin.

I scraped at the layer of fibrous fat.

She went rigid—damn near bit her tongue in half—and passed out cold.

I took one of the clean towels from the stack on the toilet seat and tucked it under the corner of her mouth, to catch the mess. And I worked quickly.

Those tight little strands of cellulose that hold your layers together—stitching them like quilting—they're what pull in the dimples. If you snap those like elastic, separate the layers, they'll hang smooth.

It will all grow back, eventually—stitch itself back together. A small miracle. But, in the meantime, you suck out all the fat, every swollen cell, and the skin lies smooth as the surface of a lake.

I ripped every stitch under her skin. All over her stomach and butt and thighs. A few extra incisions, to get those hard-to-reach places. Bruises blossomed purple in the wake of my wand as I waved it through her, making her shame vanish into the bag at my knees.

Magic.

The bag swirled with fat and blood, rose gold.

When I finished, I stitched her up with super glue—like we learned at camp. I put my tools in the dishwasher. I crushed pain pills and stuffed the powder past her swollen tongue. I poured the contents of the bag into the toilet—a little at a time—and flushed it all away. I filled sandwich bags with ice and draped them over her.

She slept until Wednesday, but the pain pills were running low, and she'd see red if we ran out.

It's all about portions.

The internet said swelling is normal. But try telling that to a girl with bright fever eyes who just sees herself getting fatter.

I kissed her and told her she was beautiful.

There's hardly an ounce of fat left on her body, and if she's still not happy with it, well. She's got a problem.

By Friday, she could almost get out of the bathtub. The purple faded to yellow and the swelling had gone down.

On Tuesday, she leaned against my shoulder while I slid the camp skirt over her narrow hips. We turned, so she could see in the mirror. She beamed and her eyes sparkled.

She let go of my neck and smoothed the crisp pleats over the angles of her hip bones. Her eyes watered at the pressure of her palms against the tender flesh.

She lifted her skirt. Scars mottled her legs—a shiny network of pink and ivory. They rippled, just like the cellulite.

She moaned against the gauze packed around her tongue and threw herself toward the doorway, hobbling to the bathroom.

I followed, chasing after her swaying skirt.

She rummaged in the first aid kit and pulled out the little Swiss army knife. Her eyes burned brighter than I had ever seen them as she carved away her scars.

Long strokes, curling strips—like we learned at camp—falling around her in a pile like rough pine bark. Till her flesh flowed slick with blood and I couldn't tell where her wounds ended and her soft skin began.

She lay back in the tub, shivering. Her eyes dimmed as all the drugs, the fever, the hate bled out of her. The drain gargled like laughter as it swallowed the swirling vortex of her red.

I kissed her and told her she was beautiful—my small miracle.

I slipped the knife from her shaking fist and carved a thin line—skinniest line you've ever seen—across her creamy throat.

And I ordered her an extra large coffin, with rose gold ornaments.

SCAVENGERS

THERE ARE PLACES in the world where the dead are not buried. They're left for the elements, for the vultures and eagles. Beak by beak, the dead are cleaned away, their spirits carried to the heavens on scavenger's wings or their bodies erased, conveniently. Perhaps both, but Mallow only needed the latter.

"And you mightn't be dead, yeah? How's a bird supposed to know? But you're dead to me." Mallow tightened the rope.

Darcy sputtered, choking on the tears running down the back of her throat, on the bile climbing up it—and she wailed till it all mixed to froth.

Mallow stepped back from the stone table and Darcy's trussed form. The old woman's skin glowed red where she'd been dragged up the trail. Her knees and elbows wept almost as much as her face did, though none of it moved Mallow as much as it might have, once. She stood as cold and resolute as the funeral rocks that dug into the bones of Darcy's back.

She pulled the bright red slippers from Darcy's feet and hurled them over the cliffside, to be lost among the boulders or tangled in the trees. Their red would fade to grey, just like the meat on the rocks.

For miles around the cliffs, the birds' nests shone with the tresses of the dead. Soon Darcy's curls would shine like silver ribbons, woven through soft beds for delicate hatchlings.

Mallow threw one final rock at Darcy, spring a bit more blood to scent the air, then turned her back and began the long trek around the mountain. On the far side of the cliffs, the valley stretched out, open and welcoming and everything Darcy wasn't, at least not anymore. And above the valley perched the Elevated School for Diminishing Young Ladies. Darcy's kingdom, once. Not anymore.

Mallow wondered if Darcy's soul would ascend to heaven on the birds' wings, as the rite intended. But that wasn't why she had done it. It wasn't done out of respect. It wasn't done for the birds, or for the safe passage of departed spirits. It was done because she had it coming, and because she'd seen too much.

There had never been any overt violence. No great wrongdoing. It was a slow brew of poison. A cruel jab here and there, any chance. Just enough to draw a bead of blood between them and keep Mallow always anemic.

Toxic, she was. And Mallow suddenly feared for the birds that had already gathered to feast on that heap of vitriol. Perhaps it would poison them.

Mallow tightened the straps of her pack. It was much lighter without the coils of rope, but her neck and shoulders ached from hauling the struggling woman up the trail. *Should've given her more of the morphine.* She'd been shocked by how hard the woman had fought. *But was there ever a day we didn't fight, once we made up our minds to do it?*

A scream tore down the trail from above. Mallow wasn't sure if it was Darcy or the birds.

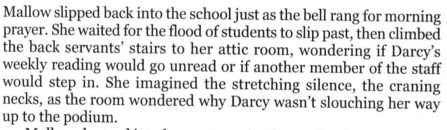

Mallow slipped back into the school just as the bell rang for morning prayer. She waited for the flood of students to slip past, then climbed the back servants' stairs to her attic room, wondering if Darcy's weekly reading would go unread or if another member of the staff would step in. She imagined the stretching silence, the craning necks, as the room wondered why Darcy wasn't slouching her way up to the podium.

Mallow changed into her grey service dress. She slipped into her apron and tightened the knot of fair hair at the back of her head. She wouldn't be missed. She had no podium, no speech to give. Not anymore—she'd given it to the birds. Perhaps they'd carry that on their wings—take her curse up to heaven with Darcy's soul.

Joseph might notice them missing. Both gone. And he might know, then, that the thing was done.

She pulled white gloves over the ragged scrapes of her palms— rope burns and rock gouges. They'd burn in the dishwater. But no one cares what's under a housemaid's gloves.

Chapel ended in a parade of chesty coughs. A river of pale young women with their hair tied back in austere ribbons, all hacking a deep baritone through their consumption-rattled frames. Sucking desperately at the mountain air that was meant to do them so much good, to prolong their fragile lives. They came to die as slowly as possible, and to live out their last days in rote luxury.

Mallow kept her eyes down, sliding over the textured shine of their satin slippers. *Mustn't shock the sick young ladies by—what? Reminding them that I exist? That it isn't a ghost that scrubs the bloody phlegm from their pillowcases?*

Joseph's gleaming leather shoes followed the procession of dainty slippers, and Mallow let her eyes dart up his figure to his thin face. His green eyes held forward, focused on the tied curls of the girls in front of him. *Look at me*, she willed, but he didn't. Later, then. He would look later—in his office, maybe, or in the library as she scraped the ash from the hearth.

By the time Mallow had swept the crumbs of tea cakes out from under plush chairs, the school hummed with the search for Darcy. Mallow gripped the broom handle till her white gloves were dotted red from her torn hands. *They'll come clean in the dishwater.*

Mallow knew the search would begin in the valley bars and taverns. Everyone knew about Darcy's secret medicine. Eventually they'd think to check the cliffside trails, but she doubted they'd check the funeral rocks at the very top. None of the young ladies had died that week. No one needed a funeral. The birds would be hungry. Sooner or later, a girl would die, and they'd take her in procession up the cliffside to the funeral rocks for her body to be consumed— and her sickness consumed with it, where it could no longer reach her family, her neighbors, the whole village. By then there shouldn't be any trace of Darcy. Even the ropes would be plucked away for nesting fibers.

Mallow jabbed the broom against the wall and dragged it through the corners of the room. Swept clean. Every inch. *Don't miss a spot.*

She gathered the table linens to her chest—heaps of fine napkins spotted with a delicate spray of blood, where the fine young ladies' lungs had crumbled out of them. *Out of their soft, round little chests and into my hands, poor dears suffering in overwhelming comfort.*

The housemaids gathered in the attic hall outside Darcy's door like birds huddled over stained rocks.

"Think she'll be back? Will they hire a new matron, or promote one of us?" They flustered around the door. It hung ajar, lock sprung where it had been picked by the groundskeeper's son. Scandalous, to have a boy in their hall. A boy who could pick locks, no less, and the silly girls nearly forgot poor Darcy, for all their wild imaginings. They all wanted their locks picked.

But when they swung open the door, Darcy wasn't there—not ill, not dead in her bed. But her things were there—or some of them. Not her bright red slippers, and not her diary. That was in Mallow's pocket.

In March, the rains come, even in the mountains where the clouds are so often pooled at the foot of the cliffs. The damp throws the school into tragic disarray as scores of fine young ladies are finally overcome by their malady. They drop like hunting birds, and their rooms are stripped and scrubbed and filled again with the next young ladies from the deacon's list.

There's always a thing or two to be found, when the rooms switch over. Something to slip into a pocket. A silver button, or a vial of morphine.

The maids spend March fighting over dead girls' rooms. A new term begins in April.

It happened, now and then, that despite a tested immunity, a maid would start to cough. To pale. To waste. Sick above her station. But then, there's not much to be found in a maid's room, save for what she'd scavenged from others—and she'd no doubt have worn it out or worn it dull or somehow made it low or common. But the head housekeeper, their matron—different story.

It was Darcy who had final say over which maid got to strip and pack a room. Often, she did it herself. With Darcy gone, the maids all looked ready to shoulder through her doorway—to pick up a set of new darning needles, perhaps, or the music box they all swore they'd heard one day—a flagrant breach of the school's regulations.

They'd not find the chocolates Darcy always had as gifts from the headmistress. Mallow had eaten them, sitting on Darcy's bed, while she waited. *Don't need a boy to pick a lock.*

Mallow shut her door against the chaos in the hall and peeled the gloves from her hands. Sticky dried blood and the crisp, jagged edges of her skin snagged at the fibers as she pulled. She reached for the vial of morphine. Still some left over, to soothe her. It had taken most of the vial to level Darcy. She didn't relish the taste of it, the way she'd seen the fine young ladies do, but she welcomed the spreading fuzz, the cozy dull. A down quilt for the mind that muffled the world.

Mallow curled up on her creaking, threadbare cot and pulled out Darcy's diary. If she hadn't been so sure of what she might find, she might not have had the stomach for looking. Dull. So dull. Outraged missives on the misuse of dish soap. Lamentations over starch. Heavy praise of a new brand of sponge. Impossible. But there, among the housekeeping drivel, was the scandal.

Mallow had been her favorite maid, once, in the beginning. Her skill with the polishing rag, dusting dexterity, her mopping footwork. Darcy indulged in her help. Empowered her. Delegated important tasks till Mallow was more a partner than subordinate. Till Mallow became essential to the school's function, and when Mallow barked an order at a fellow maid and the maid scampered, a switch flicked in Darcy. Then Mallow was competition, and Darcy wanted her gone. But she'd had no reason to dismiss her, no grounds for firing.

Not till the night Darcy ran out of morphine and couldn't sleep, walked halls where she shouldn't be and saw things she shouldn't see.

Like Mallow, slipping free of her duties and visiting Joseph in his study. The diary confirmed it—Mallow had been seen, followed. And not just Mallow would suffer if Darcy flapped her jaw. Flapped—just like a vulture's wings. Let her carry that secret to the sky.

Mallow ripped the pages from the diary a few at a time, as many as she could tear at once with her sore hands. She crumpled the papers in her fist and dropped them into the bottom of an empty coal bucket. Before dawn, she'd cover them over with coal. She'd visit all the fine young ladies and fill their hearths with coal and secrets. Light the fires to warm their shivering, feeble frames. A little piece of Darcy in every room, in the nest of every little featherless bird.

Mallow smiled and listened to the maids in the hall disperse.

149

Heard the rickety doors close all along the corridor. Would they all lie awake, concerned for their missing monarch? Mallow supposed not. Surely they each remembered their time as the favorite. Remembered the turn, the shift—the lunatic feeling of falling from favor. It isn't something one forgets easily, or forgives, ever.

~

They found one of her slippers after a few days, once the search reached the mountain trails. It had landed, exposed like a beacon on the cliffside. They assumed she fell. None ever guessed that she flew.

Mallow cinched her pack straps. The somber party gathered at the foot of the trail. They linked arms, not just to ensure all ground was covered, but also to bear each other up over the rough terrain of the gorge.

It was all Mallow could do to keep her eyes on the rock at her feet and away from the cliff face above, where birds circled the discolored splash of rocks.

No one with any sense looked for Darcy. They looked for pieces. And no one looked at the sky.

Mallow watched the toes of her shoes scuff the rocks and tried to enjoy the hike. Breathed deeply and savored the sun on her neck. Listened to the rhythmic flapping of Joseph's coat tails in the breeze.

Mallow had counted on the eagles and vultures, but she hadn't allowed for crows. They didn't often come to the mountain, when they could do so much better in the village below. But there in a crow's cache—in a heap of fractured glass and tin—there were Darcy's glasses. The birds were in on it, and now everyone knew it. Eyes drifted skyward.

Mallow felt sweat run under her collar, smelled it dissolve the starch. *Not a giveaway in this sun. Natural to sweat out here.*

The search line broke apart, and they scattered like a convoy of ants with a stick tossed in their path. They scampered through the cracking dry brush and dusty rock, scraping through anywhere that might hide a clue.

The maids all wanted to return to the academy. To get into Darcy's room and be the scavengers there. They had no use for the dead, only for what was left behind.

That evening, they had their way with Darcy's room and were disappointed. No morphine, tools missing, music box broken. They stripped the lace from the pillowcase edges to frame their aprons, made her dresses over into handkerchiefs, and wondered where it all had gone.

None were surprised when Mallow took her place as head housekeeper. Now they would call her Matron, and none would question where she walked and when, or why. She didn't need to pick locks anymore. She held the keys to everywhere.

Joseph toyed with the empty, tattered diary cover. "You're sure she told no one?"

"I'm sure. A secret like that wouldn't last an hour in an attic full of maids." Mallow pulled the scrap of leather from his fingers.

"The maids shouldn't gossip so much. The school doesn't pay you to gossip."

"Or do things worth gossiping about?" Mallow smiled and perched on Joseph's knee.

"Not paying you for that, either. That would make you a whore. Do I look like a man who needs whores?"

Mallow shook her head, heart fluttering like bird's wings.

"You're paid to clean. You still do that, don't you?" His green eyes were as cold as bottle glass.

Mallow nodded.

"Then you'd best get to it. The search party tracked in an awful mess."

Mallow stood and felt the pinch of a blister on her foot. Too much hiking, of late.

"Mallory," Joseph called as she twisted the crystal doorknob.

"Yes, sir?"

"Are you working tonight?"

"I'm not, sir."

"See that you do."

She smiled as she slipped out the door. Not so cross with her, then. She walked with a spring, bursting blisters down the hall.

Mallow's needle flew through the fabric. The thread hummed as it whipped around each stitch. It didn't have to hold forever, just for tonight. Just a touch of lace for around her camisole—a bit of something pretty to brighten the drab swath of linen. Tack it down, and she could have the lace back before it was missed. She folded over the bit of lace that was stained with blood and hid it in a seam. Much more blood out of that fine young lady and she might not have to return the lace at all.

The lace itched against her sweaty chest as she hurried through the corridors. She'd wrapped her new ring of heavy keys in wool to muffle their chime. She felt for the right one—knew it by touch, even in the dark, and slipped it into the lock. She was early. Joseph hadn't come yet. She waited, beads of sweat tickling her back and behind her knees, till she heard footfalls in the hall. It wasn't the soft leather touch of Joseph's shoes. She hid behind the desk.

The door swung open and she saw boots appear. Above them, Joseph's voice.

"Come. We're going for a walk," he said.

Mallow had dressed for a tryst, not a hike. She followed the flap of Joseph's coattails up the trail and rubbed at where the lacy underthings chafed her. They might not be in any condition to return now.

She knew this winding trail better than he did, and stepped over the rocks that caught his toes. The ones that had raked Darcy on the way to her last rite. Mallow's shoes tightened over her refilling blisters.

"Where are we going?" she asked, though she knew, and he knew she knew. "Or, I mean, why are we going?"

"To see that the job is done. That the last of this mess is cleaned up. Every trace gone."

Mallow heard a slice of the air. Stars overhead blackened and sprang back to light in a cyclone of silent shadows. The birds didn't usually scavenge at night. They were sunlight creatures—should be back at their nests, heads tucked under wings, over warm eggs. *They must be hungry. They must have learned that food follows when people visit the cliffs.*

Mallow shivered. She felt like a mess. Like a trace.

The scrape of Joseph's boots silenced ahead of her, and she nearly walked into the back of his dark coat. She could feel the warmth of him through the narrow space between them. The birds seemed to feel it, too. The breeze that kicked up around them wasn't the cool pine wind, but something musty, cast off carrion-stained wings.

Fire flared, and Mallow stumbled away from Joseph's warm back. She raised her arm to shield her eyes and felt his hand close around her wrist. He drew her to the stained rock. She opened her eyes.

Only Darcy's skull remained, too slick and round and heavy for the talons to hook. But their beaks had been at it, and there was nothing much left of it but pale stone, like the pit of a peach, but with no hope of sprouting.

"It's done, then," Mallow said.

"It isn't done."

A rank gust puffed out the delicate flame. The mountain sky fell to blackness traced with the remnant specters of fire.

The *tok tok tok* of the skull bouncing down the mountainside echoed off the cliff faces.

Tidy the last of the mess.

Joseph's grip on her arm tightened as he fumbled one-handed for another match in his pocket.

Something swift and sour knocked the knot from Mallow's hair and she felt it tumble down around her shoulders, tangle round her neck and slip under her collar. She crouched, and the thing came again, this time knocking into Joseph.

He shouted, released her arm, and she heard his breath bellow out against the stone table.

Mallow lowered herself to the stony trail and slid toward the scrub-covered slope that fell away to the valley below.

"Mallory!" Joseph called. His arms blackened the stars like the silhouettes circling above.

She slunk further into the sage, gripping the fine branches to keep herself from sliding all the way down to the gorge.

Another fire blazed and Joseph spun around it, searching for her, searching for whatever had knocked her free of him. He searched low, across the rocks, while above, the light glanced off the spreading points of talons, off the shine of oiled pinions slick with old blood.

Mallow's drab grey dress hid her in the sage.

Joseph's warm beacon drew them, and they began to pluck. They grasped at his coat, and he slipped free of it. He dropped the long match, and the length of it burned in a trench of dust at his feet. They went for his hair, for the twisting coil of rope he'd had at his hip, concealed under the coat. His shirt fell away in red ribbons, then so did the flesh of his chest, that warm back, the soft middle of him Mallow had cushioned herself against. He fell away, beak by beak, into the mountain air. His cries carried up to the heavens on wings slicked in a fresh shine that steamed in the cold air.

Till he was gone. The last of the mess tidied up.

Save for his torn coat that had fallen away against the rocks. Mallow pulled herself back onto the trail and lifted the dark fabric, inspecting the damage. It would be mendable, with the whip of her needle. It was warm, still, and felt heavy over her shoulders. Pockets full of bright treasures she could inspect in the light of his hearth, add to her own little nest.

The coattails flapped behind her like birds' wings, carrying her prayers up to the heavens as she moved down the mountain, against a backdrop of stars, toward her domain. She pulled the wool from around her keys and let them chime, sealed the rite with her bell.

THE EYE
LIARS

BENDING OVER THE CORPSE, leaning against the cold steel table on which the body rested, Dan squeezed the black spots at the corner of the rotting eye. The blackness oozed out of the pores. It collected in the basin of the temple, pooling as it drained, then evaporating into a black mist. It rose into the air around us, circling the lamp hanging low over the workstation.

"Don't breathe, Greg," Dan said.

The swirling shadow dissipated as it rose, spreading to the dark corners of the ceiling, deepening the shadows. The air tasted sharp and bitter, like dad's batteries we used to lick in the garage when we were kids.

Dan breathed first.

Looking down at the dead man between us, there were more dark spots, pinprick-sized swellings, reservoirs of foul ink collected under the skin.

"What the hell was that?" I asked.

Dan turned to his tray of tools, waving his gloved hands over them, divining which to use.

"I'm not really sure," he said, rotating the scalpel in front of his face, examining an edge too fine to see. "My guess would be that it's a waste product of some undocumented parasite. It's always around the eyes, presents as liquid-filled black spots—but the substance vaporizes almost instantly. It's organic, but I haven't been able to collect enough to run any real substantive tests. Once it's vapor, it doesn't test as anything. Nothing."

I rubbed my forehead. The film of sweat had started to cool in the damp basement. I shivered.

"It's just . . . dark air," he said.

He bent back over the body. His face tensed. He always looked ten years older when he cut, like the focus drained the life from him. He looked more like Dad than me, then, but maybe that was the grey lab coat, him holding Dad's tools, bent over Dad's table.

He removed an eye and placed it on a small steel tray. His hand

157

barely moved, but when he straightened, the eye lay open, unfolded between us, a cloudy marble nested in layers of waxy wet tissue. He looked up at me, smiling.

My tongue curled inside my mouth and my throat tightened. The muscles at the back of my knees turned to turbulent water. I tasted bile, felt it burning through my chest, at the back of my throat.

"You don't have to look," he said. He always said. I never wanted to look but I always did, always watched, first Dad, then Dan. He held the tray out, tapping the bottom of my chin with its cold edge, the eyes sliding across its stained surface.

"Why did you need me here for this?"

"I want you to know what to look for. I need research subjects."

"Dan, that's not really okay. I can't just do that—there are rules."

"Check the dementia patients first—anyone who might be exhibiting visual hallucinations or delusions. Ones who reach a crisis in their condition, then present a few hours of lucidity right before death. The spots start appearing then, during that brief lucid state. I need you to watch them. And bring me the bodies."

He pulled the caps off of glass vials and lined them up, rattling them against the tray, drowning out my protestations.

"Dan, I don't get to decide where—"

"Hold your breath."

I slapped a hand to my mouth. I tasted the powdery residue of the latex gloves I'd been wearing.

He squeezed a black spot against the rim of a vial, collecting the trickle of ink and ramming the cap in place before the plasma turned to smoke.

He exhaled. I didn't.

He held the vial up between our faces. The dark liquid inside sucked light from the room. He swirled the glass tube. The ooze coated the glass, sliding back down it in writhing swirls.

"Whatever this is, it's killing people, Greg. I can't stop it if I can't research it."

"Dad didn't leave you this place so you could play mad scientist."

"Dad didn't leave *you* this place at all," he said, picking up an eye and rolling it in his palm.

"You're supposed to be taking care of these people, for their loved ones. And you're supposed to be taking care of the business."

I swept my hand toward a section of crumbling wall, groundwater seeping in through the cracks in the cinderblocks.

"Greg, this stuff's contagious. I don't know how, yet, but it is. Who gives a shit about upselling casket hardware when people are seeing things that aren't there? People are hallucinating, tearing each other apart, dropping dead, and you don't want to help?" He tossed the eye back onto the steel tray. It splashed and rolled, leaving a trail of humor.

"Well, talk to their doctors, put it in your reports."

"No one is going to look twice if I don't bring examples. I need data before I can make a claim like this."

"Your data are *people*, Dan."

"Dead people. And if you don't bring me what bodies you do have, we'll end up with more *data* than we'll know what to do with." His eyes narrowed like the tip of his scalpel, cut into me.

I sighed and stared at the ooze. "Where does it come from?"

"How should I know? That's the point. Where do fleas come from, or rats? It's just the fucking circle of life." He picked up the corpse's arm and shook the limp hand at me.

I stepped back, stumbling over my foot. "Well, someone else has to have seen it; it can't just be here."

"Some old anthropologists in Asia mention something like it, and in other places where they don't embalm or bury or burn the dead. They called them evil spirits, and started burning the people alive at the faintest hint of hallucination.

"We soak our dead in chemicals, infuse them with toxins, and stick them in the ground—hardly ever get to see what grows when we leave well enough alone." He squeezed the man's jaw and pulled down on his chin. The scent of raw meat and blood rose from the pale mouth.

"Damn," Dan said. "He didn't just *bite* his tongue off, he *chewed* it. Look." He wrenched the neck, aiming the blank face at me. A thin black line of old blood trailed from the corner of the mouth, running over Dan's thumb and dripping onto the table.

I drove back to The Village, hands shaking on the wheel, pressing my chin to my chest to get a better view through the narrow tunnel of my vision. My scrubs stuck to the sweat on my back and legs. My skin secreted a slippery puddle in the vinyl seat of the van. The plan to stop for lunch on my way back was trashed. I couldn't get out of the van like this. It'd look like I'd wet myself.

The van's parking space sat close to the back entrance of the clinic. I could sneak into the locker room and change, grab lunch in the dining room with Miss Bessley, who could tell me, again, about the dog she'd had when she was eight.

As my sneakers squeaked across the white tile threshold, Tracy walked by, her slate hair pulled back in a braid, the edge of her clipboard pressed against her stomach as she read and walked. The walkie-talkie velcroed to the shoulder of her scrub jacket crackled and beeped, her left eye flinching each time, deepening the grooves that branched across her temple.

"Tracy." She stopped and looked up. Looked me over. I'd forgotten about the wet. "Do you know when those school kids are coming back—the ones with the dogs? Do you remember if they have a collie, like Miss Bessley's?"

"Who? What are you talking about?" She looked back to her notes, scribbling across charts.

"The group with the therapy animals, are they coming back soon? Miss Bessley's been lonely, and I thought—" I picked at the damp fabric clinging to my chest, chafing my neck.

"I wouldn't know, ask the desk." She drew her eyebrows down. "But change your clothes first." She hurried away, her braid swaying, slapping each hip in turn.

In the locker room, I stripped off my damp scrubs and dropped them in the canvas laundry bag, and held my underwear under the blow dryer.

There were no XL scrubs left. Stuffing my legs into an L, my balance wavered when the floor nurse called a code grey over the intercom. I pulled on my shoes, grabbed my badge lanyard, and sprinted for the stairwell door.

Floor 3, suite H—Mr. Brunner.

The ruckus echoed down the yellow-painted brick stairwell. I scanned my ID at the top landing, pushed the bar, leaning against the heavy door.

A breeze whipped against my exposed ankles, and the scrub

160

seams strained against my thighs as I ran past the row of closed doors to the source of the noise.

"I'll kill you for this, you bitch!" Mr. Brunner had Tracy by her braid, feebly swinging it. "Give it back!"

My hand covered Mr. Brunner's, prying his fingers from Tracy's hair. His hand came away webbed with extracted strands.

"Can I help you find something, Mr. Brunner?" I asked, pushing his wrists down.

"That whore took my lamp. I can't read here in the dark without my lamp!" Sweat collected in the deep lines of his face, beading and dripping from his hairless pate. The loose skin at his neck shook, scattering droplets.

Holding his wrists to his sides, I nodded toward the bedside table. "Is your lamp blue, Mr. Brunner? I see a blue lamp over there—maybe we moved it when we cleaned? Or let me get you settled by that nice bright window."

"No—the leather one, with the brass. It was my father's, from the war. It's very valuable, and *she took it*." He threw himself against me. I wrapped my long arms around him, careful not to squeeze.

The nurse raced into the room, blue gloves in place, flipping a syringe. I tightened my grip as she came up behind the old man and gave him the Ativan.

He writhed against my chest. My shirt split between my shoulders. He went limp. Squatting to scoop up his legs, the seams on my pants gave.

"For chrissakes," Tracy said.

I carried Mr. Brunner to his bed and laid him down.

"Go home and do some laundry. Come back for second shift to make up the hours." Tracy straightened her hair and picked up her clipboard. Her left eye twitched, her cheeks flushed. She flipped to a fresh incident report sheet and turned her back.

Back in the locker room, I pulled on my street clothes. I grabbed the canvas laundry bag on my way out.

The tattered too-small scrubs fluttered into the dumpster in the parking lot. No need to fill out a material damage report—Tracy would mention it in hers.

Folding myself into my Civic, I headed home, rubbing at the dark shapes floating across my tired eyes.

The new scrubs were itchy, starched for store-freshness and smelling like dust. I sat in the dark clinic room, watching the blipping lights of Mr. Brunner's monitors, feeling the "do not resuscitate" orders clipped to the foot of the bed stare back at me. The new lamp I'd picked up sat in its box at my feet.

Rubbing my neck, trying to push the soreness out, warm blood rushed into the muscle behind the pressure of my fingers. Thirty minutes left. Then home, sleep for six hours, and come back.

I squeezed a tight muscle in my shoulder. Bright lights flashed in front of my eyes, then the negative, dark spots filling my vision. I pressed my fists to my eyes, opening them to solid dark. Undulating, freezing black clouds rolled around me, and a sharp ringing lanced my ears. Shrill sounds drove through me like knives as the dark wave turned me upside down.

My face hit the cold tile floor, jarring my vision back with a white-hot burst of light. Shoes pounded in front of my eyes, smelling like wet rubber and disinfectant. My hands slipped in my sweat as I pushed myself off the floor.

People filled the room, their backs to me. Above their heads, the monitor broadcasted Mr. Brunner's distress signal, emitting the shrill alarms that had cut through me. Squeezing my eyes shut, I rubbed my hands over my face, painting it with salty wet that stung my dry lips. I backed out, watching them do next to nothing, making him comfortable as he passed.

At home, I spent the rest of the night apologizing to the shadow whispering behind my bedroom door.

I studied Mr. Brunner's face. Leaning over him, staring closely at his temples and the bridge of his nose, I reached out and smoothed the cold wrinkles, inspecting the depths of the crow's feet. There was one, two—another on the other side. I texted Dan and then zipped up the bag and rolled Mr. Brunner to the parking lot.

I strapped him down and loaded him up, securing the gurney to the van. Climbing into the driver's seat, my coffee sloshed out of the spout of my travel mug.

Dan's funeral home sat just down the road, built close enough to The Village for convenience, but not so close as to be suggestive. Dan waited for me outside, wringing his hands. A cigarette butt smoked on the crumbling pavement at his feet, torching the parched weeds growing up from the cracks.

"What took you so long?" He tugged at the back door, pulling the gurney down as I got out. "Hurry, get him downstairs."

In the dark basement lab, leaning in, shining a light in Mr. Brunner's face, we counted spots. Dan pushed and pulled at the skin.

"Gentle," I said.

"What?" The corner of Dan's mouth twitched. "Why, exactly?"

"I know him," I said.

"Not anymore." Dan prepared his vials and blades.

I smoothed the sheet over Mr. Brunner's chest, brushed his hair back from his cool forehead. I could hear his voice, whispering about the things his dad had done in the war, asking if I could sneak him another Bond DVD from the office, promising he wouldn't tell Tracy if I watched it with him.

"What the hell are you doing?" Dan pushed my hand away and moved in with a vial.

"He doesn't have as many spots as Alan did."

"Who?"

"The guy from yesterday."

"Oh, no. He hasn't been dead as long. There will be more tomorrow. This is good, really good—I can watch them develop."

I looked away and held my breath as Dan held the vial to Mr. Brunner's eye.

Another body lay stretched out on the next table: a young woman, naked, her eyes removed, barely visible through the darkness. Walking closer, I saw her eyes sitting on a tray next to her head, milky black. The skin around the eye sockets swelled with black pustules.

My breath forced itself out with a moan.

"That's after five days," Dan said. He had sealed his vial.

"She's been lying here for five days?" Her hair fell around her empty face, dark and soft, dry leaves caught in its tangles. The bruises on her throat and thighs were as dark as the shadows where her eyes should have been. The skin along her jaw was red and blue, distended around a small oval with a cross in it.

"No one's waiting for her. I can take my time and get the data I need. I haven't had the chance to observe them this long before—to see what they do when left alone."

"I hope it doesn't hurt. What's this mark here?"

"That's nothing, leave it. And of course it doesn't hurt, she's dead." He shook his head.

"That looks like—"

"I said leave it."

"Is that Dad's ring? Fuck, Dan, did you hit this girl?"

"She already had the spots, Greg, she was as good as dead already. I needed her to come to the lab. She was raving, she wouldn't listen."

"So you killed her?"

"I brought her here to watch her die, to see how it happened."

"You're sick. She's lying here in Dad's room with Dad's ring punched into her face, and you can't even see how sick this is."

"That still bothering you, Greggy? That Dad didn't want his ring pawned for booze? You think you should have it now you're cleaned up?" He pulled it from his finger and held it out. I smacked it out of his hand. It bounced, ringing, rolling into the glue trap in the far corner.

"Wouldn't fit you anyway," he said, bending back to his work. "There was no saving her, but I could learn from her. It's for the greater good, Greg." He pulled one side of his mouth back in a crooked smile.

My fingers flexed. I could feel my heartbeat in my temples. My tongue scraped the dry roof of my mouth, sticking to my clenched teeth. I counted and breathed. Thirty to one, a breath every five seconds. *I can't change this, I can't change him.*

"Did you run more tests? On Alan?" I asked.

"Who?"

"Alan!" Another ten seconds, another two breaths.

"Right. Yes, look." He went to a cupboard and pulled out a tray of black vials. No. Vials filled with black. "The liquid samples have turned to gas. It appears that the lack of oxygen in the vials slows the reaction, but it doesn't stop it. However, there's no increased pressure in the tube. The reaction doesn't seem to have released any energy." He held the tray under my nose, his eyes rolling with excitement.

"So . . . "

"That's not possible. All reactions have some sort of energy exchange involved. You can't go from a liquid to a gas without it—this is *outside* the laws of chemistry." Saliva collected at the corners of his mouth as he spoke faster, fogging the glass vials with his rapid breath.

I took a step back, tearing my eyes from the tray of dark tubes, and looked for the clock. It perched hidden in the shadows, high up on the wall.

"I need to get back to work. I can't be late again."

Dan lowered the tray, sneering. "Or what? Another job you can't hold down?"

"No. I promised Miss Bessley lunch today."

Dan shook his head, turning to put his tray of dark vials away.

Collecting The Village body bag, folding it, I watched the girl on the table. "What was her name?"

"Don't know," Dan said.

~

Alice Stowe ate three pounds of gravel from the garden. Sometime in the early hours, she left her room in her best dress and hat, sat in the gazebo, and ate rocks from a chocolate box. She died that evening, without a single tooth left.

I clocked out, changed, and went to the clinic. She was there, in the cooler, in one of my black bags. I rolled her out and unzipped the bag.

The spots were already there—huge, this time, and swollen. The skin felt cold and taut under my fingertip.

It ruptured. The dark liquid spilled over my finger, filling the space under my nail and pooling in my cuticle. It felt like my finger had been encased in ice. The black smoked off my finger with a soft hiss, the vapors sucking in toward my mouth and billowing on my breath.

I slapped my other hand over my mouth and ran, slipping over the waxed tiles to the sink. Cranking the hot water lever as far as it would go, I held my hand under the steaming stream. The inky shadow mixed with the steam, one swirling around the other, a cyclone of hot and cold. The heat returned to my skin in an agony of needles as vessels rapidly dilated and burst.

When all the black had washed away or turned to smoke, I breathed again, panting through my tight throat, a high whine echoing off of the sterile walls and steel cabinets. The battery taste of the toxic smoke mixed with the chlorine cleanliness of the clinic.

My fingertip swelled white like a maggot soaked in water. The back of my hand blistered with red, angry burns.

I groped the darkness. The air swarmed thick with shadows that flowed and eddied on unseen currents. My stomach burned as I swallowed the acrid cloud. Black smoke poured from Alice's face, billowing up as if from a chimney, burning the fuel of the darkness inside her.

With my good hand, I grasped the bar of the gurney and shoved her back in the cooler, slamming the door shut.

I swept my hand in front of my face, trying to clear a path through the shadow. It sighed as my hand cut through it, swirling back in to fill the space, caressing my cheek and whispering.

My legs crashed though steel carts of equipment on my way to the back door. I pushed out into the air. The daylight split through me, savaging my eyes, the setting sun hot on my burned hand. Lying on the pavement, I coughed shadow from my lungs.

I pulled my phone from my pocket to call the front desk and tell them to seal the clinic.

There was a text message from Dan, from that morning.

Not waste, eggs. Faces are spawning. Get me out. Nine hours ago.

I rolled over, forced myself up, and rushed to the clinic van. It was just a mile down the road—a mile and nine hours too late.

Darkness filled the windows of the funeral home. Pulling up to the back entrance, I turned the headlights on bright and pulled a flashlight from the glove box, using it to break the grimy window by the back door. Wisps of shadow licked the jagged edges of broken glass. Reaching in, my injured fingers fumbled to unlock the door latch, my armpit scraping against the sharp glass.

The high beams penetrated three feet into the darkness and hit a moving wall of shadows. Shapes appeared in the shifting darkness. Faces and shoulders and hands and thighs emerged from the cloud, beckoning. I walked into the middle of it all.

It stung like jumping into a deep lake at midnight in February. The shadow clung to me, sliding across the surface of my eyes, dragging itself over my skin. Whispers started in one ear and finished in the other, too many of them, fading in and out, incomprehensible. I held out my hands and walked toward the basement door. My knees knocked into a stack of caskets, sending the tower crashing, lids flying open. I dropped to the floor, dodging corpses, digging my fingernails into the carpet fibers, tracking the familiar geometric patterns of my childhood. I followed its diamond floral maze to the back wall, sliding my fingers along the chair rail, searching for the door.

I found it. When I pulled it open, the whispers turned to moans.

Clinging to the banister, I felt the edge of each splintered step with my toes.

Halfway down, the thick cloud broke. Above my head, a cumulous of shadow roiled. I thundered down the remaining stairs.

"Dan?"

He wasn't there. Alan, Mr. Brunner, and the young girl were lined up on tables: their faces concave, drained, covered in black ash. I walked over to the girl. No one would ever recognize her now. It was as if her face had been dead weeks before the rest of her. I turned, gagging.

There. The window of the walk-in freezer gleamed black, opaque as a submarine porthole. Dan's face pressed against the glass. The skin around his eyes was torn apart by erupting fonts of shadow, his eyelids flayed back. His jaw hung open, askew.

I retched. Fell to my knees and puked. Choking, coughing up gobs of tar. Moans rolled out of me, building deep within my center, rattling my bones. I pushed myself back from the caustic puddle, away from the window. The back of my head banged against the edge of Mr. Brunner's steel table.

Mr. Brunner? I forgot to tell The Village.

The cloud on the stairs had risen further, concentrating itself in the highest reaches of the house. I pressed through the thickness of it, feeling cold fingers rake my skin, malevolent hissing in my ears.

The headlights hit me like a hurricane wave. I swam through the light and climbed in the van.

A mile back and too late again.

The Village seethed, a pit of hell. Each lost in their own shadow world, they ripped each other apart—some already bursting at the face, filling the air with spawning smoke.

I took a long roll of plastic wrap from the kitchen.

I held their frail frames as they ranted nonsense and I wrapped their heads in plastic, sealing in the darkness, stemming the flow of shadow. Their eyes pressed against the clear film, rolling in their sockets, spilling ink into the folds of membrane.

I wrapped them up and zipped them into my black bags, dragging them to the clinic, piling them up in a squirming heap.

Tracy stood at the nurse's station, naked, writing notes across her stomach. Her hair hung loose, crimped from the tight braid. The twitch-line by her eye flowed like a river delta of liquid evil. I wrapped her up—all of her, in case the darkness found another way out.

I closed the clinic door and taped around the edges. I poured out the bottles of ethyl alcohol and rolled the carts of oxygen tanks from the gas storage and barricaded the door with them. Down the hall in the kitchen, I lit the burners on the stove, turned on the oven and left it open.

I ran. The air, already dark from those that burst before, swarmed me, raking at my skin with icy fangs. The shadow slithered up through the bowels of the building, collecting on the third floor, a writhing mass of nightmare. Moans echoed down the stairwell.

Walking out into the night, backing away from the building, I watched smoke surge from the chimney, streaming into the sky, obscuring the stars. Out of the corner of my eye, every shadow moved. Black tears ran in smoky tracks down my aching face.

I turned my back and walked, a mile down the road and too late. The ground concussed, a gold light spreading, casting my shadow at my feet. A hot wind flew up behind me, pushing the shadows ahead. I chased them.

Sirens ripped through me, scattering red lights cutting through the dark. They streaked past me, toward the gold glow.

I stumbled into the back door of Dad's mortuary, Dan's, mine. I shuffled down the stairs, to the corner of the basement, and pulled the ring from the dusty, sticky glue. I pressed it onto my little finger, forcing it over the knuckle, twisting it into the groove at the bottom joint.

I pulled open the freezer door, catching Dan's body as it fell. He hardly weighed a thing with the evil boiled off. I carried him to a table and laid him out.

I took my knife from the tray. Just like Dad, like Dan. From each shoulder to the base of the manubrium and down to the navel, I cut him open, separating the ribs from the breastbone, laying wide the chest cavity. I pulled the heart from its place and weighed it.

MAGNIFYING GLASS

OUTSIDE OUR NEW HOUSE, the sun flashed off of the wall of windows, and it looked like it was filled with liquid fire. But inside, the air was milky, dim with dust that floated on those relentless sunbeams. By the time we had the windows clean, we were wearing sunglasses inside, squinting at the wall of trees that held us in on all sides. Like a fortress of pine and glass. Safe. Hidden.

Warren looked at me, his face gaunt behind wide tinted lenses. "This house is like a fishbowl," he said.

"Well, swim to your room and unpack."

"Mom, do we really have to keep all this shit?"

"Watch your language. And no. Maybe the furniture. But we'll take the rest to Goodwill or something. In a few weeks, once things have calmed down. We'll get curtains, too, as soon as it's safe to go out."

Warren held up a vaguely phallic ashtray. "No one wants this old guy's shit. Not even his kids did."

"Watch your language! His kids all died before he did. And we'll throw that one away."

If the sun hadn't been so bright, we might have turned on the overhead light then, and that's probably when it would have started to flash.

"That old guy must have really liked windows," Warren said, mac 'n cheese pushed into his cheeks. He was still wearing sunglasses.

"It's a nice view, though," I said. My eyes drifted from the bowl of electric orange noodles to the ridge of pines past the yard. "Safe and hidden. They won't think to look for us here." I smiled.

The sun dipped below the tree line, granting us relief from the glare.

I flicked on the light switch. It fluttered, weak, then grew brighter, blinked out, then swelled.

Warren buried his face in his elbow. "This place is awful."

My throat constricted. I felt our fresh start turning sour. "It'll be good. We just have to make it home, that's all."

"Dad bought a condo in San Diego," Warren said. "You can see the ocean. Walk to all the shops."

"Yeah, well, Dad can go fuck himself. We can't go to a city—there are too many people. Too many cops."

"Watch your language." Warren cracked a smile.

"Drag that chair over, and I'll change the bulb."

Warren slid the chair under the blinking fixture. I flicked the switch off. The light continued to flash.

"Well. Maybe we just shouldn't use this one," I said. "How about you go get some sleep?"

I dragged the chair back to the table as Warren trudged down the hall to the room he had picked. For all his complaints about windows, he'd chosen the best view.

~

"Mom! MOM!"

Adrenaline surged as I fought off my blankets, trying to think through the stupor of panic—*Where am I? Where is Warren?*

I chased his screams to his room. "What's wrong?"

"There's someone walking around the house—past the windows!" He was curled up at the head of the bed, pillow clutched to his chest.

"Was it the police?" I cupped my shaking hands against the glass and peered out toward the line of trees. "I don't see anyone, sweetie. Are you sure? Were you dreaming?"

"No—it was a person, walking."

"Maybe it was a neighbor." I thought back to the map of the property. Isolated. Nothing for miles. Perfect. "Stay here. I'll check it out."

I ran back to my room and pulled the .22 from the nightstand drawer.

I walked through the house, peering out into the night. The light in the living room still flickered—growing to a glow almost blinding before plunging the room into darkness. My pupils were in spasm. Any ability to see past the glass was lost. But I could see the kitchen chair—not where I had left it—under the errant light fixture.

172

"Warren? Come out here, please."

He crept out from the hall, his blanket over his head and framing his face, like he always used to do. For a moment, he was five years old again, until he came up next to me, eye-to-eye.

"Did you come out here and mess with this light?"

"No."

"Warren, it's not safe to mess with shit like this!"

"I didn't!"

The light blinked out and stayed dark. Warren's breath sounded in fits, in the rhythm that the light had left behind.

"Mom, I don't like it here."

I closed my eyes, let my pupils stretch—and when I opened them again, I could see his silhouette against the dark windows.

Then the light swelled, and he was gone. His bedroom door slammed, and the sound echoed off all that glass like a bell.

～

Sunglasses, again, at breakfast. Still, the light above us blinked, its pattern lost in the flood of sunlight.

I nursed my coffee, rubbed my temples. "I'm just going to take the bulb out. I'll be careful."

I climbed onto the chair, screwdriver between my teeth.

The fixture was coated in dust. Cobwebs laced away from it to the textured ceiling.

I handed the screws down to Warren. "Stand back."

The light flashed in my face as I tugged at the glass dome. It pulled away from the metal base, and then the whole fixture slid out of the ceiling, dropping into my arms. The bulb still blinked as a tide of grey and brown spilled from the hole in the plaster. Warren shouted and stumbled back.

I looked at the puddle of dark particles pooled in the broken fixture—moths. Dead and dry, an army of them collected above the light. "I guess we know why it wasn't working." I looked up at the hole in the ceiling. A piece of brown paper stuck out from the attic crawlspace.

I balanced the heavy fixture against my chest and reached up, careful not to brush the exposed wires. I pulled down an old envelope. It was brittle and coated with the dusty fuzz of moth wings.

It was sealed, nothing written on the outside. I shoved it into my pocket and heaved the light fixture back up through the hole in the ceiling. The bulb continued to flash, casting momentary light on the roof beams and the drapes of cobweb hanging from them.

I climbed off the chair, feet crunching in the moth husks, all curled into paper crescents.

"Gross," Warren said. "What did you find?"

"Just a piece of paper. Get the broom, for chrissakes."

"It's probably that guy's will. He left his penis art to his secret porn buddy."

"Warren, will you sweep the goddam floor already? God, you've spent too much time with your father."

He pushed the broom through the pile of moths, but watched me as I stuck my thumb under the envelope flap and pulled the old glue apart. A cloud of dust danced in the sunlight as I unfolded the letter.

My heart hammered so hard, I thought it might scatter the dust motes.

7/11/2001
Susan,
Don't break the glass.

And that was it.

"Warren, did you put this up there?"

"What?"

"Did you put this note up in the ceiling?"

"And bury it in bugs? No. Why, what does it say?"

I handed him the paper.

"It's for you?"

"Look at the date."

"My birthday?"

"Now, tell me you didn't put it up there."

"Mom—I didn't. Explain how I could have possibly done that."

"I don't know, but it would be a lot more convincing if you'd remembered to put the chair back. Clean up this mess."

I left him with the broom, the moths, and that infernal light.

By the afternoon, the flickering had stopped.

"I guess I must have knocked something loose."

Warren pushed his sunglasses onto his forehead. He looked up at the dark hole, and then out at the trees—the last bit of sun glowing from behind their bristles. "This house creeps me out," he said.

It was hard to breathe as deeply as I needed to. "I'm sorry, honey. But you'll get used to it. It's a good place for us, for now."

"I want to sleep with my light on, but it's like the whole forest can see me. Like whoever was walking around is watching me."

I reached across the table for his hand, but he pulled it back. Dropped it into his lap. "Mom?"

"What, sweetie?"

"I want to go back to Dad's."

And it was like all the windows fell in on me, like every one of those wires had been alive and angry, like I'd taken them into my mouth and chewed. I kept that feeling between my teeth—held it in my mouth to keep it from welling up in my eyes.

"Can you give it a week, please?"

He looked at me—those wide hazel eyes disappearing into black circles as the last of our light faded, and he was four years old again, reading my face for an answer, all those times I didn't have one. No excuses. Only apologies. He nodded, and sulked away to his room.

I sat at the table and stared into the woods. The room was dark, but I still felt the flash of light behind my eyes, throbbing with the rhythm of the pain I kept trapped between my teeth—so I wouldn't scream and shatter the whole house—

Don't break the glass.

I was squinting into the darkness when the shadow crossed my vision. Just beyond the glass, a figure walked past—a dark form against the black backdrop of the woods.

My thoughts slammed closed as a cold sweat crept over me. Slowly, I stood from the chair and walked down the hall, following the glass wall. I poked my head into Warren's room. He slept, blanket pulled over his head, like when he was three.

The shadow slipped past his room, around the corner of the house.

He's right, there's someone here.

I grabbed my gun and returned to Warren's room. The blanket had slipped from his face, and his hair had dampened against his sweaty forehead. He frowned and sighed in his sleep.

I lowered myself to the foot of the bed and sat, facing the windows, gun resting on my thighs.

I must have dozed. The moon had risen over the tree line. The yard—empty—seemed almost bright. Not enough of that light pierced the glass, and the bedroom seemed darker than ever.

I turned to check on Warren.

His face was inches from mine, pale in the darkness, pupils wide and black. He sat rigid. His breath felt cold against my face.

I sprayed him with spit as I choked back a scream. He flinched.

"Warren?" I sputtered his name. Remembered to pry my shaking finger off the trigger.

"What are you doing here?" he asked. His voice was hollow with sleep.

I held my breath steady. "Just checking on you, sweetie. Back to sleep."

He watched me with those black eyes as I backed from his room.

~

The light woke me, slipping under my eyelids like bright water.

I tiptoed to Warren's room. He leaned against the wall, snoring.

And when I saw his window, I screamed.

Warren flailed awake and fell from his bed in a tangle of blankets. I reached and pulled him toward me. He sobbed and pushed me away, turning to look where I looked.

The entire window—from ground to ceiling—was smeared with hand prints.

Warren let out a low moan and let me pull him into my arms. I pressed his head to my neck, and he was two again, me with a hand over his ear to shut out the violence, to mask the yelling with the sound of my heartbeat. Until he raised his eyes to mine, hazel and watery, and his face twisted and he shouted, "I TOLD YOU!" so loudly my vision went white.

And by the time I could feel my feet again, he was locked in the bathroom, the only room with no windows.

The entire glass side of the house was the same—painted with hands. Some prints dragged finger trails that turned my thoughts dark.

I tapped on the bathroom door. "Warren? I'm going to have a look outside."

The door swung open. "No—Mom, you can't." He shook his narrow head.

"I have to. I need to see what's going on."

"Can't we just call the police? Please?"

The live wires between my teeth flared again, and I squeezed to keep from shaking. "You know I can't."

His eyes spilled over.

"I can't lose you again." I swallowed the tightness in my throat. "Look—let me see if I can figure this out. Take care of it. If I can't, we'll hit the road. If you want, I'll drop you at a hotel. You can call the cops. They'll take you back to Dad. Just give me a head start, okay? Please?" That word again. *Please.* Every time it comes, something ends. I lose. *Not this time.*

He nodded. His face folded as he swung the door shut again.

I slid to the floor.

Everything felt broken.

~

There were no footprints in the grass, no depressions in the flowerbeds, no sign of anyone. I stared at the handprints. They seemed to be on the inside of the glass, and bent the light as if they were scratched into it. Scrubbing at them did nothing.

Warren slept in the bathtub that night. I sat in the living room, practicing my aim at the crude ashtray. *Just give me a target.*

In the attic, the dismembered light began to blink. And in its erratic strobe, I saw the shadows—figures passing by the window wall, trailing dark fingers along the glass, leaving dark stains in their wake. The glass scratched—etched, as if their fingers bled acid.

"Warren!"

The bathroom door cracked open. I pulled the pre-pay burner phone from my pocket and slapped it on the counter. "I'm going out there. Stay inside. Make the call, if you have to."

"Mom, please—don't go out there!" With every flash of light, the angles of his face grew deeper.

I turned away—and he was one again, and more than I could handle—until his hand, bigger than mine now, curled around my wrist.

"Don't go," he said.

I didn't deserve this—another chance. Until I remembered that it was my last chance. And fuck-all if some creepers were going to take it from me.

I pulled away from his thin fingers and slipped out the door.

I swung the gun around, trailed it across the windows where the shadows had walked.

They were gone.

Inside, the light flashed. Warren's face was pressed to the glass, eyes wide and black—pupils starved for light, long fingers splayed. Behind him, shadows walked, black silhouettes in the shock of light.

I shouted to Warren. Screamed for him to run, and I pointed the gun at the largest shadow looming behind him. I squeezed, and the glass shattered, the pieces flew, catching the light as they flashed, catching the dark as they fell around me. And around Warren.

And it was the day he was born again, and I held him, precious and terrifying in my arms and he wailed, pink face screwed up with rage, until his face wasn't pink anymore but white, and his rage went quiet, wrinkles smoothing to a mask. A dark stain spread around him.

And I stayed there, holding him, sitting in broken glass until there was nothing between me and the sunlight. Moths danced around the flaring bulb, raining dust from their wings and casting wild shadows over the walls, and over me.

In the shards that shone like mirrors, figures moved and pressed themselves to the glass, before slipping around the jagged edges and out into the world, into the light.

CROSSWIND

JACOB STOOD HIS ground, feet planted, windbreaker whipping against his body. His microphone was useless in the wind, but he kept reporting. The other trucks, the desk-jockey weathermen, had all left—retreated to studios and green screens. *The story is out here in the sky. This is why they watch. Live, now. And later they'll share it to their timelines, text it to their friends. See the storm?*

Footage of the twister that had killed Paula still creeps up in search results. The people who watch it "ooh" at the debris cloud—oblivious that one of those zooming specks liked pineapple on her pizza and sang along to opera in languages she didn't know. *Maybe she knows them now.*

Even magnified on the wall-sized screen in the studio, he couldn't tell which speck was her. Couldn't see where she learned to fly—tasted the storm in ways he never had. Maybe never would. The closest he could get to her now was here on the beach, telling everyone to take shelter. *Take cover,* the last thing he'd said to Paula, but too late.

"Took an unexpected turn," is what he said—what the storm did. What so many storms do—unpredictable, always reminding him *I was wrong I was wrong I was wrong.*

They still called him Radar. He was right more often than not. He saved lives, the anchorwomen reminded him. *And sometimes they die anyway.*

Blowing sand sounded like angry snakes against his cinched hood. The earpiece broadcasted static. He recited the same wind stats again, rambled about currents. They couldn't hear, back at the desk, but no one cared—they just want to see him stagger, watch something heavy blow away in the background. Good TV.

When he felt the wind shift, saw it was on the move, he wrapped up.

Ten years ago, I'd have thrown the camera in the van and hit the road—gotten ahead of the thing and seen if that spin of warm air had more fight in it up the coast. He'd watch his laptop radar for that trailing hook—like a bullseye—storm chase treasure.

But this camera wasn't his. Neither was the van.

If you blew up the old footage, you could tell which speck was *his* van. Watch it arc off the ground, up and around, bright in the light angling in from beyond the angry system.

An unexpected shift in the wind.

The studio van rocked over wind-whipped sand dunes back toward the road. His hearing hadn't recovered from the roar of the storm. He turned up the radio—his competitor's station.

"Maybe if Radar spent more time at his station and less time playing at the beach, he'd have seen this one coming," their weatherman said. The blonde anchor laughed—he could tell it was the blonde one, recognized the laugh.

Jacob punched the button, silenced the station. His team wasn't broadcasting now. Wouldn't be for another two hours. They shared the airwave with the local church and school district. If he tuned in now, all he'd get is a sermon. Maybe a song—if he was lucky, Becky Merriweather at the mic. She always joked that if they married, he'd have to take her name. She was nearly old enough to be his mother. Didn't know he'd been married before. Thought a nice young man like him ought to be.

Back home, he flicked the TV on, saw his own face—or what he could of it, cinched inside his hood, behind a pair of ski goggles that kept the rain and sand out of his eyes. His lips moved, words unintelligible, but it looked impressive. Torn awnings whipped around the boardwalk behind him, birds flapping like mad, unmoving in the sky. But no vans. No wives.

People would be watching, more interested in the storm than the goons on four making fun of him.

He left the TV on through the night.

At the station in the morning, faces were grim. He returned his camera to Phil—he wouldn't need it today. No one tunes in for blue skies. Phil poured sand from the case, popped the disc, handed it to him wordlessly, and side-eyed him as he packed the gear away.

Jacob returned the look in kind as he stepped through the glass door into the open, shared office.

The grating voice—the wide, ugly face of the anchor from four took up the whole screen wall.

" . . . could have been a local disaster not unlike the storm from years ago that took a life here in Miranda County . . . "

"The fuck is this?" Jacob said, waving at the screen. The sound cut, the anchor's lips still flapping.

"Sorry, Jake. They're making a thing of it—the storm you called wrong."

"It was just a thunderstorm. No one was hurt. Right?" His heart fluttered.

"One lady can't find her dog." Susan looked down as she said it—her face the waxy clay color left over from the morning show.

Jacob patted his hair. It always stood up, forever in the wind. His head always in the storm.

Dan came forward, the remote in one hand, ratings in the other. "They said your miscalculation was dangerous. That you're still just a storm chaser. That you belong on the side of the road and not in a newsroom."

"Those fucking jerks."

"Yeah. People ate it up. Stupid always sells."

Jacob grabbed the remote and hurled it at the screen. The duct tape from the last time held it together.

"I've been storm chasing for twenty-three years! The fact that I'm even still alive means I'm good at it. I can read a radar—I can read a fucking storm."

"We know that, Jake."

Paula's ghost hung in the room, pushing everyone's chins to the floor.

"Why don't you take the day? Get some rest. Weather's clear here now." Dan forced a smile.

"How do you know?"

Susan's eyes shot to the screen. Of course. The news.

Jacob stalked out of the room. A day would be good. Maybe that storm was still within driving distance—rough and gorgeous.

He checked the camera back out.

It had moved northeast, those warm winds from the south hitting the cold Canadian front and stirring up a cataclysm. The sort of storm that leaves little ambiguity for meteorologists. No one needs a weatherman to tell them to take shelter when the trees begin to bend.

Jacob went north along the beach, just a few miles out ahead of it. He dug the tripod legs deep into the sand, pointed the camera at the sea, across a marina where the boats bucked like angry bulls.

The world needs a new waterspout video. Something viral. Bury the old clip, like I could never bury her.

Conditions were perfect. If they held, it would work this time.

Wisps of funnels dangled from the underside of the cloud, forming, then spinning out. The twisting ropes stretched closer and closer to the foaming swells offshore. Lightning stabbed, whiting out the world, snapping it back to a different view.

One of the funnels dropped, gaining strength, rotating so fast its body seemed as smooth as glazed porcelain.

Jacob let the video roll and lifted his still camera, taking shots. Paula used to do this part. He felt the vibration of the shutter—the wind howling too loud now to hear anything but the relentless engine of nature.

The hair on his body rose. The world went white and split with a roar, then concussed into silence. His body burned with its own friction, everything the flavor of ions.

When his vision returned, blighted with dark erasures, the funnel churned in front of him—its smooth surface now scarred with sand, sea rock, the silver flash of unlucky fish. The wind pulled the breath from his lungs like a greedy kiss. He tried to scream, but the sky left him nothing. All air belonged to the storm.

Behind a veil of debris and vapor, he saw a face—lean and cold, with eyes the color of heavy clouds. He stared into those deep shadows, trying to read their currents. His mouth hung open, filling with sand and salt spray.

"Paula?" Sand grated across his tongue as he spoke.

He squinted against the whipping sand and shells, and reached into the funnel, toward the glowering face. Rocks beat his wrist and forearm. The heat of his blood ran cold in the biting wind. His fingers closed on something rough and solid. He clenched his grip around the thing and pulled, drawing it out of the eye and back through the whipping wall of storm. He leaned against the draw of the vortex. His hand reappeared through the sheet of vapor and he fell back onto the sand.

The funnel roped, twisted erratically, losing stability until it broke, wisped, and disappeared back up into the churning clouds.

Jacob lay panting in the sand. He reached to wipe debris from his eyes and found the strange thing still clutched in his fist. A handle of driftwood—light and smooth. From it protruded a carved scrimshaw blade.

He sucked air into his lungs, and the gasp echoed beside him.

A woman lay shivering, naked in the sand. A mane of hair fanned around her in tangled silver dreadlocks. Her skin was grey as a fish's belly, and her roving eyes were white-gold as lightning.

She coughed as if the air abraded her lungs.

Jacob scrambled to sit and peeled off his windbreaker. He fished his phone from the pocket and draped the jacket over her.

"You're okay—it's okay; I'm calling for help."

The phone felt hot and wet against his cheek. He pulled it back, long strings of dark plastic trailing between his face and his hand. The glass of the screen fell away as fine sand.

The woman shrieked, then coughed like thunder. She reached out from under his jacket and grabbed for the knife that had fallen next to his leg.

"Oh—no, no, it's okay. I want to help. Are you hurt?" He tucked the knife into his camera bag. Paula's camera bag.

She thrashed and threw his coat aside, reaching for him.

"Stop!" He grabbed her arms. "Where are you from? Did you get lost in the storm?"

How had she survived and not Paula? Why not Paula?

She leveled her eyes at him. He felt the hair on his arms rise in her yellow glare. She began to shake.

"You're in shock. I'll drive you to the hospital. They can contact your family."

He scanned the roads along the beachfront—no cops, no cars at all. "I'm sorry, but you need a doctor." She was light, but fought him, biting his hands and arms. He set her on a seat and slid the door shut. He grabbed his bag and the tripod. The video camera belched a black line of smoke.

A pattern crossed the sand. The wide, twisting line where the funnel had come ashore had melted—the sand fused into a glossy crystalline sheet. He pressed a foot onto it, shattering the glass like pond ice.

He turned to the van to see the back window spidering, cracking like the sand. The woman's bright eyes refracted through fissures, her pale hands pressing against the glass.

Jacob slid into the driver's seat and started the engine.

"Just calm down, please—I'm going to take you to the hospital."

She opened her mouth, gasped, and her sternum collapsed against a cage of bones. She screamed a clap of thunder that shattered all the windows. The car alarm yelped, and the airbag knocked Jacob back against the seat.

A funnel of cold mist shot from her mouth and blasted the side of Jacob's face. Icy water ran down his shirt and pooled in his seat.

Jacob wiped the water from his eyes and stared at the woman. Her mouth closed and her sternum reflated. Eyes cooled to a muddy grey.

Droplets of rain shook from Jacob's hair. "Who are you?"

She watched his mouth. Licked her lips with a scaled tongue.

"I'm a tempest," she said, in a voice like swelling wind.

Jacob stared at her, at how clouds seemed to pass through her eyes. "You're a storm. *That* storm?" He gestured to the sky, now void-blue, the raging system gone. Now in his back seat.

"Give me my blade," she hissed.

"Are there others like you?"

"We are one storm. We are many. Give me my blade so I may return. I was not finished. I have a gale yet in my throat."

Jacob ran his eyes over the creature's anatomy. "But you're a woman. Where does the wind come from? Where does it go?"

"It came from my sister to the south. It goes north and east."

Jacob's eyes widened. "You know the wind. All of it. All the time?"

The charge of yellow was rebuilding in her eyes. "I am the wind."

Jacob turned and wrenched the van into gear. "I know where to go. Someplace safe."

He backed over dunes toward the seaside road. The gutters flowed with runoff rain. He splashed onto the street and headed for the highway.

"Do you have a name?"

She concussed the car with a roll of thunder.

Jacob swerved, hydroplaned, regained control. He glanced in the mirror. She sat slouched in the seat, eyes slits, irises the color of fog.

He pulled the van into the garage and lowered the door before he dragged the storm woman, half-conscious but still struggling, from the backseat. She'd shaken the van three more times with her thunder on the way to his house, each time growing weaker.

Jacob hadn't opened the door to Paula's studio since The Storm. She'd always kept it locked. The key hung on a nail by the door. There had been a second key on her keyring. They never found that, either.

Jacob hurried down the basement stairs, clutching the tempest. Her body reverberated like distant thunder—the feel of it against his chest made his heart race, then slow, then race again. He held her awkwardly against himself, fingers slipping over skin the texture of fine-grit rubber, as he fumbled for the key and opened the door.

The smell of Paula nearly dropped him. Her robe lay draped over the back of the chair. Her slippers under the desk. Four tubes of her lip balm at the base of the desk lamp—always handy to soothe her storm-chapped lips. The scent of film and the fluids used to develop it. All of it hit him at once—as if she'd been in this room all along, working the months away while the world went on without her.

But she wasn't here.

A storm took her.

The storm bit Jacob's arm, and his flesh froze at the touch of her mouth. He screamed and pushed her into the small room. Her eyes turned amber again—the cloudy grey clearing.

Jacob pulled the robe from the chair and tossed it to her. "What do you eat?" he asked.

She smiled, revealing the inky interior of her mouth. "Everything," she said. Her eyes sparked yellow. Her chest concaved over her ribs.

Jacob slammed the door as thunder exploded. The wood jumped against his shoulder.

When he caught his breath again, when the ringing in his ears had faded, he cracked the door. Everything glass in the room had shattered. All of Paula's lenses and plates turned to razor sand.

The storm lay on the floor, gasping, eyes dark. Her face twisted as he looked over her.

"Take me outside," she growled. "Give me back my blade. I need the sky."

Jacob closed the door and turned the lock.

He unloaded his bags. The video camera had practically melted, but the chip appeared intact. He popped it into the reader.

The funnel twisted across the screen—pale and beautiful, impossibly smooth. It roped and bent closer to shore, tossing debris. He saw himself walking toward it, reaching for it, then all went white.

He pulled the strange knife from his bag. The driftwood handle curved into his palm, its surface smooth but fibrous, polished as if by a hundred years of holding. The scrimshaw blade arced away from the wood, fiercely serrated, carved with strange symbols. Some resembled waves, funnels, and branching lightning; others were impossible to discern.

He slid open a drawer, lay the knife on a messy stack of files, and locked it.

He watched the video again, and again. It never showed the face deep inside the wind. It stopped before he'd pulled the knife from her center, pulled down the storm. None of the debris looked like Paula.

He clicked over to a live feed of the news.

No one reported the storm. It was as if no one but him had even seen it.

Beneath his feet, the storm raged.

~

Thunder shook the house every few hours through the night. By dawn, the pulses became less frequent, less urgent. Jacob sat in bed watching layers of feathered ice spread across the insides of his windows.

He revived his old phone and scrolled through the overnight weather maps and radars. His frown deepened with every refresh of the page. The currents were all wrong. The hot gulf winds arced west, dropping rain storms across Arizona. Arctic fronts sank like rocks across the east and well into Florida. Windsocks across the Midwest hung limp.

Climate scientists around the globe sweated against green screens, stumbling over words like "unprecedented," "anomaly," "unpredictable."

Jacob's heart hammered. *Unpredictable. They can't predict any of this.*

He grabbed his notebook and ran down the basement stairs just as his phone chirped a series of texts from Dan asking him to hurry—they needed him live ASAP.

He unlocked the studio door and peered inside.

His heart cartwheeled for a moment at the sight of the empty room, till he saw the storm plastered to the ceiling, glowering down at him. Her eyes were nearly full gold. He swallowed the lump in his throat and spoke quickly.

"I'll give your knife back—not yet, but soon. Just, first, tell me everything. What's happening with the wind? Where are the storms? Where will they be?"

~

The vapid anchors of channel four weren't laughing anymore. They were tuned in—watching Radar. Everyone was. Not just locally, but nationally. He put off questions about his sources, muttering half-formed information about studies he and Paula had conducted on the road.

"There's no better way to understand a storm than to chase it. Corner it and see what it does."

He saved lives. Hundreds. He sent people to basements before the clouds even began to spin—and they listened.

Jacob called the shots till his voice gave. Near midnight, he reached the end of his notes. The end of the storm predictions.

He slid his notebook in his pocket. Said he needed a break. Sleep, food—time with maps, then he would be back, he promised.

The media team's devices lit up with angry calls and tweets.

They—the public—wanted him to stay. They needed him. Relied on him—their lives depended on his forecast.

He needed the storm.

"I'll be back soon," he said.

He sped home, listening to the broadcasts and weather reporters who tried to pick up where he left off, but who mostly talked about how he couldn't know what he knew, instead of addressing the needs of their communities.

He ran inside, slipped and fell down the hard wood planks of the basement stairs—ice a half-inch thick coated them. A cut above his ear bled into the frost on the floor, congealing into a red slurry. He pressed at the wound, the inevitable headache already blooming.

Thunder boomed and shattered the ice sheet, sending him back to the floor, where icicle daggers pelted him from the ceiling. He covered his head till the world stilled again. The barometric pressure dropped, his ears popping as a wave of vertigo hit.

Jacob pulled himself up; small cuts across his body stung as he waded through the ice shards to the studio door.

The storm was inside the eye of a debris field. Everything was broken, every speck of it a little bit of Paula. Her scent was gone, replaced with the cool ions of lightning and snow.

Jacob's temper rose like an updraft. He stomped through the room, pieces of his past, of his Paula, crunching underfoot. Here, all the debris was her. Every speck.

He lifted the storm by her hair.

"What have you done to this room?" He tossed her back down into a pile of broken glass.

She laughed and it blew the hair back off his forehead. "I do what I do. There's nothing else that I can be but a tempest. Trapped in your teapot." She laughed again and the blood in his lacerations froze.

His phone beeped and rattled against the keys in his pocket. More storms, unseasonable and unnatural, twisted across the country.

"Call off the storms."

She smiled her ink-in-water smile. "I can't call them. I can only meet their winds with my own. We push and pull each other through the sky."

"Push them, then!"

"I can't take my place in the pattern from here." Her breath grew faint, her eyes more milky than stormy, not yet taking on the slightest cast of yellow.

"Then tell me what happens next. Those storms are deadly. I need to know where they're going."

"All storms are deadly." The storm's eyes roved in her head, shot through with white-hot lines. Her arms shook, scattering drops of rain around the room. She collapsed.

Jacob grabbed her and shook. "Where are the storms going?"

"To sea. All storms go to sea."

He dropped her on the floor, his phone already to his ear as he locked the door and raced up the stairs, kicking aside chunks of melting ice.

He burst into the newsroom they'd prepped for him. The cloud map imposed across the wall screen, circulating in digital blips over the world map. He jumped in front of it.

"The system will continue to head southwest across southern California, moving out to sea. Expect continued rainfall as it progresses—there could be some flash flooding in the hills and burn scars. Don't try to drive through deep or moving water, plan an evacuation route to high ground—"

As he spoke, the swinging arm of the stormfront moved eastward, churning north—directly away from where he had just indicated.

The anchors in his peripheral vision exchanged confused looks.

He froze, watching the system as it pulsed closer.

"We'll be right back," he said, nodding to Dan. Dan cut the feed.

"Can I get a computer?" he shouted into the shadows offstage. Phil came running with a laptop.

Jacob called up all the satellites and radars, the wind maps and thermals. The storm was moving east. Quickly. Not to sea, but straight back into the Midwest.

"That's not where it was going . . . " he said. Susan and Dan looked at him, shook their heads. Not even Cathy's makeup magic could hide the circles under their eyes or the way their furrowed brows cracked the flesh-toned paste.

He opened his storage drive and grabbed the video clip from the previous morning.

"Show them that. Distract them. Stall. I need to . . . I need to go talk to the storm." He left before their incredulous faces could fully form.

The ice in the house had all melted. He splashed down the basement steps and unlocked the door. The storm was crumpled on the floor where he'd left her, her wild hair strung in clumps through the broken glass. She wasn't moving.

Jacob knelt next to her, his pants soaking up the icy water.

The thunder in her chest sounded far away. A storm receding.

He pulled her hair off her face and gripped her shoulders. He squeezed and her scaly eyelids fluttered.

"You were wrong about the storm," he said, unsure she could even hear him.

She struggled against his grip and tried to sit. "I can't see . . . "

"Your eyes are closed."

"I can't see the sky."

"You need to see the sky? You need to go outside to predict the storm?"

"I need the wind."

She was too weak to fight or run or stop his heart with thunder bursts. Her eyes were as milky as cataracts—not a trace of lightning yellow.

"I'll take you outside, just tell me what's happening."

She was easy to lift. She hung in his arms like seaweed.

The sun crept lower toward the tree line. Wind pulled and pushed at him. He staggered to the grass and lay the storm down on his overgrown lawn. She quivered as the wind raked over her cold skin.

"Bring my blade," she said.

"I can't. Not yet. I need you to tell me—"

"Bring my blade! Set me free. I'll grant your knowledge." Her voice gained strength already.

"First tell me where the storms are going."

Her eyelids fluttered and peeled back from swirling charcoal irises. "They aren't going. They're coming."

He stared at the sky. A dark line stretched across the horizon.

"Free me. Let me go and I will have the wind whisper secrets to you."

He looked back. She'd pulled herself up into a crouch, her fingers twisting in the grass.

"You can do that?"

"If I want to."

"Why would I need that if I have you?" A gust nearly swept him from his feet. He looked up again at the darkening sky. "The storm is coming here?"

She smiled weakly. "All of the storms are coming here."

"You said you couldn't tell them what to do!"

"I can't. But they're coming anyway. Storms are unpredictable." Her legs trembled as she pushed herself to stand.

His face heated. The wind felt even colder.

"Are you the one? The storm that took Paula?" His nails cut into his palms.

Her smile grew. "I've had a thousand Paulas."

"You'll never get that blade back. You'll never kill again. I'll shake the knowledge out of you till you blow out, till you're nothing but mist—a sneeze," he shouted over the roaring wind.

She laughed, and her ropes of hair twisted in the sky. "It will be easy enough to pluck it from the rubble. I'll have it either way." She held out her open hand.

Lightning streaked across the sky in a jagged branch. It exploded against a tree on a nearby hillside. Thunder knocked him to his knees.

Jacob squinted at the silhouette of a funnel against the black sky.

"The time for choices is over . . . "

He ran back into the house, grabbed the knife, and headed for the basement, sheltering in the ruin of Paula's things.

Out of the roaring wind, he heard his phone, crowing like a gull—every notification pinging at once. He thumbed open an app and started a live feed.

"Get to shelter! A basement or interior room! A severe storm—multiple systems converging, tornadic—"

His electricity cut with a pop.

"Storm's here—shelter now!"

They couldn't see him, but they could hear him. He kept broadcasting, watching angry comments scroll against the dark rectangle where his face was hidden.

—you said west

—don't have a basement . . .

—are we gonna die

—you were wrong

You were wrong you were wrong you were wrong . . .

His voice stuck behind the lump in his throat.

The wind came up like a jet engine. He shrunk down as beams shrieked and split overhead.

"Storms are unpredictable," he croaked into the mic just as the ceiling lifted away and the basement filled with the strobe of lightning. His live viewer count ticked down one by one, then all at once, before the house came back down on him.

~

Wind licked his face.

Faint light filtered pink through his eyelids. He peeled his eyes open. Thin ropes of white twisted around him like the bars of a cage. Behind each swirling veil was a face.

He struggled to sit. Wind pinned him on his back.

"This one would have all knowledge of storms," a familiar voice cooed.

"Ahh," they all sighed, their voices circling him, the long sigh blowing his wet hair.

"To save his people?" Another voice circled him, cycling around behind and back again.

"No."

"Guilt."

"Ego."

"Power."

He tried to track a single face, but his eyes rolled.

"Shall we?"

"Tell him?"

"Show him?"

"Make him?"

"Pin him to the sky on the end of a blade."

"Turn his tempest inside out."

"Make him into what he is."

Faces leaned in through the vapor veils—all dusky and heavy with rain, eyes hot and static, charged with bright energy.

"But what is his blade? Which is his first kill?"

"So many died in the night, but which was first?"

The storm—his storm—paused her cycle to stare into his eyes. "His first kill was called Paula. Here is his blade."

The long, silver studio key rose above him.

"Paula?" he croaked, his voice lost—pulled from his mouth into the vortex.

The key dagger fell into him. Impaled him, driven by a hammer of wind. He felt it twist, moving hot through him like a spear of lightning. His head spun. His gut swirled. He twisted in pain and rage, writhing, till he lifted against the wind and joined it—turning, roping, raging.

A storm. Full of thunder. Destruction.

The funnels peeled off, away in every direction, tracing scars across the earth. The storms were everywhere. Unpredictable.

Jacob twisted and twisted, a tight knot of air, digging a hole in the ground.

RENOVATION

A BLANKET OF SPRING snow surrounded the hulk of flaking wood, frosting broken windows, sagging the ancient roof. Wetness seeped into the seams of Laurel's new boots and soaked her socks, numbed her toes. Ashley had disappeared around the side of the broad building. The whole place seemed to lean, though not in one uniform direction. It splayed, as if something inside was pushing its way out.

Ashley appeared around the far corner. Her smile was visible even at a distance. She had their mom's smile, the one people called infectious. Laurel was immune.

Ashley's smile was trained toward the sagging façade. Her voice echoed off the rock faces of the surrounding mountains. "Don't you want to take a closer look? The carriage house over there is where the shop will be." She reached Laurel's side, breath shooting streams of fog in the cold mountain air.

Laurel ran her eyes over the row of boarded-up windows. "I guess I just don't see how you're going to turn that"—she nodded at the derelict outbuilding—"into what you described. Even with all of Mom's money."

Ashley's white teeth disappeared behind a thin line of dark lipstick. "Don't start, Laurel. We agreed; it's a fresh start."

"The only thing fresh up here is the snow. Where are we going to sleep?"

"There are over 50 rooms in there. You can pick your favorite."

"Ash, that building does not look safe to sleep in."

"It's fine. I had it inspected. It's rundown, but it's sound. Just needs a little spit-shine."

Laurel watched a tattered curtain wave in one of the third-floor windows. Broken glass caught the light glaring off the undisturbed snow. She did not feel comforted. The structure might have been sound beneath all that rot, but something about the place—the matte shadow of the windows, the cracks between boards that seemed to heave as if breathing—its hollowness felt like her hollowness. She had too much in common with this ruin. She knew what she would find inside, and she didn't want or need to see it.

"Ashley, it needs a gas can and a match."

"Fine. Sleep in the truck. I'm going to go pick the room with the best antiques. The furnishings are all still there, you know. From 1906. And we didn't have to pay a dime for any of it—just the cost of the land."

Ash started back toward the house, snow sticking to the wool lining of her boots. Warm boots. Not like Laurel's. Laurel followed her.

"They're for the shop. You can't keep them there, Ash. I need to get them out before you start tearing the place apart."

"Then get your ass inside and stop whining."

Ash bent to the space beneath the porch steps as Laurel climbed them. "Foundation's good," she said. "Set right on top of the rock." She ran her hands over a sloping pillar. "It's built on quartz, you know. Can't you feel the incredible energy here?" She closed her eyes and breathed deeply. "Quartz holds on to its past," Ash said. "This place is rich with history."

Laurel shook her head and wondered what those broken windows meant for the antiques inside. *Holding on to history isn't always a good thing. Not when the past is broken. Not when everything rots.*

The bright sunlight that leapt off the snow banks barely penetrated the currents of dust inside the old building. Laurel's boots crunched over shadowed debris on the floor. The air smelled of damp wallpaper, old plaster, and rancid wood varnish.

Ashley pressed the wire handle of an LED lantern into Laurel's hand. A button on the top created a rim of cold light around them. Dust motes circled them like curious moths.

Laurel held the lantern higher, and the light stretched farther across the wide entryway.

Ashley pulled a hammer from her bag and went to the front wall. She began prying nails from grayed planks, pulling the wood away from shattered windows. The crack of brittle boards echoed dully off ancient plaster walls.

As the light crept in, shapes emerged in the shadows.

Laurel walked to the dusty mound of an old secretary desk. She lifted the hinged handle and lowered the heavy writing surface. It was a dark-grained wood coated in crumbling leather that peeled away from tarnished brass tacks. She ran her fingertips gently across the rich grain, tracing the hand-carved grooves. The back wall of the desk was a honeycomb of cubbies and chambers, each stuffed with brittle, yellowed papers. The desk held the scent of old paper trapped for a century, and Laurel breathed it deep, a concentrated hit of endorphins.

Laurel set the lantern down and reached into the first enclosure, pulling out a handful of crumbling correspondence. She settled in the tilting wooden chair and shuffled through the papers. Ledger after ledger lined in red; bills for repairs, lumber, and unfinished labor. Red everywhere.

Ashley's chin pressed down on her shoulder. "Shall I leave you two alone?" She giggled.

"Actually, that would be great," Laurel said.

Ashley smacked her arm. "Bitch."

"Why don't you go see if you can find us a room that doesn't smell like dead things?"

"You can find your own room. We're not kids anymore; we don't have to share."

Ashley stepped onto the sweeping staircase. Laurel set down the papers, grabbed the lantern, and followed Ashley's light around the curve of the stairs. There weren't likely to be many habitable rooms. She'd have to claim a space or be left sleeping in a pile of damp rot.

The second-floor hall stretched long in either direction. The floor warped like a twisted ribbon, and the ceiling sagged and bulged with whatever secret damages lay on the floor above. Ashley's light glowed from a room to the right. Laurel went left. Barely half the rooms had doors, and most of those hung from a single crooked hinge. Dusty furniture sagged under the weight of years. Ashley had been right about the antiques—there was a goldmine here—a lifetime of restoration. A lifetime of work.

Laurel felt a pull in her chest. *Hope? Probably asthma.* She couldn't tell the difference anymore. Both hurt.

The second-floor rooms were derelict, as were most on the third.

The fourth-floor rooms with their sloped ceilings and small windows—servants' quarters, clearly—had better withstood the elements.

Laurel found a bare interior room with a stooped ceiling and no window—nowhere for nature to have slipped its erosive fingers into the walls. An empty iron bedframe stood in the corner, a small table next to it. A hook-latch held a narrow closet door closed. On a shelf inside the closet lay a dark picture frame. Laurel picked it up and blew dust from the glass. It was an embroidery of a copse of aspen trees in autumn colors, each outlined in fine lines of yellow, orange, and brown, with black and silver tree bark. Laurel held the light closer, let it play over the impossibly fine lines. They shined in her light, reflecting back in delicate frayed curls.

Laurel gasped and tasted the dust of the place on her tongue. The picture was embroidered in human hair, from the bright yellow and orange leaves to the silvery tree bark. Beneath the trees, she could make out tiny figures, poised as if in dance, each a different color of hair, only a few strands thick. Silver grass formed a meadow at their feet.

She carried it from the closet and scanned the walls. There was a nail by the door. It was bent and rusty, but a gentle tug showed it to be sturdy. She slid the frame hook over it and stepped back to admire the piece. At a distance, it almost looked like a watercolor. She'd never seen one wrought so finely.

Laurel walked to the bedframe and slid her pack from her shoulder. She'd lay one of the fallen doors across the metal and sleep in her sleeping bag. There might not be any sweeping mountain views, or sunlight dazzling off snow, but this room was hers. She relaxed her shoulders and let out a long, deep breath.

The battery in her lantern died, as if she'd blown out the light. The walls of the room felt closer in the dark—pressed in on her, hiding her, keeping her safe. *They'll never find me here.* Safe and small, like sink cupboards or under beds. *No one is looking anymore,* she remembered.

"The chambermaid's room? Is this some sort of martyr complex?" Ashley leaned closer to the huge fireplace, rotating her skewer of veggies.

Laurel stabbed a second sausage onto the end of hers and leaned across Ashley to the flames. "No, it's just a nice room. Not all moldy like the others. And there's no gaping hole in the floor."

"I can walk around a hole. Mine's still the Presidential Suite." Ashley slid a red pepper off her kebab with her teeth.

"Talk about a complex." Laurel leaned back in a rickety chair and chewed her sausage.

"Seen any ghosts yet?" Ash asked.

"Ash, please. Don't start with that stuff. Not now."

"Let me know if you do. We can charge extra for those rooms." She grinned.

"And what will we charge for the rooms with no floors?" Laurel chewed cold sausage. No matter how long she held it to the flames, it wouldn't heat. The house and everything in it had committed to cold.

"You have no imagination, Laurel. You see the place the way it is now, and I see what it will be. Give me a few months, and this place will be *swank*. People will pay top dollar to stay here. And extra for ghosts."

Laurel shook her head. Her teeth started to chatter.

"We're going to need more firewood," Ash said.

"This whole place is firewood." Laurel tossed a scrap of debris into the hearth.

The flames surged.

"Laurel, go to bed. You sound like a cranky toddler."

"I just think this place is a mistake, okay? Yes, it's a neat building. The location is gorgeous. But I don't think you're going to get it fixed up in time for the summer tourists, and I definitely don't think Mom left us enough money to make it into what you want." She didn't think all the money in the world could fill the pit of her sister's wants. It had been a long time since she, herself, had dared to want anything. Wanting was too close to hoping. "And I should have more say in it."

Ashley set down her dinner and folded her hands in her lap like an elementary teacher. "Mom left you no say for a reason, Laurel."

"Damn it, Ash, she wrote that will two years ago. I've been sober ever since, and Tyler's gone. Things are different now, and I deserve a chance to make some decisions about my future. Just because she left you everything doesn't make you the new Mom!" *Look after your sister. You're in charge. Set an example.* Mom had always left Laurel in charge. Just because she had failed miserably didn't mean they had to trade roles.

"Let's talk more about it tomorrow, okay? After sleep. You can take a look at the shop building. That space is all yours, remember? Whatever you want in there, we can make it happen."

Laurel got up and walked toward the grand staircase. The light from the fire behind her cast her shadow dancing along every step. As she turned onto the landing, she thought she could hear the hiss of whispers from below—the way Mom and Ash would whisper whenever she left a room—secret judgements they thought she couldn't hear, or maybe they knew she could and wanted it that way, wanted her to know they disapproved of her.

Or perhaps it was just the snap of the fire.

The door to her room had been left open, though she remembered closing it—having to push hard to force the swollen boards past each other. *Could it have swung ajar as the building settled?* She chewed her lip and spread her sleeping bag over the door she'd salvaged for a mattress. As she went to pull her door shut, she noticed the wall by the doorway was bare. Heat flared from her chest to her throat. Had Ash searched her room? She stomped to the closet to throw her pack inside.

There, on the shelf, sat the picture—right back in the exact same space in the dust.

Laurel took it out again and hung it back on the nail.

"She can't have the antiques." She ran her fingertips over the glass, tracing the hair stitches. "She may have everything else, but she can't have those."

I could nail a board across my door. That would keep her out. But I'd probably burn to death when this place goes up in the night.

Laurel slid fully clothed into her down sleeping bag.

She swore she could still hear Ash whispering. *Was that even possible?* She must have called someone, or she was reading her tarot cards. Ash sounded happier with her gone. Everyone was always happier after she left. She bet Tyler missed her, though. *Good.*

She pulled the sleeping bag up to her chin, closed her eyes and drifted off to the sound of the wind slamming boards against the empty window frames.

She felt a sharp pain in her scalp. A tug on her hair and the digging tines of a comb against her skin. The sting of hairs plucked and yanked, the ice-cold steel of scissors, the warm spread of blood down her neck. She heard her mother's voice. *This is what happens, stupid. You ruined your hair. Now see how ugly you are?* She heard Ash's quiet sobs from behind the bathroom door, remembered the smell of burning hair, the curls dropping around her in piles to the floor, the strawberry-red blister on Ash's mouth where she'd bit down on the curling iron—how it stood out against the terrified blanch of her face.

She ran her fingers through the hair trailing from the picture on the wall, pulling the stitches free, clearing the tangle of knots, untying all those memories. Long strands in every hue wrapped around her wrists in silky curls. *Let's play hair salon*, Ash said. *I'm going to make you beautiful.* She braided the hair from the picture in a long plait that trailed from the frame as though from Rapunzel's tower. White crossed over red, red over yellow, yellow over black . . . *I'm going to make you beautiful.*

Laurel opened her eyes to darkness, unsure in her windowless room if morning had come or not. There was a scratching at her door. A hiss of nails against wood.

"Coffee?"

Ashley, with truce coffee. It must be morning, then. And it better be good coffee.

"Yeah," she called. She pulled her arms from her sleeping bag and struggled to sit up. Her back felt as stiff as the board beneath her. She stretched, and felt each vertebra slip and pop along her spine.

Ash stepped into the room and handed her a tall mug. Laurel breathed in the steam and couldn't resist a smile. French press.

"That's pretty," Ash said, nodding at the picture by the door.

"Haven't you seen it already?" Laurel's dream floated back to her.

She reached up and ran her fingers through her hair. She flinched when they caught on a snarl. A headache bloomed at her temple.

"No." Ash shook her head and leaned in close to the picture glass.

"I think it's the best of its kind I've ever seen." Laurel took a long drink. "So you weren't in here last night?"

"Best of what kind?"

"Look closer. That's all human hair."

Ash stepped back. "Oh, gross."

"Relax, it's behind glass. That's probably locks cut from all the women in the family. Several generations, I bet. Moms cutting the first locks of their babies, or their children that died of fevers. Maybe the last from a deceased matriarch. They were mementos. Usually they're wreathes or flower baskets. I've never seen trees done like that before."

Ashley was leaning in close again. "Looks like a lot of different people in this one."

"Well, there was a lot more to die from back then."

Ash shuddered and held her mug close. "I guess they didn't take each other for granted, at least. They probably all felt lucky to be alive, to have each other."

"Shame so many had to die so the rest could feel appreciated." *You're all I have left, Ash.*

"Well, you're going to die when you see what I found down the hall."

Laurel kicked her feet till she was free of the sleeping bag. "What?"

"Only a library."

"Shut up."

"Never." That infectious smile. Laurel could feel her heart mounting an immune response.

"Are there books?"

"They've seen better days. But some are okay. It's the shelves I think you're going to love. I've already rigged a pulley system to get them down the elevator shaft. They're all yours. For the store."

Laurel squeezed her mug, trying to soak in some measure of warmth. "I'm sorry I lost my temper last night. I am excited about the store. And a fresh start. It's just hard to have to rely on you." *I promised to look after you. Now look at us.*

"Yeah, well. You took care of me a time or two."

Should have been four, five. A hundred.

Laurel smiled over the edge of her mug. "I'm not sure hiding you from Mom in my toy chest really counts."

"It counts more than you think." Ash scraped her foot through the dust on the floor.

There was a loud crash from down the hall. Ash's face paled. She leapt into the hallway.

Laurel grabbed her stiff new boots and pulled them on, feeling the hard leather squeeze at the spots still sore from yesterday.

"I must not have tied something right. I'm still working out how best to get all these down." Ash led Laurel through the long corridors to the hall outside the elevator shaft.

"In one piece, preferably," Laurel said.

"I'll see what I can do. Go down to the lobby and help. You can guide the cases and unhook them when they're down."

Downstairs, Laurel stared at the open mouth of the elevator shaft. She reached in and pulled a tall, swinging oak bookshelf out onto the floor. It had vines carved along the top and sides in ornate scrolls. Even through the dust, Laurel could tell that the grain was beautiful. It had crashed into the side of the elevator shaft, one side scraped and split. *More work. I'll never be out of work again in this place.*

"How many of them are there?" she called up the shaft.

"A lot."

Laurel grinned. "And what have you done with the books?"

"Left them for you—in huge piles you can swim through if you like."

Laurel's smile grew.

"You're starting to get it, aren't you?" Ash asked.

"I don't give a shit about your crappy hotel. But I'm going to have an awesome antique store."

Ash laughed. "Okay, next!"

Laurel adjusted the boards Ash had laid across the shaft, creating a platform level with the floor. "Lower away!"

A loud crack sounded as something landed at Laurel's feet in a cloud of dust. Wood splintered. Ashley screamed.

"Ash?" Her head spun. Panic clouded her thoughts. She raced

up the stairs to the fourth-floor hallway, kicking up a cloud of debris behind her. Ashley writhed on the floor, her foot pinned under one of the massive shelves.

Laurel shouldered the shelf off Ash's foot, knelt beside her shrieking sister, and pulled the knot from the laces, yanked the laces from the eyelets, carefully slid the boot off Ash's foot. Ashley twisted in pain, leaving marks like snow angels in the dust. *Dust devils.*

Ashley's two smallest toes were already turning black.

Laurel had only seen a broken bone once before: her forearm. She rubbed at the scar that wound down her arm. Somehow, this was worse. This was Ashley.

Laurel pulled off her scarf to wrap around the twisted toes. Blood had begun to bubble up from where the toenails had torn from their beds.

"Not your dirty rag! Go get the first aid kit from my room."

Laurel willed her feet to move. She darted down the stairs to the suite and grabbed Ash's bag. As she left the room, the door slammed behind her. She jumped and yelped, but kept running. *Just wind.* The breeze tugged at her hair, the snap of it stung her scalp. *Yellow over red over red over red . . .*

She ran back to Ashley. "We're going to need to set the break before we wrap it," she said.

Ash nodded. Laurel could see her throat working to hold back panic. She'd always shown her fear there, in the front of her neck, tendons tight against the skin. She lay pale on the floor.

Laurel gripped the cooling ends of Ash's toes. They were slick with blood. She pinched hard, pulled the toes straight. Bone scraped against splintered bone until the break aligned and settled in place. The jagged plates of Ash's toenails came away in Laurel's hands.

Ash's scream shook dust from the plaster around them. The floor groaned under the arching of her back as if she might thrash the whole place apart.

Laurel squeezed her sister close and felt the tremble in her shoulders, tasted the dirt in her hair. *Just like when we were kids.* She combed the dirt from her hair with her fingers. *I'm going to make you beautiful.* There was never anything they could do to make Ash's hair curl. It hung straight as wet yellow satin, always. *I bet it would glide through the eye of a needle. Lie smooth against the embroidery backing*. Ash had always wanted to play with Laurel's hair—to tame its wildness. *Mine would snarl before you could pull a single stitch. It would tangle in the rest and pull out all the work. Ruin everything.* She had hated acting the doll. She remembered when Ash had set the iron too hot and burnt the locks of her hair clean away. Remembered the smell as she pressed the iron to Ash's mouth. How her eyes widened. How her burnt lips split when her mouth stretched to scream.

The echo of Ash's screams sent a chill down Laurel's spine. She gave Ash a teary kiss and left blood smeared across her cheek. She gripped her close until her hands hurt, her knuckles white like the snowy peaks outside. "Sorry," she said, and released her sister.

"You're right," Ash said.

"About what?"

"I can't do this. It's too much."

Laurel fought down the impulse to agree, to say that her injury was the natural consequence of her cockiness. That she should have listened to her big sister. *That's what you get.* Mom had said it often enough. *That's what you get for being stupid. For not listening. For not minding your own business.* For a moment, it was like she was there again, whispering it in her ear.

Laurel wrapped the toes in soft gauze, then a protective layer of thick tape.

"How about a nap? You can use my room. It's dark and quiet." Laurel helped Ash up from the floor. "I'll get some snow, so we can ice that foot."

"Yeah, I think that would be good."

"You can have one of my pills."

"You brought pills? What pills?" Ash looked ready to fight, broken toes or not.

"For my *headaches*. They should help your pain."

"Oh. Yeah, I want some."

With Ash tucked into her sleeping bag, a bitter pill dissolving in each of their throats, Laurel crept from the room. She tiptoed down the long hallway, avoiding piles of dust and debris that had all taken on a uniform shade of grey-brown. She turned a corner, and the black hole of the elevator shaft yawned to her right. Ash's faulty pulley swung overhead, a scrap of broken bookshelf still tied to the line.

At her feet, a dark pool of blood crept across the floor, running along the gaps between boards. Laurel frowned. She knelt at the edge of the puddle. She hadn't seen this much blood here before. It thickened in the dust till it became a dark paste and slowed under its own weight. She pressed her fingertip into the mess, and it came away wet and reeking of whisky, not blood. Laurel lowered her face to the puddle and sniffed—spirits and grit. She resisted lowering her tongue. Imagined the dust stuck between her teeth if she lapped up the liquor. She pulled away and stood, steadying herself against the wall as her head spun. She looked at her finger again. Blood. Definitely—red and sticky as she wiped it on the knee of her jeans. *Maybe I should nap, too.* But the call of the library was too strong.

One of the elegant bookshelves leaned on a dolly against the wall on the other side of the opening. Laurel stepped over the blood. She felt the hair along her arms rise. The quality of the light in the hall changed as if a dark cloud passed in front of the sun. The dry chill of the mountain air stiffened her neck.

There were trenches carved through the debris along the floor, tracks through the dust. They led from the base of the bookcase down the hall to an open set of French doors. She stepped onto the cleared path. Bright scraps of threadbare carpet showed through the dust. *This place must have been amazing once. It hasn't held on to its past; it's buried it.*

Beyond the French doors was the library. Well over a dozen of the carved cases lined the walls. In the center of the room, piled over and around a sagging velvet couch, was a mountain of old books. Laurel ran her fingers over the rough, woven covers. Most were beyond saving. Damp and dust had tarnished the embossed titles so that each book was anonymous—every one a mystery. She'd have to read them all just to figure out what they were. She felt the corners of her mouth pulling upward, imagined herself perched on a sunny mountain outcrop, working her way through a stack of these old books. Penciling a price inside the covers—stashing some away for herself.

She plucked one from the pile and opened it. The dry fabric spine crackled, the brittle pages fluttering like dead moth wings.

"*. . . everything within my view which ought to be white, had been white long ago, and had lost its lustre, and was faded and* *yellow. I saw that the bride within the bridal dress had withered like the dress, and like the flowers, and had no brightness left but the brightness of her sunken eyes . . . "*

I feel you, Pip.

"Damn it, Laurel!" Ash's voice bellowed down the hall.

Laurel jumped and rushed back out to the corridor. "Ash? What is it? What's the matter?"

"You tell me to sleep, but I don't know how the hell I'm supposed to do that if you won't shut up!"

Laurel froze. Those were Mom's words. Was that her voice? " . . . Mom?"

Ashley stormed around the corner, hobbling on her bad foot, and stopped in front of the elevator shaft. She glared at Laurel through the thin light of the hall.

"Ash, stop, you're standing in—"

"Who were you yelling at?"

"What?" Laurel shook her head, partly from confusion and partly to try and clear the fog that throbbed at her temples.

"And why were you laughing? I want to know what's so fucking funny about today."

"Ash, I wasn't laughing. I wasn't talking at all."

"I heard you!"

"I've been right here! Looking at the books, quietly, I swear."

Ashley's brow drew down. "You're serious."

"Yes! Now will you move? You're standing in blood."

Ash looked down. "Where?"

"All over! I think we should probably get you to a doctor."

"I don't see any."

"What are you talking about? It's everywhere." Laurel walked over to Ashley.

The floor was dry and grey. The dust was disturbed only where their boots had kicked furrows through the debris. "It was here. There was a huge puddle."

"Are you sure?"

"Of course!" Laurel knelt, running her fingers through the dirt, digging as if a hundred years of dust could have settled over it while she read.

"You saw a pool of blood, and now it's gone?"

"I was sure it was here, right by the elevator. Blood, or . . . or something. Is there another elevator shaft?" She looked at her knee, saw the smear still there on her jeans. "I touched it, and I wiped my finger here." She pointed to the stain.

"That's probably from when you wrapped my toes."

Laurel pressed her fingertips to her temples and tried to squeeze the headache away for a moment so she could think. Her hands smelled like blood and books and whisky, her skin the texture of grit.

Ash shook her head. "I heard screaming. You didn't say anything?"

"No!"

"Laurel, do you know what this means?"

"It means I'm calling the police. There must be someone else in the building. Squatters. Druggies. We do *not* want to run into them out here."

Ash reached for Laurel. "Shhh, no, Laurel, there's no one else here. Just us. And we are *so* going to charge extra for your room."

"Ash, this is not the time for this—"

"What's time here, anyway? Laurel, we're frozen in time here! Just like the ghosts. I knew they'd be here. It's the quartz in the foundation—it acts like a battery, storing energy."

"I think my pills may be too strong for you."

"I think we've got some ghosts." Ash grinned. "I was hoping for ghosts."

Laurel stared at her. "Ash, no."

"What's easier to believe, Laurel—that this old building is haunted, or that we're both simultaneously losing our minds?"

"Are you seriously asking me that?"

"I'm going to smudge with some sage." Ash headed for the stairs, limping. Laurel followed.

"That might help the smell. But will you at least let me get the books out before you burn the place down?"

A bang sounded behind them. They looked back around the corner and saw that the French doors had slammed shut. Small panes of glass lay shattered where they had fallen from their frames.

"I think that's a 'no,' Laurel." Ash's eyes twinkled.

"Ash, it's ridiculous. The whole thing is—this place, these plans, your ghosts."

Ashley turned back as they reached the Presidential Suite. "You either need to stay by me, or get out of the building while I do this."

Laurel followed her into the room, stepping around the ragged hole in the floorboards. The floor was broken clear through to the ballroom below.

"Why don't you go out to the carriage house?" Ash handed her a long key. "Start envisioning your future there. And maybe you'd rather stay there if things get weird here."

Laurel looked at the tarnished key and at the tied bundle of herbs in Ash's hand. "If? We are so past that."

"Take your attitude and get out. I need to stay positive for this, and you're pissing me off." Ash's eyes were bright and manic. Determined. Lit with the sort of fire Laurel was never able to look at for too long.

Laurel stomped down the stairs, her untied bootlaces snagging on stray nails that seemed to reach out and pluck at her, tacking her to the floor. As she reached the lobby, sweet smoke began to tickle her nose. Wind rattled the shutters.

She hoped it was wind.

~

The frozen stab of outside air cleared her head of the oppressive fog. Her head ached, but now from light and clarity and cold. Not from dust and squinting through angled shadows, from straining to hear nasty whispers.

The carriage house sagged across the sloping field, dipping down the side of the hill as if it might slide through the snow all the way to the lake at the bottom of the valley. Laurel chipped away at the ice in the lock with the end of the key. Even after she'd managed to grind the frozen tumblers of the mechanism, the door stuck fast—boards bloated with damp and ice swelling to fill every gap of the opening. *This isn't a way in anymore. There isn't a way in to places like this. No way in that you don't have to break.*

She pulled a hammer from her case. The windows were already broken, but the boards had been nailed in place from the inside. If she hit them hard enough, they should break loose.

A shelf of heavy snow slipped from the roof and poured onto the ground at her feet, burying the toes of her thin boots in piles of frozen wet. She stepped back. The door popped open.

The snow was weighing it down, that's all. It's physics. Everything has an explanation.

She waded into the new snowdrift, plowing a path through to the door.

The wide plank floor buckled like the surface of a lake frozen mid-wave. The floor had clearly been submerged at some point—twisted as it dried, then was soaked, and dried again. Just like her. It was useless now. Dangerous. Would have to be replaced. *This is beyond fixing.*

She stepped carefully across the splintered boards, avoiding nails, aiming for the visible support beams underneath. One misstep and she'd fall through to the basement—if that darkness underfoot was in fact a basement at all. She might drop straight through to the foundation, to that quartz battery that gave this place whatever power it was that lit Ash's eyes like lanterns.

Laurel could barely see. She wedged the hammer over the head of a nail and leaned, pulled. It squealed as she drew it out and moved on to the next and the next, for she didn't know how long, until the wall of windows was opened and light drove in.

She had been hoping for actual carriages, but the vast room was empty save for a few shattered crates and a tilted piano in the corner. Even at this distance, and despite its missing leg, Laurel could see the shadow of its opulence. The echo of its elegance. It was a beautiful piece, and far enough from the windows that she almost dared to hope . . . until she remembered the way the floor heaved, and that the piano, too, must have once been submerged. But she had to see.

She stepped from beam to beam across the room, hammer held like a counter-balance. *All those sobriety tests would have been easier if they'd put an antique Steinway piano at the end of the road.*

Up close, she could see where the legs had weathered away to kindling. The housing, though, was intact. Damaged, but it could be refinished. New strings, new dampers . . . The Bavarian spruce and ivory keys could be cleaned, but never replaced. She ran her fingers over the keys, but they didn't respond. Time and inattention had silenced it. But she could make it sing again. It would be her first project, after the floor.

Glass shattered against the door of the carriage house. Screaming followed it.

"You lying bitch! I've done nothing but try to help you, but you don't give a shit! You're just like Mom—you're going to die like her, yellow and alone!"

More glass hit the door. It shook against its hinges. The reek of alcohol reached Laurel's nose, a scent like balm and acid all at once. A puddle grew at the gap at the base of the door.

"Ash?" Laurel made her way across the floor as quickly as she could, the floorboards rattling just like loose piano keys, and she swore she heard the music of them, the tinkle of song in her steps, creeping up behind her as she hurried toward the sound of screaming. Once, she would have run, or hidden—climbed inside that piano housing and waited till the smell of alcohol faded. She opened the door a crack.

Ashley stood in the snow. Her hands and face were covered in soot. A crate of old liquor bottles sat at her feet. Tears carved ashen trails from her eyes. She hurled another bottle at the building.

"Ash, what the hell?"

"You're right—none of this is going to work. Because of you. You ruin everything." Ashley's lip trembled, the white scar on her mouth bright against the red cold of her face. *I'm going to make you beautiful.*

"Slow down, Ash—I have no fucking idea what you're talking about."

Ash kicked the crate with her good foot. "I found your stash."

"That isn't mine!"

"I trusted you!"

"Keep trusting me, Ash, and please shut up and listen."

Ash stood silent. Her chin shook.

"I swear to you that isn't mine. I don't know how it got here, or where you found it, and I haven't touched a drop since I left Tyler." *At least, not since that next morning.*

Ash looked back into the crate.

The liquor fumes made Laurel's head spin, or maybe it was the adrenaline. She felt like a shark swimming through chum, not allowed to take a bite. Ice and glass crunched under her boots as she walked to her little sister.

Ash still looked ten years old, face fresh but creased with the worry she'd always carried for their mother, and then for her. Laurel hated to be the cause of those worry lines. That face had kept her sober.

"Ash, do you believe me?"

Ashley ran her fingers through her hair, leaving dark cinder streaks in the blonde strands. "I'm not sure. I guess—you're a little hard to trust, Laurel."

Laurel felt the lump in her throat tighten. "I know. And I don't know how I can prove it to you. But I swear those aren't mine."

Ash nodded.

"Where did you find them?"

"In the service tunnels. They were all over down there. Like there had been some kind of party."

"Tunnels? Creepy."

"It was totally creepy." Ash cracked a smile. "We could charge for tours."

Laurel reached into the crate and pulled out a bottle of Jack Daniels; an inch of liquid still sloshed inside. "Oh, Ash. I had way better taste than this." She hurled the bottle at the building. It shattered. The glass joined the ice, and amber liquid slid over the cracked white paint of the wall.

"Mom loved it," Ash said. She picked up another bottle and threw it.

Bright mountain sunlight refracted through the broken glass, casting small rainbows over the snow.

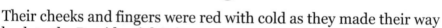

Their cheeks and fingers were red with cold as they made their way back to the Presidential Suite.

"Can I have another pill, Laurel? My foot hurts."

Laurel's smile crumpled at the memory of those jutting bones, of her pale face, of the vanishing pool of blood. "Yeah. Of course. I still think you should see a doctor."

"It's only my toes. They don't do anything for toes."

"They could give you something stronger for pain."

"I won't have any of that shit in this house."

Laurel tried to swallow the lump rising in her throat.

They stripped off their coats and laid them across a broad wooden desk. Laurel ran her fingers over the carved drawer faces. "This is a nice piece. Good shape. Just needs a fresh finish."

"So you're still on board?"

"Yeah. I mean, as long as you're not afraid I'm going to ruin everything."

"I'm sorry, Laurel. I didn't mean—"

"Yes, you did. And you're right to be afraid. I do ruin everything. Or I have, so far. But I'm going to try harder." Laurel pulled at the iron ring on the drawer face. The wood stuck, then groaned as it gave. The smell of old varnish cut through the smell of dust and sage.

"Ash, what's this doing here?" A flush of blood warmed her cheeks. She pulled her journal from the drawer. "Did you take this from my room? Are you reading my journal?"

"No! I didn't even know you still kept a diary."

"Well, how did it get here, then? You're spying on me?"

"No! No, I'm not, Laurel."

Laurel's fingernails ached as they dug into the worn cover of the book. "What the fuck do I have to do to make you trust me, Ash?"

Ash's face hardened. "Try harder. Like you said. But I swear I did *not* take your diary."

Laurel focused on breathing. She tasted the sage smoke. "Mom used to take my diaries all the time."

"I remember."

Laurel ruffled the pages with her thumb. "I used to lie in them. Because I knew she was reading. I knew what to write to make her proud of me, or to make her hurt. Whichever I felt she needed at the time. Or whatever I needed."

Ash's brow furrowed.

"I only just started writing the truth again."

Ash looked at Laurel. "It's Mom."

"What?"

"Our ghost, Laurel—it's Mom."

"It's not Mom."

"It is—it's just like her."

"Ash, I'm not sure it's a ghost." Laurel searched her sister's face for signs of fever. Had her toes become infected already?

"The Jack Daniels. The diary. The voice that sounded just like you."

"If it's Mom, why's she trying to talk to us?" The whispers screamed in these rotten halls had been the closest thing Laurel had heard to her mother's voice in five years. Since she ran away with Tyler. *Tell that motherfucker he can pay for your funeral, then, I never want to see you again.*

"Maybe she's trying to apologize."

"She's got a funny way of showing it."

"See? Just like her."

Ashley settled into a leather chair by the fire. Laurel had discovered the piece in a fancy office in the basement near the tunnels. She had wrestled it up to the lobby, cleaned it off. They'd done their best to make a comfortable space. Fixed the room up so that it looked more like a dingy parlor than a condemned rat trap.

Laurel busied herself hooking up a generator to an old-fashioned boxy TV that was crowned with an elaborate antenna. "We'll at least get some football and the news."

"Good," said Ashley. She reached into a box at her feet.

"Is that the stuff to repair the fireplace?" Laurel asked.

Ashley slid the lid off the box. "No. I want to have a séance—to try and make contact."

Laurel squeezed her eyes shut and took a slow breath. The smell of gasoline reminded her of Tyler—of sleeping in his car, of hiding in the trunk when he made deals, reading the gas can label over and over while she waited, wondering what the gas would taste like. "That is a super weird idea."

"C'mon, Laurel. Maybe we can get some closure. Make amends," Ash said.

"We don't even know if it's Mom. We don't even know if it's a ghost."

"So if there's no ghost, what harm can it do?"

"I can't believe you still have that," Laurel said as Ash set the ragged old Ouija board on the table.

"I can't believe you still keep a diary."

"It's a journal."

Wind rattled the shutters. *Of course.* The fire, despite its mountain of scrap wood, guttered and bent the light across them in strange shadows. They tuned the TV to soft static to try and cast more light into the room. The flicker set Laurel's teeth on edge. Ashley had scattered candles around them, but they wouldn't stay lit in the drafts that cut like saw blades through the building.

Ash laid her fingers on the planchette. "Come on, Laurel," she said.

Laurel sighed, scooted up to the low table, and placed a few fingers on the old plastic game piece.

"Now." Ash closed her eyes. Her voice was deep and barely above a whisper. "I need you to focus. Breathe, and think about Mom."

Laurel thought about her mother all the time. Too often. She didn't need any special reason. She thought about the nights filled with shouting and thrown toys, when Ash would creep into her room and they would sit in her closet and color on the back wall until the storm of their mother had blown over.

She thought about early mornings spent cleaning up reeking puddles of sick before Ash could see them. About her desperation to escape, and how Tyler was right there, with an open door and a closed fist. About her own journey down the neck of a bottle, and how she finally understood her mother on a new level—the one at rock bottom.

And how, by then, it had all been too late. And her secret guilty relief that she could stop seeking resolution. She didn't need closure. The door was closed in her face years ago.

The planchette jumped.

They gasped.

"Mom, is that you?" Ash's voice shook.

Glass shattered somewhere in the dark of the lobby.

"Do you have something you'd like to tell us? Is there something you need to say?"

The planchette continued to rattle across the board, spelling out gibberish. It squeaked over the board, then carved grooves in it where the felt feet of the planchette had long since worn away.

"Can you be drunk when you're dead?" Laurel asked. "Maybe her speech is slurred."

Ash shot her a pained look.

A loud crack—a shattering splinter sounded from the ballroom behind them. Laurel raced to the ballroom and slid open the pocket door.

"Jesus," Laurel said, and stumbled back. Another crash sounded from the dark room.

"What is it?"

Laurel's face paled. "There's furniture falling through the hole in the ceiling."

"That's the hole in the suite. In my room," Ash said.

Laurel refocused on the shards in the dark center of the floor. The handsome grain of wood. The desk from Ash's room. *I could have saved that. I could have brought it back to life.*

"Mom, are you mad about something?" Ash called out behind her. "Don't you want Laurel to have the furniture here? So she can start over?"

A soft cascade of flapping thuds came from the elevator shaft. The books—hundreds of them—tumbled down, pouring from the dark mouth and spilling across the lobby floor.

Laurel backed toward the rattling front door. "Maybe you should stop asking questions," she said.

The generator died. The TV screen went grey and faded to black.

"Mom, stop it!" Ash screamed.

The toxic scent of liquor filled the room. It rained down on them, dripping all over the floor. It ran in rivulets down the walls, curling the scraps of wallpaper and soaking the plaster. It burned in Laurel's eyes. Danced on her tongue.

With a loud slam, one of the carved bookcases crashed out of the elevator shaft and shattered into splinters.

Laurel's face grew hot. Her vision went white, and her fists shook—nails carving crescent cuts into her palms. *"That's fucking enough!"*

The crashing stopped. The wind stilled. A soft slithering sound filled the room. Laurel felt something brush her cheek. She flinched away. The light from the fire played off shining curls of hair growing from the fractured plaster. Brown and black and red and yellow, bright silver—all growing from the walls and ceiling. The tendrils coiled on the floor.

Ash sat, weeping quietly into her hands, just like before. *Like always.*

Laurel's rage only grew. "Proud of yourself? Still the big, scary alpha bitch? Think this place is yours because we bought it with your leftovers? Well, fuck you. You can't have it. You've shit all over the past—there's no way you're getting any piece of our future. You're gone. You're done. We're done with you."

The planchette shot off the table and raked Laurel across the face. Blood trailed from her cheeks and forehead where the plastic had cut. Laurel dabbed at the wounds. She wiped the blood from her fingers onto a clump of yellow hair that swayed toward her as if drawn by static.

Ashley reached for a tied bundle of sage.

"Still throwing toys? Think we'll go hide in the closet again?" Laurel slapped at the long scar on her forearm. She remembered the way time had seemed to slow as she watched the arc of the metal doll stroller through the air, as it came down on her—remembered the look on her mother's face through those metal bars as they crashed into her. Not fear or regret—satisfaction. The lies whispered to the doctor who set the bone, who stitched her up.

The seam of her scar split, layers of flesh and fat peeling away from bright bone. Brown liquid poured from the cut and ran sticky down her fingers. It smelled of spice and sweet rum.

Ash's bundle of sage smoked. It hissed and flared where the liquor dripped, fueling the embers. The forest of curls brushed the flames and filled the room with the reek of burnt hair. Laurel felt the tug on her scalp, the scrape of the comb, the burn of the iron. *I'm going to make you beautiful.* Her own hair tangled with the locks falling from the plaster cracks. Stitched in with them, embroidering a forest all around them.

Laurel pulled Ash to her side and linked an arm though hers.

"Go away," Laurel said. "This place is ours. It doesn't belong to you. *We* don't belong to you. We never did. We were never yours." She pushed against the force that seemed to squeeze her and heard the house groan. Felt the spaces between the boards heave. Laurel felt her lungs stripped of air as the house itself drew a breath, walls bloating; then it exhaled in a rush, a scream, and all the dust and hair and ruin lifted, spinning in its wake. The walls sagged inward.

She could breathe again. She coughed on the grit in the air. Ash coughed beside her. The pressure eased.

The dripping slowed. It stopped. The fire crept further up its kindling and filled the room with light. Clumps of hair fell from the ceiling, detached, into piles of silk in the dust.

Ash panted, blowing her sage smoke out across the lobby. "Is she gone?"

The secretary desk slammed open.

Ash screamed.

Papers shot from their cubbies and scattered across the room like a flock of startled birds. They settled in the debris, sticking to the pools of booze. Red ink bled from the pages, spreading into the liquid.

Ashley bent to pick up a sheet. "What are they?"

"Legal papers, mostly," said Laurel. "Records of how this place has ruined everyone who's ever tried to run it."

A twisted wood frame fell from a web of hair, landing with a soft splash in the soaked locks.

Ash pulled it from the damp clumps of hair at their feet. "She ruined your antique."

"It was a memento." *A memento mori.* Laurel took the warped frame. The fabric fell away in strips. The hair stitches had all pulled free into a tangled mess. "Maybe it's not so healthy to hold on to the dead like that." She tossed the wrecked picture aside.

Ashley let a cascade of papers fall from her hands. "This place is going to ruin us. It is, isn't it?"

Laurel kissed the top of her head. "I'm sure Mom would like you to think so. I'm sure she'd want us to cut and run. Burn it all. Give up and hide. We'll sink every penny into this place and go absolutely broke, probably. But it's not going to ruin us. It takes a lot more than that to ruin us."

Ashley shook her head. "What are we going to do?"

Laurel kicked at the piles of hair on the floor. They tangled across her boots, caught in her laces.

"Clean up. Do our thing. And if it doesn't work, we'll start over. Over and over again." *Yellow over silver over black over red over red over red.*

ACKNOWLEDGMENTS

Thanks are due to Jess Landry, Scarlett R. Algee, Christopher Payne, Sean Leonard, and Mikio Murakami—my publishing dream team. You make magic happen.

Thank you to my mentors and teachers, especially Rena Mason, Danielle Kaheaku, and Richard Thomas.

Thank you to my husband and sons, and to all my family, for their support and delightful distraction.

Thank you to my alpha and beta readers: Regina, Awilda, Jen, and Debbie. And to my critique group, the Post Apocalyptic Writers Society: Kat Köhler, Julie C. Day, Jordan Kurella, Steve Toase, Chip Houser, Carina Bissette, Marianne Kirby, Karen Bovenmyer, and Matt Garcia. And to all its former members whose hearts touched these stories, especially Bonnie, Emily, and C.

Much appreciation and gratitude to the editors who originally published these stories, with extra special thanks to Andy Cox.

Thanks to my amazingly supportive coworkers at the library. And thank you always to my Fairy Spirit, Kathryn Grusauskas.

PUBLICATION HISTORY

"Endoskeletal" first published in *Black Static*, July 2017; reprinted in *Best Horror of the Year*, Vol. 10, June 2018.

"Making Monsters" first published in *Stupefying Stories*, August 2016.

"Dead Man's Curve" first published in *Tales from the Shadow Booth*, Vol. 1, December 2017.

"In Tongues" first published in *Menacing Hedge*, Fall 2016.

"The Eyes of Salton Sea" first published in *California Screamin'*, October 2017.

"Underwater Thing" original to this collection.

"Tall Grass, Shallow Water" first published in *LampLight*, Vol. 6, Issue 2, December 2017.

"Intersect" first published in *Gamut*, October 2017.

"Grave Mother" first published in *Vine Leaves Literary Journal* and *The Best of Vine Leaves Literary Journal*, 2014.

"Thorn Tongue" first published in *Gamut*, April 2017.

"Through Gravel" first published in Behold*!: Oddities, Curiosities, and Undefinable Wonders*, July 2017.

"Still Life with Natalie" first published in *Suspended in Dusk II*, July 2018.

"Golden Avery" first published in *Black Static*, May 2014; reprinted in *Gamut*, June 2017.

"Scavengers" original to this collection.

"The Eye Liars" first published in *Exigencies*, June 2015.

"Magnifying Glass" first published in *Black Static*, May 2015.

"Crosswind" original to this collection.

"Renovation" original to this collection.

ABOUT THE AUTHOR

Sarah Read is an author, editor, and librarian living in the frozen north of Wisconsin with her husband, two sons, a cat, and thousands of spiders. Her novel *The Bone Weaver's Orchard* was released from Trepidatio Publishing in early 2019. Follow her on Twitter or Instagram @inkwellmonster, or on her website at inkwellmonster.wordpress.com.

be obtained

9
06B/37/P